The Croaking Raven

By Guy Hale

The Croaking Raven draws DC Toby Marlowe and DS Fred Williams into the dark world of Hamlet, not on the stage but on the streets of Stratford Upon Avon. Oliver Lawrence has returned and he's looking for revenge.

'Wildly entertaining, darkly funny. Hamlet as you've never seen it. Had me gripped and gasping. Outstanding!'

Rob Parker (author of the Thirty Miles Trilogy)

'Dexter meets Shakespeare in this dark and twisted tale of revenge.'

Christie J. Newport (Joffe Books prize winner)

'Masterful plotting, a dark and funny take on Hamlet.'

Blair Kessler (The Birmingham Film Company)

'I loved this book. Very atmospheric. This Hamlet is extremely good but also very bad!'

Imran Mahmood (author of I Know What I Saw)

'Fresh, funny and fiendishly clever. The Croaking Raven is an absolute triumph. A deliciously dark gem of a read.'

A.A. Chaudhuri (Amazon bestselling author)

'Shakespearian tragedy on the streets of Stratford Upon Avon. A dark, sassy, revengers tale, wicked and funny.'

Paul Burke (Crime Time FM)

By Guy Hale

The Comeback Trail Trilogy

Killing Me Softly
Blood on the Tracks
All the World's a Stage

The Shakespeare Murders

The Croaking Raven

*This book is dedicated to the memory of
Laura Zito and Jayne Evans.
The most beautiful human beings.
My life is better for having known them.*

Chapter 1
Return Of The Prince

Oliver Lawrence lay on his bed. In the distance he could hear the sounds of Casablanca. The call to midday prayer had begun and the voice of the Muezzin floated from the top of a nearby minaret, borne on the warm winds of the Sahara as they headed for the north west coast of Morocco.

Oliver was a long way from home. Fifteen long years away. Forced from a great future by a web of jealousy and lies, a bitter crop that had been planted by those he trusted most. They had nearly destroyed him and he had run. Run until he could not hear their lies or their taunting. Run until he had found a place to shelter, recover, and plan his revenge.

It had taken fifteen years. Years when he should have been confirming his reputation as the greatest stage actor of his generation. He had not wasted his time. In the quiet beachside community of Ain Diab, he had sheltered from the seething turmoil that was Casablanca. As the early May heat had begun to rise, so had his desire for revenge. Now was the time to return to England and deliver his justice to all those who had plotted against him.

The list was a long one. It would take time, but time was his friend. No more deadlines driven by success, a shattered career, a reputation in tatters. Nothing could rebuild it now; too much time had passed. He was just a once illustrious footnote in the history of the British theatre. The bright new talent upon the Shakespearian stage who had burst like a shooting star across its firmament, only to be destroyed by the lesser stars of those who feared being cast in his shadow.

Jealousy is a terrible thing. For Oliver Lawrence, revenge

would be his answer. An eye for an eye was insufficient payment for his loss. This bill would be paid in blood; no mercy, no forgiveness. He knew who had betrayed him; they were listed in the letter he held in his hand. The paper was now mottled with age but the clear handwriting of Felix Richards was still legible. He had sent it to him as his career began to fall around him, the one true voice that remained in his hearing. He would find Felix on his return and seek his help.

Felix, like him, had been betrayed. Cast aside by the Fleet Street mafia for daring to stand up against the growing howls of derision that had been aimed at him. The two of them would show them. They would use the cold heat of a long-suppressed rage.

Oliver looked down at the tickets on the table. The ferry to Faro, three trains up through Portugal, Spain and France. A ferry from Caen to Portsmouth. In Portsmouth he would buy a second-hand car and then, in anonymity, drive up through Hampshire and then the Cotswolds, all the time moving inexorably towards Stratford-upon-Avon and his final solution. He had no plans to return, this would be a one-way ticket. The cast list he had drawn up would all be joining him in the play he had constructed for them. A play in which nobody survived. A tragedy in three parts.

Oliver looked into the mirror. He was still a fine-looking man, forty years old and in the shape of his life. In his eyes burned a fire, a madness that could only be extinguished by blood. The smile that had played upon his lips faded as the veil of hatred possessed him. His eyes narrowed and familiar words from long ago hissed from his mouth.

'And Caesar's spirit, ranging for revenge,
With Ate by his side come hot from hell,
Shall in these confines with a monarch's voice
Cry "Havoc" and let slip the dogs of war,

That this foul deed shall smell above the earth
With carrion men, groaning for burial.'

The grave digger was going to be busy.

Chapter 2
Strange Bedfellows

Toby Marlowe awoke with a spring in his step. He had just turned twenty-six and had landed his first post as a detective constable at Stratford-Upon-Avon, his dream station. After four years of patrolling the not so mean streets of Kings Heath, Toby was convinced that his future lay in CID. He had once had to break up a fight outside of Wimbush's, the bakers, during the great mince pie shortage of Christmas 1971. For his trouble he had received a nasty gash above his left eye from Mrs Howard's umbrella. He learned a valuable lesson that day; never get between a group of angry women and a pile of mince pies.

He looked in the mirror. The scar from Mrs Howard's umbrella was still visible. He had fostered the legend put about by his friend, Sergeant Dusty Rhodes, that he had been slashed with a razor as he broke up a fight outside The Maypole pub. He'd protested, but Sergeant Rhodes had insisted.

'Listen, son, to do well as a copper you need a reputation. We pressed no charges and, in the melee, could not identify the perp. That's how I wrote it up. You sign the report and you're a hero.'

Toby had tried to dissuade him, but Rhodes just gave him a knowing look. 'Imagine it gets out that you got clobbered by an umbrella while you were trying to break up a bunch of housewives during a mince pie riot. Not going to look good, is it?' He had a point.

Toby checked the clock. Ten past eight. It would only take about twenty minutes to get to the station in Stratford from Alcester, he wasn't expected until nine. He hated being late and so he grabbed the keys to his car and headed down the stairs of his little terraced cottage, eager to begin his new role.

In Stratford there was a debate going on at the station as to who would have the honour of being lumbered with the rookie detective.

'Well, I'm not having him. We've just got a puppy and I haven't house-trained him yet.'

'I'm pretty sure DC Marlowe is house-trained, Ken.'

'He's from Birmingham, Tony, how can you be sure?'

'Point taken. Maybe we could put him with a uniform, just while he settles in.'

'Beeching wouldn't go for that. You know how he likes to keep plain clothes and uniform separate. Easier to apportion blame.'

Tony knew that Ken had a point. Inspector Beeching was very protective of the CID unit he was building in Guild Street. Beeching was a man on a mission; he wanted to get to the Met. London was where all the big jobs were. Stratford was just a stepping stone, but a very nice one.

He was forty-eight and still fit enough to row for Stratford boat club. Coming from Northampton to Stratford had been a calculated risk, but Sidney Beeching was a clever man. He knew that Stratford had a profile that belied the actual size of the town. Here would be a good place to build a reputation.

With Oliver Lawrence heading inexorably across Spain and France towards Stratford, little did Inspector Beeching realise just how big that profile was about to become.

Back in CID, Tony Parsons had been hit with inspiration. 'Let's pair him up with Williams.'

'Fred wouldn't take that, he hates working with a partner.'

'He hates everyone,' said Tony. 'But he can't just do what he likes.'

'Well, he has done for the last few years.'

'Look, Beeching will want to pair the new guy with somebody. We don't want him, so why don't you suggest to Beeching that Fred would be the man?'

Ken White didn't look convinced. 'Fred gets results, that's why the boss leaves him alone.'

'Worth a try though, isn't it.' Tony smiled. 'Can you imagine Fred being teamed up with a rookie?'

Ken had to admit that it would be funny. The swearing would be heard in Shipston. 'Maybe I could have a quick word with Beeching, suggest that as Fred is the only DS working without a DC, he's the logical candidate.'

Tony began to laugh. 'That would be priceless.'

Ken White held up a folder containing a couple of sheets of typed A4. 'Have you read his file?'

Tony shook his head.

'He's only a theatre nut, does am-dram and everything. Says that one of his reasons for wanting to be based in Stratford is his love of Shakespeare.'

Tony grabbed the file from him. 'You're kidding me. He's a bloody luvvie!' Tony scanned through the papers and a broad smile spread across his features. 'We have to make this happen, it's gonna be Romeo and Juliet all over again.'

Tony Parsons was wrong; it was going to be more like Hamlet.

Half an hour later, White and Parsons looked out of the window and saw Toby pull up.

'Flash little git's got an MG,' observed White.

'Did you manage to convince Beeching to pair him with Fred?'

Ken turned to Tony and smiled. 'Oh yes.'

Parsons slapped him on the back. 'You're a bloody genius, Ken. Can't wait to see his face when we break it to him.'

A couple of minutes later, a PC showed Toby into CID. Ken came over to him with his hand outstretched.

'I'm DS Ken White and that plonker over there is DS Tony Parsons.'

Tony nodded. 'Welcome to the Avon retirement home for detectives who don't want "too much" crime.'

This wasn't what Toby had wanted to hear but just being a DC and based in Stratford was enough for now. 'Will I be working with one of you?'

They exchanged a glance.

'No, Toby, the boss has put you with our top thief-taker,' said White.

'Great.'

'Hold that thought, son.'

Toby didn't understand but, before he could ask, the door banged open and a bull of a man, who appeared to be in a state of simmering rage, burst into the office.

'Some twat's parked a hairdresser's car in my spot.'

'Morning, Fred. Not come in the tractor today, then?' asked Ken.

'Sod off, Ken.'

'I'll take that as a no then, shall I.'

Fred Williams shrugged. 'You can take it any way you like, just tell me who parked that hairdressing monstrosity in my spot.'

White and Parsons turned to look at Toby.

'Have you met your new partner?' said White.

'I don't have a partner,' snapped Williams.

Toby cleared his throat and approached Williams with his hand outstretched. 'I'm Toby Marlowe.'

Fred looked at the hand like it was a wet fish. 'If you say so, son.' He turned back to his sniggering colleagues. 'What's amusing you two idiots?'

Parsons pointed at Toby. 'This is our new DC. Beeching wants to partner him with you.'

Williams turned to Toby. 'No offence, son, but I work alone, mainly because the rest of CID are about as bright as this pair of idiots.'

'Toby drives a Red MG,' added White.

Fred paused and then slowly turned his gaze on Toby. 'That true, son?'

Toby nodded.

Fred Williams considered the facts for a moment. 'It's not been a good start, has it. Why don't you toddle down to the car park and move that … thing out of my place.'

'But the place wasn't marked.'

Williams shook his head. 'You're supposed to be a detective. The rear car park was full except for one space right near the entrance. Why do you think it wasn't occupied?'

Toby shrugged.

'Because, DC Marlowe, no bugger who knows me would dare to park in my spot. Now, there's an overflow car park round the corner. Why don't you toddle off and stick it in there while I sort this problem out.'

'What problem?'

Fred Williams stared at him with a vague expression of mystification. 'You, son. I don't have time to nursemaid a rookie.'

For a moment Toby considered debating the point, but DS Fred Williams had a distinct edge to him and he was also a big bugger. Maybe a few pies past his peak, but still a formidable figure.

'I'll just go and move the car then.'

'Here, take these with you,' Fred Williams threw him some keys. Put mine where yours was when you've moved it.'

Toby caught the keys. 'What car is it?'

DS Williams gave him a sickly smile. 'You're a detective now, son, see if you can work it out.'

Toby glanced across at White and Parsons, who were struggling to contain their smiles. He backed out of the room. It had not been the start he had been hoping for. As he walked down the stairs, he heard an eruption of laughter, which was obviously at his expense. He hurried out into the car park praying things would get better.

Back in the CID offices, Fred confronted his colleagues. 'I suppose you pair of prats set this up, paired me with the rookie.'

They shook their heads in unison.

'No, Fred, it came from on high. Beeching wants him trained by the top man.'

'Bullshit. You pair of hyenas have set me up.' Fred smiled. I wonder how young Toby is getting on.'

'Why, what are you driving today?'

Fred grinned. 'Well, my dad's farm does have dairy.'

Out on the car park, Toby was struggling to find a vehicle that could belong to DS Williams. There were four unmarked Mark 3 Cortinas, which would belong to CID, and several marked cars including a couple of Rover 2000s and an Escort. All the other staff cars had been on the car park when he arrived. The only other vehicle was a milk float. What the hell was that doing here? It bore the legend 'Loxley Dairies'.

Chapter 3
The Odd Couple

Inspector Beeching swept into the office like a house-trained bear. 'Where's DC Marlowe?'

White and Parsons looked at Fred Williams.

'He's trying to find a milk float.'

For a brief moment Beeching hesitated as he tried to comprehend what DS Williams had just said. Beeching, despite being deskbound, had lost none of his investigative skills.

'Why?'

It was both incisive and succinct, but DS Williams was his equal. 'Because, like a mountain, it's there, sir.'

Beeching looked to White and Parsons for clarification. 'What's he talking about?'

White shrugged. 'DS Williams sent DC Marlowe to move his vehicle.'

'You've come in a milk float?'

'Yes, sir,' DS Williams nodded. 'We are supposed to serve the community, so I delivered their milk on the way in.'

Beeching shook his head. DS Williams was eccentric to say the least. He was also well known for beating confessions out of criminals, some of whom were guilty. The problem for Beeching was that Williams got results and he needed them.

'I realise you still live at the family farm, Williams, but could you try and confine your agricultural vehicles to their rural location. We are trying to create a serious investigative team here and tractors and milk floats are not the mode of transport for a senior detective to be seen in.'

'On, sir.'

'I beg your pardon, Williams.'

'On, sir. You ride on a tractor or milk float, not in it.'

Beeching sighed. 'I haven't got time to discuss the semantics of your varied means of transportation. I'm putting you with DC Marlowe.'

'But I work alone, sir.'

'You're not on a tractor now, DS Williams. You are working with DC Marlowe until further notice.'

There was a brief outbreak of sniggering from White and Parsons, which Beeching quelled with a withering stare.

'Right, lads, there's crime out there, go and solve it.' Beeching turned on his heel and swept from the office.

The three detectives waited for the door to close behind him.

'There's crime out there, lads.' They all laughed.

'How would he know from behind a desk?' asked DS Parsons. He looked out of the window at Toby, still wandering round the car park. 'You going to call him in, Fred?'

Fred shrugged. 'Let's give him a few more minutes, see if he notices the "Loxley Dairies" logo on the keyring.'

Some ten minutes later, Fred heard a rattle of gold tops as his milk float juddered to a halt outside the office. The brakes on that float were fierce. He opened the window and called down to Toby, 'Bring us up a bottle of milk. Full- fat, I don't want any of that healthy muck.'

Toby nodded. He had been a milk monitor at his primary school long before, 'Thatcher, the Milk Snatcher', had supervised its withdrawal. Now, on his first day as a detective, it seemed he was once again a milk monitor. Surely things could only get better.

As Toby walked back into the CID office, Fred greeted him warmly.

'Well done, lad, you've solved the puzzle of the mystery

vehicle and you've got the right milk. You may make a detective yet.'

Toby held out the bottle, but Fred held up his hand.

'You hold onto that, Toby, because I have another bit of detective work for you.'

'And what might that be', asked Toby suspiciously.

'See if you can find the kitchen, there's a kettle in there.'

'You want me to make the tea?'

Fred pointed at White and Parsons. 'Well, we are all detective sergeants, and seniority dictates that a DC makes the teas.'

Toby poked Fred Williams in his ample stomach. 'I'm guessing you know where the biscuits are too.'

As Toby headed off in search of the kitchen, Fred Williams turned to his smiling colleagues.

'Nice to see he's got a bit of spirit in him.'

Fifteen minutes later, the three DSs and Toby had been joined by DCs Dave Dalton and Kinky Bernstein for the morning briefing. Unlike at Kings Heath Station, the pace of life in Stratford seemed decidedly sedate. Fred Williams stood up in front of the whiteboard, uncapped the board marker and took a sniff.

'That's better. Right, I've got the morning briefing notes,' he glanced through them dismissively. 'According to these we don't have any crime today. Any questions?'

Toby put up his hand.

'Yes, young Toby.'

'What do you mean, "there's no crime". There must be.'

Fred Williams frowned. 'There's a couple of burglaries and somebody's reversed into the butchers on Bull Street and driven off.' Fred threw the briefing notes down on the desk. 'It's hardly worth leaving the station for.'

'But …'

Kinky Bernstein put his hand on Toby's shoulder and shook

his head.

'Fred only likes crimes of a violent nature; he's longing for a murder.'

'I might be able to oblige him,' whispered Toby. He was beginning to think that his dream posting was in severe danger of becoming a nightmare.

Fred Williams took another sniff of his marker pen, it seemed to galvanise him.

'OK then, Ken and Tony can take a burglary each and me and young Toby will take a look into the butchers. Shouldn't be too hard with the front wall missing.'

There was a round of groans from the assembled detectives. Toby was silent, he was really disappointed that Fred hadn't allocated him one of the burglaries.

'Anything of a sexual nature?' asked Kinky.

Fred shook his head. 'No, but there was a report of a flasher on the cricket pitch at the weekend.'

'Male?'

'I would imagine so. We don't get many female flashers in Stratford, Kinky.'

'You want me to check it out?'

Fred shook his head. 'No, according to the report he wasn't well endowed, so we can class it as a minor incident.'

Kinky looked disappointed. 'What are me and Ginger going to do then?'

'You two can man the phones and be on hand should any major crimes take place. If there aren't any, you can run the milk float back up to the dairy. One of you can follow in the squad car. I promised Stan I would have it back before lunch.'

Fred turned back to the whiteboard and jotted down the allocations. He took a final sniff of the pen before putting the top back on. 'Any questions?' It was rhetorical, as all of the detectives apart from Toby were already moving.

'Is it always like this?'

Fred shook his head. 'No, sometimes it's really quiet.'

As they walked towards the car park, Fred matched step with Toby. 'Can you drive a real car?'

'Course I can, I took my advanced.'

'That's very impressive, young Toby, but have you ever been in a chase that isn't on foot?'

Toby nodded. 'Yeah, as it happens, I have.'

'Two wheels or four?'

'Two.'

Fred smiled. 'With or without peddles?'

'With.'

Fred jiggled the keys of the Cortina in his hands. 'In that case, I'll drive.' Fred whistled happily as he walked towards the car.

Toby slammed the door as he got in.

'Easy, young Toby, this is valuable piece of taxpayer funded equipment.' Fred looked across at Toby's sullen face. 'Have I displeased you in some way?'

'Why did you take a damaged butchers shop over a burglary?'

'Where there's a missing shop front, there's bound to be some damaged sausages or chops that may need to be taken into evidence.'

Toby looked pointedly at Fred's stomach. 'Should have known.'

Fred shot him a smile that seemed almost genuine. 'There could also be a more sinister reason. We've had a bit of rustling round here recently. Now, somebody that reverses accidentally into a shopfront is probably going to stop. If it's deliberate, sending a warning maybe, well, then you probably would hit and run.'

Toby began to realise that Fred Williams should never be underestimated. 'Blimey, I never thought about that.'

'Well, you'd better start then. Most things are never what

they seem.' Fred released the clutch and span the rear wheels as they left the car park. 'I was serious about those sausages, though.'

Chapter 4
Return Of The King

Sir Morris Oxford pulled up outside The White Swan Hotel in Rother Street. He turned off the engine and let out a long, deep breath. He was home once more, back in the place where he belonged. To tread the boards where he was King. A new season at the Royal Shakespeare Company and he was the star attraction. Many actors had come and gone during his long and illustrious career. Some had risen to challenge his dominance but all had been vanquished, by fair means and foul. Sir Morris would never relinquish his crown without a fight.

'Morning, Sir Morris, welcome back to Stratford.'

Sir Morris smiled. 'Good to be back, Carter. Have I missed anything?'

The little man shook his head. 'Not really. Mister Selby's Henry V was something to behold though.'

Sir Morris gave him a disdainful glance. 'Really?'

'Not a touch on yours though, Sir Morris,' he added tactfully.

'The part should have been mine. Damn director said I was too old to play young Prince Hal.'

Carter nodded. 'Well now you're in your sixties, Sir Morris, you get to play Caesar, Lear, Shylock.'

His words did not pacify Sir Morris. 'But look at me, Carter, I still look like a young man.' He pulled in his stomach several inches. 'When you're an athlete like me the ageing process goes slowly.'

Carter couldn't respond to that. The red faced, big stomached pensioner that stood before him was nobody's idea of youth incarnate. However, he was the great Sir Morris Oxford. 'Very true, Sir Morris, you'll be delighted to know we have added a gym to the hotel since your last visit.'

Sir Morris looked at him as if he had taken leave of his senses. 'I'm a natural athlete, Carter, I have no need of a gym.' With that, he swept past the porter and into the hotel with the arrogance of the deluded. Sir Morris was back in Stratford.

Chapter 5
A Pale Rider

Fifty miles away, one of the vanquished pretenders to his throne was crossing the Thames at Lechlade. The Angel of Death, Oliver Lawrence, not upon a pale horse, but in his second-hand Morris Minor van. He travelled towards Stratford jerkily, there was no synchromesh in the gearbox and he was struggling to double declutch. As avenging angels go, his progress was slow but unstoppable. He had a date with Sir Morris and all who had wronged him those many years ago. Oliver smiled and began to quote from John, The Revelator.

'And I looked, and behold, a pale horse; and his name that sat on him was Death, and Hell followed with him.'

Death was coming to Stratford, riding in a Morris Minor van, and Hell would surely follow. He began to laugh and didn't stop until he reached Burford. Burford was no laughing matter, the main street was very steep and the drum brakes on the Morris were terrible. He put the van into second gear and slowly ground down the hill towards the bridge that crossed the river Windrush.

The lorry driver behind him was unimpressed by his slow descent but Oliver didn't care, he had waited too long for his revenge. He wasn't going to risk crashing into a river less than fifty miles from his destination, there were places to go and people to kill. The lorry driver pipped his horn again and Oliver considered the idea of adding him to his list of potential victims. He pulled up at the traffic lights and decided he would pull in and allow the lorry to pass as soon as he was over the bridge; he didn't want to do anything that would stick in the memory of anyone who saw him. Death was a Pale Rider and nobody was going to notice him coming until it was too late.

Chapter 6
One Man's Meat

Back in Stratford, Inspector Beeching was looking disappointedly at the crime figures; there just weren't enough. He needed some real crimes to be solved. Petty burglaries and domestic incidents were not going to cut it, he needed something to raise his profile with the Met. If only someone would commit some murders.

His mother had always told him to be careful what he wished for; he should have listened to her.

The answer to his prayers was travelling northwards and the quiet, crime free streets of Stratford would soon be a distant memory. A time before the madness. A brief moment before the darkness descended and his face was plastered across the news.

Fred Williams pulled up outside what was once the front window of Mullens the Butchers on Bull Street. The front wall and display window lay in the road.

'That's disappointing,' said Fred.

'More like devastating. That wasn't a simple reversing mistake, to do that much damage it must have been rammed intentionally. I think you might be onto something, sir.'

Fred nodded. 'It's deliberate all right, but I just realized that there wouldn't have been any sausages or chops in the window display at night. Our hopes of a free meat feast are but a distant dream.' He climbed wearily out of the car, disappointment wrapped around him like a tramp's blanket.

Toby jumped out and followed him, keen to assess his first

crime as a detective. Glass and bricks were scattered down the street up to thirty feet away, clearly some of the bricks must have landed on the back of the vehicle that had rammed the shop front and been scattered down the street as they fled. Splinters of glass glittered in the morning sunlight; they were liberally sprinkled throughout the scene, bearing testament to the force of the impact.

'Jeez, they must have been doing twenty miles an hour when they hit.'

'Newton's third law, Toby. For every action there is an equal and opposite reaction.'

Toby nodded agreement at Fred's assertion. 'If you say so, sir.'

Fred bent down and inspected what was left of the bay wall. 'Look down here, young Toby. There are flecks of green paint on top of these bricks. I'm certain that if we look at some of the bricks that got knocked down there will be further paint flecks. Pretty sure the boys in SOCO will be able to find out what the paint is and which company use it.'

'Good thinking, sir.'

'Call uniform and get them down here. We need to put up some barriers, I don't want the scene disturbed.'

Toby nodded and went back to the car to radio in the message. When he had finished, Fred was already inside the shop and talking to the owner.

Nigel Mullen was a man who clearly enjoyed his product; thickset with a complexion of marbled beef, he was the epitome of an apex carnivore.

'I don't understand it, Fred. Why would anyone do this?'

'Well, that depends, Nigel.'

'And just what do you mean by that?'

Fred smiled patiently, which clearly didn't come naturally to him. 'Have you been buying poached meat again?'

'I would never do that,' he said, with an indignant air which would have failed an audition at the local amateur dramatic society.

Fred turned to Toby. 'Mister Mullen doth protest too much, methinks.'

Toby was taken aback. Fred clearly didn't believe Nigel Mullen, and he was quoting from Hamlet. 'Why do you say that, sir.'

Fred gestured towards Nigel Mullen. 'Because Mister Mullen, here, was convicted of handling stolen meat in sixty-nine, just three years back.'

'I was falsely accused.'

'So why did you plead guilty?'

'My solicitor is an idiot.'

Fred nodded. 'I can't disagree with you there; Ken Cadbury is clearly the product of many years of inbreeding.'

'Well, he is from Wellesbourne,' said Mullen.

'True, but you did plead guilty and there were three carcasses in your freezer with the Boffey Farm brand on them. The same Boffey farm that had twenty cows rustled two weeks before.'

This seemed to take the wind out of Mullen's indignant sails. 'I bought that meat in good faith.'

'Did you get an invoice?' asked Fred.

Mullen winced. 'It was a cash job; you know how it is, Fred.'

'Oh, I know how it is, Nigel. You going to start telling me the truth or do we need to go back and start inspecting the contents of your cold room and freezer?'

Nigel Mullen's marbled beef complexion turned somewhat anaemic. 'You want some sausages?'

Fred nodded. 'Well, that'll do for starters, nice bit of fillet wouldn't go amiss.'

Nigel Mullen knew when he was beaten. 'What about your DC.'

Fred turned to Toby. 'You like sausages, young Toby?'

Toby shook his head. 'I can't take a bribe.'

'There's no bribe. We need to inspect some of Mister Mullens' meat to make sure it's not branded from an illegal source. Once we've looked at it and handled it, we can't put it back into stock. Wouldn't be hygienic, isn't that right, Nigel?'

Nigel nodded enthusiastically. 'I'll just go and grab some from the chiller.'

'I don't want any,' cried Toby.

Mullen paused and looked at Fred.

Fred nodded. 'He does.'

Toby watched in horror as Nigel Mullen disappeared into the back of his open-fronted shop to fetch his bribe.

'What the hell are you doing, sir? It's my first morning on the job and you have got me receiving stolen goods.'

Fred held a finger to his lips. 'Calm down, Toby. I'm pretty sure that this …' he pointed to the shattered shop front, 'is a warning from Boffey. He knows Mullen's up to his old games.'

'Let's nick him then.'

Fred shook his head. 'Mullen didn't rustle the cattle; he just bought some cheap meat. The gang that did this will be selling it to dozens of outlets. They're the ones we want to catch. We nick Mullen, we stop one shop; we nick the rustlers, we stop it going into dozens of outlets.'

When Fred put it like that it made sense.

'But what about the sausage and steak? It's stolen.'

'We don't know that, Toby, that's why we are taking it into evidence. We will check to see if it's got the brand of the farm it was stolen from and if it hasn't, we will have to burn it because we can't return it.'

'So, what's the point?'

Fred winked at Toby. 'I don't know about you, but I'm going to burn mine under a grill until it's medium rare.'

'But what if it's stolen? It's evidence.'

'Freeze branding can be on the rump or the inner ear of a cow, sometimes it's inside the mouth.'

'But sausages and fillet steak won't have a brand mark.'

A broad smile spread across Fred's face. 'Oh, that is disappointing. Guess it's not stolen then. Yummy.'

Before Toby could protest, Nigel Mullen returned with two bags of sausage and steak. Fred took them both.

'Are we good then, Fred?' asked Mullen.

'For now, Nigel, but I would like you to pass a message on to your cash supplier. Stop it. We are going to be watching closely and any repetition will be punished severely. We can come back and inspect your books at any time and if they show any profits which haven't been generated from traceable stock, we are going to be forced to assume that you are at it. Do we understand each other?'

Despite the smile on his face, there was no disguising the threat in Fred's tone. Nigel Mullen knew when he was beaten.

'What you going to do about my wall?'

'Do I look like a bricklayer?'

Mullen shook his head.

'But I will let the Boffey boys know that you no longer sell meat of dubious provenance.'

Mullen's face twisted in confusion. 'I wouldn't buy French meat.'

Fred looked at Toby with disgust. 'Can you believe some people are allowed to roam free.'

He turned back to Nigel Mullen. 'It's not Provence, it's provenance.'

Mullen looked none the wiser.

'Stolen, Nigel. I will inform the Boffey brothers that you are no longer in the stolen meat market, which should reduce their desire to come around here and break things. Next time it could be your legs.'

'But what about my wall, who's going to pay for that?'

'Use the wages of sin you've acquired over the years, Nigel.'

'The wages of sin are death,' whispered Toby.

Fred smiled at him. 'He's already brain-dead, his legs just haven't realised it yet.' He turned back to Mullen. 'We done here then, Nigel?'

Mullen nodded.

'You want me to get Shaun the Brick round here? He'll sort that for you in no time.'

'Does he work for cash?'

'He's a builder, you do the maths.'

And, with that, Fred Williams turned and walked back to the car. When he reached the door, he paused for a second and looked over at Mullen.

'I'm going to put this in the book as an accident; some late-night reveller who hit your wall and didn't stop because he was probably over the limit. That suit you?'

Mullen nodded. 'Suppose.'

'Excellent. Case closed.' He opened the door and jumped in. 'Come on then, Toby, let's get these sausages round to my place and get them in the fridge.'

Toby reluctantly climbed in alongside him. 'What just happened, sir?'

Fred grinned. 'We just solved a crime by making it disappear.'

'Is that legal?'

'Do those two bags of steak and sausage lie? A reward from a grateful member of the community. No crime, so now they won't need to be taken into evidence.'

Toby wasn't so sure. 'Haven't we just taken a bribe to ignore a case of rustling?'

Fred turned to him like a patient teacher talking to an extremely dense pupil. 'We have just prevented two future crimes. Mullen won't buy any more stolen meat and the Boffeys won't have to come round here and break his legs. Crime prevention is good policing.'

'What about the sausages?'

'What sausages?' Fred started the car and began to whistle happily as they pulled away. DS Williams, like God, moved in mysterious ways.

Chapter 7
Foul Crimes Done

The Morris Minor puttered into Stratford on the old Oxford Road. As the familiar landmarks came into view, Oliver found his hands gripping the steering wheel tightly. The spire of Holy Trinity Church rose like a phoenix from the ashes of his past. The place where Shakespeare was baptised, where he worshipped and where he was buried. A holy place and a sacred spot for an actor like Oliver. He could sense William's presence. He would understand that, like Caesar, he needed to be revenged. Unlike Caesar, he was still alive to take his revenge in person. First there would be words, then blows.

As he crossed the old bridge into town, the theatre rose above the marina on his left-hand side. He slowed; it seemed like only a day had passed since he had last been here. The place where he was the prince, the heir apparent to the throne. Sir Morris Oxford had betrayed him. Lovely, kindly Uncle Morris, who had stabbed him in the back, just as he had his father. Like the Montagues and the Capulets, there was a blood feud to be settled. But first, lunch.

Crunching down the gears, Oliver turned onto Waterside and drove slowly towards the theatre, taking in the beauty of the façade and then the magnificent dome of the Swan Theatre. So many nights he had played upon that stage, the cheering of the audience still rang in his memory. He felt cheated, robbed of the crown that would have been his, and yet he still felt a love for the place. He had been happy here and would be again as he watched his enemies fall, one by one.

He pulled up outside the Dirty Duck, where he would test his new look. He had been a regular for six years; there would be people in there who had known him, but time and planning had changed him. Gone were the dark flowing locks. The warm sun and sea air of Morocco had bleached all traces of deep brown leaving a blond head of hair which he had cut short. No doubt the cooler, damper surroundings of Stratford would allow his hair to resume its natural colour. He carried a bottle of bleach to ensure that it wouldn't. The soft, slightly rounded features had also gone. Hard times and hard work had turned his jawline into something far more chiselled and muscular. He had left a boy and returned a man. His voice had changed too; deepened and hardened.

He exited the car, climbed the steps and looked up at the sign for The Black Swan. He smiled. Only tourists called it that. To the locals it had been the Dirty Duck for years. The nickname was alleged to have come from American GIs who had been based on the other side of the Avon during World War Two. The name had stuck and the Dirty Duck had become part of the Stratford legend. As he entered, he felt a sudden rush of déjà vu. Nothing had changed. The table he had sat at with Dame Suzy Tench, who wasn't a dame then, was still there. He walked across, looked at it and smiled. It still bore the signature that she had scrawled one night after a performance of The Taming of the Shrew.

'What can I get you?'

Oliver looked up. There, behind the bar, was Dick Mayrick. They had played rugby together. Dick's family had run the pub for many years and he and Oliver had been friends. He would soon know if he had changed enough to not be recognised. 'Pint of bitter, please.'

Dick smiled. The years had been kind to him, clearly, he was still playing rugby. 'You here on holiday?'

Oliver nodded. 'Sort of. Bit of a busman's holiday, really.'

'Why, you an actor then? We get all the stars in here.'

'I know. I used to act but now I'm a playwright.'

'You've come to the right place for that. What kind of plays?' Dick nodded towards the theatre. 'You got anything on at the Swan?'

Oliver laughed and shook his head. 'Nothing as grand as that. I'm reinterpreting three tragedies of Shakespeare for a modern audience.'

'Good luck with that, the folks that come here won't like it.'

Oliver nodded. 'No, I realise that. I'm doing it for TV. Taking it to a bigger audience. Bringing them alive for people who have never seen the real thing.'

Dick nodded. 'I take it back, the folks round here will like that. Taking the Bard to a bigger audience is good for business. Do a good job with it and I may end up paying for your beer.'

'I do hope so. I'm planning on creating a few waves, maybe get some news coverage.' Oliver didn't expand on the type of news coverage. The murders in his version would be real.

'You want something to eat with that?' asked Dick.

Now that he thought about it, Oliver realised that he was starving. He hadn't eaten since he got off the ferry. 'What have you got?'

'I can do you a ploughman's lunch or a ham and cheese cob. If you want something hot, I can throw a pie in the microwave.'

'What's a microwave?'

The question seemed to stump Dick, but only for a moment. 'It's like being nuked.'

Oliver looked doubtful. 'Is that safe.'

Dick smiled. 'Too soon to tell, it's bloody quick though. Got it from the US. You just sling something in, nuke it for two minutes and, hey presto, it's cooked.'

'You mean like gamma rays or something?'

Dick shrugged. 'I dunno, all I know is it's quick. Been using it for two months now and nobody's had their head fall off.'

'Well, with an endorsement like that I'd be crazy not to.

What pies have you got?'

'We've got mince and onion, mince and mushroom, and mince.'

'Is that beef or lamb mince?'

Dick shrugged. 'It's mince, mince. I buy in bulk and it doesn't specify.'

Oliver smiled. 'I'll have a ploughman's, please.'

Chapter 8
Sometimes You Have To Do Wrong To Do Right

Just a mile away from the Dirty Duck, Toby and Fred pulled up on the car park at the back of Guild Street Police Station.

Fred smiled. 'Thank God for that,' he said.

'For what?' asked Toby.

Fred pointed to where his milk float had been parked.

'Kinky and Ginger got it back to the dairy just in time by the look of it.' Fred nodded towards the big Rover 3500. 'You see that pimp wagon over there?'

'You can't really miss it,' said Toby.

'That belongs to The Supreme Lord, the Destroyer of Worlds.'

'I didn't know you were married.'

Fred turned to Toby and actually smiled. 'You know, young Toby; you're quite amusing in an acquired sort of way. Clearly, you've never been married.'

'You have then.'

Fred shuddered. 'Several times. The first time for love, she left me for a postman. The second time, the triumph of optimism over common sense, I married her for a secure home life. She wasn't a looker, but then neither am I. In the kitchen, however, she was amazing. I put on four stone in two years. If she hadn't left me, I would probably have exploded.'

'Why did she leave you?'

'Irreconcilable differences.'

Toby looked questioningly at Fred.

He sighed. 'I told her that her puff pastry needed more puff.'

'She left you for that.'

'You've never been married, Toby. Take it from me that conversations when married are like walking through a minefield; one wrong word, inflection, even praise that isn't quite full enough and it's ...' he paused, regret and sadness falling across his features like a cloud slowly covering a mountain.

'Over,' offered Toby.

'Over,' agreed Fred.

'Was it just two then?'

'No, there was a third Mrs Williams.' A huge grin split his features. 'I married her out of pure lust.'

'Did it work out?'

'Hell yes, best month of my life.' Fred didn't expand on this. His gaze had come to rest once more on the big Rover. 'The Supreme Commander is the reason I'm still only a DS after twenty years.'

'Who is it?'

'Chief Constable Wilson, the lord of Warwickshire and all he surveys. Never caught a villain in his life but acts like he's Dixon of Dock Green.'

'You're not a fan then.'

Fred shook his head. 'You could say that, young Toby. Let's get in and see what the slimy toad wants.'

Fred eased himself from behind the wheel and took off towards the station like a condemned man. It was obvious that there was history between Fred and Wilson. Toby decided to hang back and let it reveal itself.

As they entered CID, Chief Constable Wilson swung around to greet them. He had been talking to a rather pale looking Inspector Beeching. His eyes fell upon Fred.

'Ah, DS Williams. Just returning from brutalising the good

people of Stratford, I assume.'

'No, sir, not today. My knuckles are still too sore from the pub fight I broke up last week.'

'Throw anyone down the stairs?'

It was a caustic remark and Fred Williams ignored it. 'To what do we owe the pleasure, sir.'

Wilson smiled; it wasn't a pleasant look. 'Thought I would come down and see why you boys seem to be underperforming. You don't appear to be solving many cases.'

'This is Stratford, sir, not Coventry or Birmingham. We don't get a lot of crime here.'

'Just as well. As I arrived I saw Detective Bernstein driving a milk float down the high street. Not going to catch many criminals in that, is he.'

'He could creep up on them.'

Toby sniggered at Fred's joke; he couldn't help himself. It was a mistake.

Wilson's snake like eyes turned to him and looked him up and down disapprovingly. 'And who is this cackling hyena?'

Beeching stepped forward. 'DC Toby Marlowe, sir, he's just joined us from Birmingham. Comes highly recommended.'

'So why is he working with Williams?'

There was an awkward silence. Mistakenly, Toby filled it. 'DS Williams has been showing me the ropes, sir.'

'The only rope Williams knows about is the one he uses to trip his interviewees up with so they can fall down the stairs. Take it from me, lad, any advice you get from him needs to be ignored.'

There was an awkward silence. Beeching looked on, unable or unwilling to stand up for his senior detective. Fred just stood there, taking the barbs that Wilson was throwing his way without reply. From behind him, Toby could see his fists clenching. Again, Toby felt the need to fill the void in the conversation.

'DS Williams is our most decorated officer, sir.'

It was Wilson's turn to laugh and he did it loudly.

'We didn't have a choice, we either gave him an award or arrested him for assault. Not a good look when we are trying to police consensually.' He pointed dismissively at Fred. 'I advise you not to use Williams here as a role model. He's a loose cannon, a rule breaker and he's not averse to bending the truth to fit his facts.'

'I get results though, don't I.' Fred's words were harsh and took Wilson by surprise.

'Beating a confession out of a criminal isn't the way forward, this is 1972.'

'But if he's guilty ...'

Wilson cut him off. 'We follow the procedure.'

'Always, sir,' said Fred.

'Don't make me laugh, Williams. You're a dinosaur. You roam around Warwickshire like a T-Rex with a hangover. Terrorising suspects, beating up members of the community that haven't even confessed yet.'

'That's why they need beating, sir. I've always found that if you soften their features a little they tend to co-operate.'

'But what if they're innocent, man?'

'Been doing this a long time, sir, I know a guilty man when I arrest one.'

Wilson shook his head. 'Is that a fact, Williams. Well, if you're so good why do we need a judge and a jury? Let's just send them straight to jail!'

'Good idea, sir, save a fortune in court fees.'

Beeching cleared his throat. 'DS Williams has our highest clear up rate, sir. Nabbed more villains than any other detective in Warwickshire last year.'

Wilson fixed him with a cold stare. 'I'm sure you like the clear up rate that Williams here is bringing you, but what if a more stringent burden of proof gets applied? We could find ourselves getting sued for wrongful arrest. That's not going to look good on your ledger, is it?'

Beeching knew better than to argue with his superior, but if he was to progress up the career ladder he knew he was going to need Williams.

'Could you and Toby get down to the racecourse. Apparently somebody tried to rob Tommy Vaughan last night.'

Fred laughed. 'That's ironic, old Tommy has been robbing the punters for years.'

'That's exactly what I'm on about, Williams,' snapped Chief Constable Wilson. 'A total disrespect for the people we police. An innocent man is attacked and you think it's funny?'

'With due respect, sir, it is. Tommy Vaughn is a rogue. He's got a rap sheet longer than a vicar's sermon.'

'Whatever happened to innocent until proven guilty, Williams?'

'Does that apply to me too, sir?'

Again, Toby couldn't help himself and sniggered.

Wilson turned on him once more. 'That wasn't funny DC …'

'Marlowe, sir,' said Toby.

'Marlowe. You need to watch your step. Williams here is the perfect example of how not to police in a modern police force. He's a throwback to a bygone age when dinosaurs ruled the Earth. Policing is changing and you better change with it or you'll end up on the scrapheap with DS Williams here.'

There was an awkward silence, which Beeching stepped in to fill. 'Get on down to the racecourse before Tommy Vaughan forgets who hit him.'

Fred turned on his heel without saluting, nodding or acknowledging his chief constable in any way. The contempt he held Wilson in was clear for all to see. As he disappeared through the door, Toby was left standing awkwardly in front of his two superiors. He nodded uncomfortably and then, for some reason, clicked his heels like a German officer and saluted. Even as he did it, he was cursing himself. Wilson and Beeching watched him go.

'Is he quite normal?' asked Wilson.

Beeching nodded. 'Well, he is from Birmingham but apart from that his record is exemplary.'

'You need to watch him, Beeching. Working with DS Williams will be corrosive. Last thing we need is another Fred Williams.'

When Toby got to the car park, Fred was already revving the Cortina. Toby jumped in and Fred screeched from the space before he had closed his door.

'What a jumped-up twat. Never caught a criminal in his life but I'm supposed to take orders from him.'

'Chain of command, sir. You can't fight that.'

Fred looked long and hard at him. Toby would have preferred Fred to be looking at the road.

'I know I'm good-looking, sir, but would you like to look where you're bloody going.'

Fred laughed. 'If I must.' Fred slowed down and visibly relaxed. 'I really shouldn't let Wilson get under my skin but he's tried to have me prosecuted twice.'

'What for?'

'Said I had used excessive force when I beat a confession out of suspect.'

Toby tried to absorb the implications of Fred's words. 'Isn't that implicit if you "beat a confession" out of him.'

'You're a clever sod, young Toby, but you can't beat a guilty man hard enough, even after he's confessed.'

Toby was confused. 'Wouldn't that be police brutality?'

'It would be if he was innocent, but he wasn't, so he had it coming. You should have been there, Toby. He had one of those faces.'

'What faces?'

'The ones that just need hitting.'

'Oh, one of those faces.' Toby smiled. Working with DS Fred Williams was going to be educational. 'Was he guilty?'

Fred winked at him. 'Probably.'

He waited for a moment while Toby went pale.

'He got away with a nasty armed robbery in Kenilworth two years ago. Night watchman took one hell of a beating but he had a clever sod brief and he got off with a technicality. I made a mental note to nail him and when the chance came I took it. It was a case of making the crime fit the punishment, might not have been the right crime but you just do the best you can.'

Toby didn't know what to say, first day as a DC and his boss was confessing to stitching somebody up.

Fred Williams could see the confusion on his face. 'Listen, young Toby, out there,' he gestured towards the mean streets of Stratford-upon-Avon, 'the deck is stacked against us. We need evidence, witnesses, motive and worst of all, proof.' Fred almost spat the words out. 'All these scumbags need is an element of doubt and a good brief and they can get away with it. When you've been doing this job as long as I have, you just know. You get a gut feeling.'

Toby looked at Fred's bulging stomach. 'That's a big feeling.'

'Sod off, you know what I mean. When you know, you know.'

Toby thought for a moment. 'You said Wilson had tried to get you prosecuted twice?'

Fred nodded. 'Yeah. Four years back. Big Trev Johnstone, nasty piece of work. Specialised in getting drunk and then going home and using his missus as a punch bag. We knew he did but she would never give evidence against him. Too scared.'

'So, how did you get him in custody.'

'Well, one of the neighbours phoned it in so I went round. He'd given her a right going over and I knew it was time to put an end to it before he killed her. It was raining when I got him back to the station. The stairs up to CID can get slippery in that weather.'

'They're indoors,' said Toby.

'Exactly,' agreed Fred. 'Must have been the condensation.' He paused to wink at Toby. 'Long story short, he fell down the stairs. Nasty fall, too.'

'And did he confess?'

Fred shrugged. 'I had to kick him back up, to allow him to slip and fall back down but, once he realised how damp those stairs were, he saw the error of his ways.'

'I take it there were no witnesses.'

Fred laughed. 'Course not, I'd told them to look the other way.'

Toby was beginning to understand why Fred Williams' clear up rate was so high.

'Sometimes you have to do a bit of wrong to do right. Big Trev went down for five years and Mrs Johnstone divorced him and married a lovely plumber from Tysoe.'

'What about Big Trev, didn't he come looking for you after he got out?'

Fred gazed down the road, his faced filled with happiness.

'No, Big Trev never got out. He upset someone in prison and got stabbed to death in the showers.' He turned to Toby. 'Happy endings all round.'

Chapter 9
Before The Cock Crows

Oliver Lawrence placed the letter on the table. It was four pages, all in the beautiful handwriting of Felix Richards, his one true friend. Felix had been an actor. For a moment in the late fifties, greatness had beckoned. His name was mentioned in the same breath as Gielgud, Richardson and Morris Oxford before the spotlight had proven too hot and his talent had wilted under the heat of comparison. Close proximity to fame comes with fear, and Felix had succumbed.

The occasional fluffed line, a momentary memory lapse. Instead of inhabiting his character, he watched from outside, playing it safe, taking no risks. The critics were gentle at first, but they could see the acting now. Felix did not stay long, his nerve was gone and television received him with open arms and an open cheque book.

Corrupt politician in Kangaroo Court, gangland Toff in Z Cars and then his big break in How Green Was My Sally where he played friendly gentleman farmer Hugh Bony-Dent. It was a massive and unlikely hit. Martian spaceship crashes in Willow Woods, a remote part of his Cotswold farm. The Martian, keen to avoid detection, then assumes the identity of Bony-Dent's wife Sally and comedy ensues. The critics panned it but the public loved it.

Felix's bank balance was assured but his serious acting credentials were in tatters forever. He played the part for seven series and then, when the extremely thin plot lines became totally transparent, he cashed in his chips and became a journalist and theatre critic for the London Herald. He was a fair and generous critic; the actors and producers loved him. Doors that would normally be closed to the press swung open for him, he was one of their own and trusted.

Soon he became one of the most influential critics in Fleet Street. All this came after Oliver had fled to Morocco. The information in the letter had been gathered when he was acting alongside Oliver, before both of them fell from grace just a few years apart. Oliver's fall had been orchestrated though, as the letter explained.

Oliver still didn't know how Felix had found him but his letter, when it arrived, changed everything. He leaned forward and began to read.

Dear Oliver,

This letter will come as a great shock to you. I have thought long and hard about writing it. As your friend, I feel I can no longer remain silent.

You and I lost our dreams upon the stage; mine was self-inflicted, yours was a foul and wicked deed. Those you trusted betrayed you, they schemed and plotted against you, whispered lies in dark corners planning your downfall. I saw it all. From the stage and in the corridors of the theatre. Gradually I pieced it all together, every bit of the puzzle, every detail of the sorry tale on these pages.

Where do I begin? There is only one place, the man who is the very catalyst for this tale of woe: Sir Morris Oxford.

Oliver had read these words before, many times, and yet, even now he could not fully comprehend their awful meaning. All those that he had loved and trusted most in the world had betrayed him. Felix wouldn't lie. He had no reason, nothing to gain.

The warm sunlight shone through the window of his rented terrace in Trinity Street, in Old Town Stratford, illuminating the words that would release a reign of terror the likes of which Stratford had never seen. He read on.

Your loving Uncle Morris engineered your downfall, he did the same to your father. You were both too good, threats to his crown, and he cut you both down.

Oliver was only four when his father died. Richard Jenkins had had the world at his feet. In his first full season at Stratford, he had been given the role of Coriolanus. It was almost unheard of, so much responsibility for such a young actor, but the artistic director saw something in him. It was a triumph, catapulting young Richard to stardom. The following season Richard was given the role of Henry V; it had been assumed that the role would go to Morris Oxford. If he was put out, he hadn't shown it, but clearly Morris Oxford resented losing the role. Oliver read on.

When Morris found out that your father had been given the role of Henry, he was incandescent with rage and he felt betrayed. The close friendship between him and your father faded. Morris became distant and then began to plot against Richard. Despite his towering talent, your father was a sensitive man who was unsure of his abilities. His confidence was fragile and Morris laid a plan to exploit this weakness.

The terrible way that Morris Oxford had poisoned the well from which his father's talent had flowed did not make pleasant reading.

Morris had friends in the press, Terry Fibs and Gerard

Soames, and they began a series of reviews that subtly sniped at Richard Jenkins' performances, undermining his confidence. Morris had also recruited Desmond Tharpe, a lifelong pal and workmanlike actor who, as part of Morris's entourage, was protected. A proficient actor, Desmond knew his lines and didn't bump into the scenery. He relied upon the protection of Morris Oxford to keep him in the company and, because of that, he would do anything that Morris asked him to do.

On stage with Richard, he would delay a line, slightly ad lib one, anything to throw Richard off his game. With all the bad reviews, these little things added up. Richard Jenkins' fragile confidence slowly dissolved to nothing. He began to drink heavily, and the broad Welsh accent that he had worked so hard to remove from his voice began to make itself heard. After one particularly bad performance, Fibs and Soames had christened him Llewelyn V. It was a disaster. The next night Richard was stood down and Morris Oxford replaced him. In the early hours of the following morning, Richard Jenkins was found dead on the railway tracks near Long Marston.

Oliver put down the letter. He had read it so many times that he knew each line by heart. This letter was the reason he was here; hidden away in the very heart of Stratford, just a short stroll along the river bank to the theatre and yet invisible. A false name, a new look, and a rented house that did not bear his name on the paperwork. Hidden in clear sight, waiting for the moment he would strike.

The letter had detailed everything and given him the names of all who had betrayed him and his father. All he needed now was to meet with Felix and look into his eyes to confirm it was all true. He knew it was, but murder is such a permanent solution, he needed to look into the eyes of the accuser. He also needed his help. Felix had told him to go to Trinity Street, he had rented the little terrace in a false name and paid a year's rent in advance. He would get a message to him when the time was right. That time had come.

Chapter 10
A Horse, A Horse

It didn't take long for Fred and Toby to reach the racecourse. Fred had fired the Cortina through the tight twists of Shottery, and then turned right on the Bidford road.

'Shouldn't you have the siren on?'

Fred skidded to a halt on the gravel drive behind the grandstand. 'What, and let them know that we're coming.'

'Tommy Vaughan was attacked last night.'

'You know that and I know that, but you have to admit it was fun scaring the crap out of the good people of Stratford. Did you see that old boy with the Labrador? I swear they both took off when I hit the siren. He walked into the lamp post.' Fred chuckled.

'He was blind.'

'You mean that Labrador was a …'

'Guide dog,' Toby finished the sentence for him.

'Well, he wasn't a very good one, they aren't supposed to react to road noise.'

'You let the siren off right by him. And what about the cyclist?'

'He'll be safer in the hedge.'

Before Toby could comment further, Fred's door slammed behind him and he was off towards the grandstand. Toby scurried after him.

'Why the hurry?' asked Toby.

'If Tommy's still confused from the beating, we might be able to get the truth out of him.'

Toby followed Fred through a door at the back of the grandstand. It led onto a corridor and Fred hurried down it until he came to a door bearing the legend, 'Manager.' He entered without knocking. Behind the desk was an elegant gent dressed in tweed; tweed jacket, tweed trousers and tweed waistcoat.

'Hello, Frederick, you here for Tommy?'

His accent was pure Public School, the plum in his mouth must have been very large.

'Hello, Cedric. Yeah, where is the old scoundrel?'

'I put him in the bar with a brandy.'

'How is he?'

'Vague and confused.'

'No change then.'

Cedric smiled. 'I say, Frederick, that's not very charitable. Poor chaps had a good hard bash on the bonce.'

'Well hopefully it's knocked some sense into him.'

Cedric smiled. 'Oh, I don't think they hit him hard enough for that, old boy.'

Fred nodded. 'Right, better go and have a word then, any chance …'

Before he could finish his sentence, Cedric held up his hand. 'Two teas and two bacon rolls?'

Fred nodded his appreciation. 'You may be an upper-class twat, Cedric, but you're all right.'

'Damned by faint praise as always, Frederick.' He turned to Toby. 'And who might you be?'

'DC Toby Marlowe, sir, pleased to meet you.'

'Likewise, I'm sure. Have you been teamed with Frederick as a punishment?'

Fred smiled. 'I'm part of his training; they've teamed him with me because I'm such a great role model.' Fred gestured for Toby to follow.

'Only if he wants to be Genghis Khan,' whispered Cedric.

In the corner of the bar there was a fireplace. On this warm May morning it was unlit. Beside it, seated on a worn Chesterfield armchair, sat Tommy Vaughan, a bandage around his head, cupping the brandy between his hands. He looked pale.

'Morning, Tommy,' said Fred. 'Been up to no good again. Whose toes have you trodden on this time?'

Tommy looked up and scowled. 'Fred Williams, that's all I need.'

'I'm enough for most people, Tommy.'

'More than enough. What are you doing here?' Despite his head wound, Tommy had lost none of his belligerence.

'I'm here to help catch the villains who robbed you.'

'Who said I was robbed?'

Fred exchanged an amused glance with Toby. 'You were found unconscious on the car park with a big bruise on your head and your swag bag was missing. Rob yourself, did you?'

'I must have slipped and fell.'

'Did you fall twice? According to the notes from the doctor you had a blow to the back of your head and a blow to the face.'

Tommy thought about this for a moment. 'I must have fallen back and then bounced up and landed face down.'

Fred considered this for a moment. 'That makes sense, Tommy … if your head was made of rubber.'

Toby sniggered.

Fred turned to him. 'So, what do you think, DC Marlowe?'

'I think someone that Mr Vaughan knew confronted him and punched him in the face, and then someone, an accomplice maybe, coshed him from behind for good measure.'

Fred nodded approvingly. 'That all makes sense to me. Why do you think anyone would attack an outstanding pillar of the community like Mr Vaughan here?'

'Because he didn't pay out on a bet.'

Fred turned back to Tommy. 'Because he didn't pay out on a bet. Did you hear that, Tommy? It's almost as if DC Marlowe knows you.'

Tommy scowled. 'You don't know nothing. I always pay out.

Honest Tommy Vaughan, they call me.'

'You've been called a lot of things but never that.'

'Sod off, Williams, I'm not pressing charges so there ain't a case to answer.'

'And why wouldn't you press charges when you've been robbed and beaten? Don't you think that seems a bit suspicious?'

'Like you have a secret,' added Toby.

'You don't know nothing.'

'Nor, apparently, do you.' Fred turned to Toby. 'Well, if Mr Vaughan doesn't remember who hit him …'

'Twice,' added Toby.

'We might as well get off and try and find some real crime.' Fred turned back to Tommy. 'If your memory returns, you know where to find me.'

'I won't,' said Tommy, rubbing the back of his head gingerly. 'I'm just a bookie. I make my money on the horses. Sometimes they lose, folks don't like that.'

'And sometimes they win and you don't want to pay them, Tommy.'

'I'm the king of the bookies round here. If I did that nobody would bet with me, I'd lose my reputation.'

Fred snorted with laughter. 'Your reputation has about as much value as a damp kebab.'

A pained expression crossed Toby's features, which Fred noticed.

'You don't like my metaphor?'

Toby shook his head.

'What would you suggest?'

'May lose his Kingdom for a horse.'

Fred nodded. 'Ooh! Richard III reference there, young Toby.'

'Yes, sir.'

'So wise so young, they say, do never live long.'

Toby watched Fred stroll from the room and realised there were depths to Fred Williams that had not been plumbed.

As they returned to Cedric's office, they found him bent over the photocopier trying to retrieve a piece of paper that had been chewed by the inner workings.

'We're off then, Cedric.'

Cedric looked up from the copier. 'That was quick. Tommy got amnesia?'

'Apparently. Seems he attacked himself.'

'He probably had a motive.'

They both laughed.

'I'm guessing he hadn't paid out on a bet again,' said Fred.

'That would make sense. Any suspects?'

'Half the male population of Stratford.'

'Case closed then?'

'I guess. Probably mark it as a suspicious fall. I can close the case file with a question mark for future reference.'

'Story of your life, Frederick.'

'Bugger off, Cedric.'

'You may want to reconsider that remark.' Cedric pushed two cups of tea and two bacons rolls wrapped in silver foil towards Fred.

'Consider that insult retracted, you are a gentleman and a scholar.'

'Apology accepted.'

They both laughed and Fred marched out of the office and headed for the car park with Toby in his wake. As they sat in the car, eating their bacon butties and slurping their tea, Toby felt the need to clarify the Tommy Vaughan position.

'Is that it?'

Fred shrugged. 'He says he wasn't attacked.'

'But he was.'

'You know that, and I know that, but without any proof or a

desire to press charges it won't go anywhere. If Tommy is happy to be hit, I say we should let him be hit. A few more of those might knock some sense into him.'

'There's something more to it, sir. He's hiding something, I can feel it.'

Fred stopped and turned to Toby. 'You can feel it, can you?'

For a moment Toby thought he was in for a lecture but a smile slowly spread across Fred's face.

'And you'd be correct, always listen to the facts but make sure you pay attention to your instincts. An experienced copper can always sense a wrongun.' Fred got into the car and fired up the motor.

'Where we off to now, sir?'

'We're going to the Green Dragon to find the lesser spotted Whomper.'

Toby didn't know what the lesser spotted Whomper was but he knew the Green Dragon was the toughest pub in Stratford.

Chapter 11
The Croaking Raven

Oliver did not have to wait long for Felix to get in touch. As he lay on his couch reading the local paper, he heard a click as something was posted through his letterbox. He froze. Only Felix knew he was here. He waited for a knock; it never came. Cautiously, he opened the lounge door and looked up the short hallway. On the doormat was an envelope.

He walked quietly along the hall, all the time listening for movement outside. When he was sure there was nobody there, he bent down and picked up the envelope. It was sealed but bore no name or address. He tore it open. He recognised the beautiful handwriting immediately. There were just a few lines.

Dear Oliver,

Our moment is at hand. Tonight, I will prove to you that all the accusations I made are true. We must be careful, Morris Oxford has his spies everywhere. He is a powerful man and Stratford is his base. We cannot be seen together in town.

Meet me at midnight at Kenilworth Castle. I will be at the top of Mortimer's Tower. You can park on the track at the south side of the castle, there is a footpath that leads to the gate at the base of the tower. I have a key; the gate will be open.

Felix

Oliver smiled. Dear Felix hadn't lost his love of theatrics. What an old luvvie he was, on the battlements on top of Mortimer's Tower. Clearly, he intended to be good King Hamlet. Well, if that's what he wanted, who was he to say no? If he convinced him tonight that his accusations were true, he would be set upon a path from which there was no return. There would be Ravens in the Mortimer Tower. Oliver gazed into the mirror in the hallway.

'The croaking raven doth bellow for revenge.' A dark smile passed over his features. Tonight was the start of something and the Raven would have its vengeance.

Chapter 12
Pleasure And Pain

In the Green Dragon, the clientele looked like part of the furnishings. Grubby and well worn.

'What does this Whomper look like?' asked Toby.

'Imagine a Hells Angel but not so angry.'

'A greasy biker then.'

Fred frowned. 'Not your normal greasy biker, Whomper took English Lit and Philosophy at Oxford. This makes him an interesting chap, and also a pain in the arse. You've been to university, haven't you?'

'Birmingham College of Art.'

Fred raised his eyebrows. 'What the hell did you do that for?'

'I wanted to be an actor,' said Toby, sheepishly.

'Well, congratulations, you have achieved your ambition. You can go over to Whomper and pretend to be a detective.' Fred paused for a moment. 'Do you need a second to get into character?'

'Sod off.'

Fred smiled. 'Sod off, sir, if you don't mind.' Fred turned and pointed into the dark recesses of the bar to a table that seemed to be engulfed in a fog. 'Whomper's in there somewhere, he smokes Gauloises.'

'Can I have a gas mask?'

'You were told in training that police work could be dangerous, just get over there.' Fred gave Toby a shove to help him on his way.

As Toby's eyes adjusted to the dark, smoky interior of the Green Dragon, he began to make out the figure of a biker. Jeans and a leather jacket that bore many badges and looked like it had lived many lives. Whomper was about forty, although it was hard to tell behind the droopy moustache and long dark hair that fell across his face like a weeping willow. A Gauloises glowed in the dark and Toby could make out intelligent eyes watching him.

'Are you Whomper Smith?' asked Toby.

The Gauloises glowed again. 'Depends who's asking.'

'I am.'

Whomper looked Toby up and down. 'And who might you be when you're at home?'

'Detective Constable Marlowe.'

Whomper nodded. 'So that beast in the shadows must be DS Williams.'

Fred stepped forward. 'Hello, Whomper, you want another pint?'

'That would be most acceptable, they also do a ploughman's which is survivable.'

'What about you, Toby. Pint and a ploughman's?'

'We've just had a bacon buttie.'

'That was a mere aperitif, a ploughman's is more of a main course, with a pint,' he added.

'A pint? I'm on duty.'

'You're in a pub, blend in.'

Before Toby could object any further, Fred was off to the bar.

'How are you finding working with Fred?'

Toby shrugged. 'It's my first day.'

'Still in shock then,' Whomper grinned. 'He's not your average cop, but he is the best around here.'

'I'm starting to understand that.'

'He moves in mysterious ways.'

Toby suddenly realised that he didn't know what Fred wanted him to ask and he was aware that Whomper was looking at him expectantly.

'Do you come here often?' The words were out of his mouth before he could stop them.

Whomper stared unflinchingly back at him, the smoke shifting around him, like a gorilla in the mist. 'Only on days with a y in them.'

Toby nodded. 'That's a lot of days.'

'All of them,' agreed Whomper.

Toby sat there as an awkward silence grew between them. It was only awkward for Toby, though, Whomper seemed amused. To Toby's relief, Fred returned carrying three pints.

'You managed to squeeze anything out of Whomper yet?'

'He's doing great, Fred, made me admit that I come here every day.'

'Did he have to beat that out of you?' Fred handed Whomper his pint.

'No, I just coughed it up, he was so intimidating.'

'That's because he's an actor, a man of a thousand voices.'

Toby tried to become invisible, which wasn't hard given the atmosphere in the bar. Both of them were laughing at him. He was grateful for the beer which gave him an excuse not to talk.

Fred did it for him. 'What Toby here wanted to ask you was if you heard anything about Tommy Vaughan's little problem last night?'

Whomper sipped his pint. It was a big sip and half of it disappeared.

'What problem?'

'Somebody hit him on the head, twice.'

'Sounds reasonable. To be fair the list of possible suspects would be a long one.'

Fred nodded in agreement. 'This one's different, Whomper, he was covering something up. I got one of my feelings.'

'You can get ointment for that.'

'I'm serious, Whomper, something's off.' Fred laid down a crisp ten-pound note. 'You heard anything?'

Whomper took his second sip and the rest of his pint disappeared. At that moment a call from the bar informed them that the ploughman's had arrived. Fred nodded to Toby to go and get them; the Green Dragon didn't do table service, it barely did any service.

When Toby plonked them down, they were surprisingly fresh looking. The miniature cottage loaf was a decent size. It was accompanied by a heart-stoppingly large chunk of cheddar, a pickled onion the size of a bull's scrotum and a generous dollop of chutney. There were also two mini packets of butter thrown in for good measure, just in case there wasn't enough animal fat to cause a coronary.

Fred nodded approvingly. 'Well, what do you think of that, Toby?'

'It looks like a suicide pact on a plate.'

'And therein lies the dilemma, can things this tasty be good for you. What do you think, Whomper?'

Whomper considered his ploughman's for a moment. 'I guess that depends on whether you follow the writings of Sigmund Freud.'

'Why, is he a food critic?'

'No, that's Clement, but Sigmund did propound the pain pleasure principle. Basically, we are all applying that to our everyday lives. We do things we like, say drinking too much or eating rich food, knowing full well it's bad for us but the pleasure overrides the potential pain. Our whole lives are predicated upon it.'

Fred took a huge bite into his cheese. 'I'm definitely in favour of the pleasure bit.'

Toby looked at Whomper. There was much more to him than there appeared at first glance.

'Why are you called Whomper?'

'When I run, I tend to express gas in a southerly direction. My ex-wife once described it as whomping. I try to avoid running these days.'

'He still "whomps" though,' added Fred, through a mouthful of cottage loaf and pickled onion.'

Toby nodded at the plate of food that Whomper was about to attack.

'Well, that lot's not going to help, is it?'

Whomper shrugged. 'Pleasure and pain, I've made my choice.'

The three fell silent as they devoured their lunches. Fred and Whomper like a committee of vultures, and Toby pecking at his like an anorexic budgie. The two watched Toby eat, they had finished minutes ago. Like vultures, they were waiting to pick up the scraps from Toby's plate.

Toby pushed it away. He had eaten the loaf and a third of the cheese with a bit of chutney. The pickled onion and the majority of the cheese sat there unmolested.

'You finished?' asked Fred.

Toby nodded.

Fred pulled the plate towards him and cut the cheese in half, he did the same with the pickled onion and then scraped half the remaining chutney onto his knife and dropped it on his plate. He looked up at Whomper. 'Fifty, fifty?'

Whomper nodded and the feeding frenzy resumed.

'So, what have you heard?'

Whomper wiped his mouth with the sleeve of his leather jacket. At the Green Dragon, serviettes were not provided.

'Tommy's been doing a Shylock.'

'He's Jewish?'

Whomper and Fred looked at Toby with amusement.

'No, he's been money lending again.'

'Who to?'

'Well, that's a good question, DC Marlowe. Who is Shylock's Antonio? The word is that he may be a high-ranking police officer.'

Toby and Fred looked at each other. If this was true, the repercussions could be very damaging for someone.

'You must have an idea, Whomper.'

'It's going to take a lot more than a lump of cheese and a pickled onion to get that kind of information. Besides, I need to verify it for myself first. All I can say is that if you look at your force it's someone near the top, in uniform.'

'Not Beeching,' said Fred. 'He's too ambitious to risk bending the rules.'

'It's not Beeching,' said Whomper. 'You have to go higher.' He leaned back into the shadows and lit up another Gauloises; the information hotline was clearly near closing time.

'Can you give us a clue?' asked Fred.

Whomper thought for a moment. 'Word is that the officer in question has a younger wife with expensive tastes. When I say younger, I mean much younger.'

'That should make him easy to trace,' said Toby.

'It should. Chief Constable Wilson recently married a young lady twenty-six years his junior!'

Chapter 13

Let's Talk;
It Is Not Day

Oliver chugged along the dark Warwickshire byways towards Kenilworth. He had avoided the main road and, as he traversed the quiet back lanes, passing through the attractively named hamlet of Haseley Knob, he could feel the anticipation building within him. Ten minutes later, he pulled up on the rough track that lay to the south of the castle. As he did so, the moon broke through the cloud cover and the castle walls were bathed in a phosphorescent light. A perfect night for a midnight rendezvous. Felix really did know how to put on a show.

As he walked ever closer to the outer wall of the castle, the mighty battlements of Mortimer's Tower rose above him, dark and foreboding. Despite the warmth of the May evening, he shivered. He reached the gateway that Felix had told him would be open. The chain was still wrapped around the bars but the padlock was unlocked; Felix was here already.

Oliver slipped through the gateway, careful to wrap the chain around the bars to give the impression that it was locked. He didn't think there would be any night watchmen but he had come too far, waited too many years, to take chances.

From above him came a hissing sound. He looked up. Silhouetted against the night sky was a head.

'Up here, Oliver, the stairs are to your left.'

Oliver waved a hand and headed into the darkness of the inner tower; despite the moonlight, he couldn't make out the steps. He pulled out his trusty Rayovac Sportsman and clicked it on. A beam of light illuminated the dark stairwell and he headed up towards the top of Mortimer's Tower, his footsteps echoing through the ancient walkways, following the ghosts of nearly eight hundred years. As he neared the top, Felix's voiced hissed once more from above.

'Turn off the bloody torch before you reach the battlements, someone might see it.'

He smiled. If Felix was so worried about being seen, why had he arranged to meet on top of a tower? As he reached the top, he turned off the Rayovac and emerged into the moonlight.

Felix was on the far side of the tower some twenty yards away. 'Welcome back, Prince Hamlet.'

Oliver chuckled. 'You are such a luvvie, Felix. Couldn't we have just met in the Dirty Duck?'

Felix shook his head. 'Too risky. I'm well known and, even with your new look, which by the way is very fetching, someone could have recognised you. Morris Oxford has his spies everywhere.'

'Isn't he a Knight now?'

Felix curled his lip. 'Unfortunately, little toady has smarmed his way to the top. Arse licker.'

'That's not all he's done, according to your letter.'

Felix moved to the edge of the tower. 'Remember me.'

'Course I bloody do, we've acted together.'

'Context, Oliver, the ghost of old King Hamlet tells young Hamlet to remember him. Who was the ghost of the old king?'

Oliver shook his head. 'What the hell are you on about, Felix?'

'If you are Prince Hamlet, then your father would be …?'

Oliver rubbed his head. 'Did you bring me up here so that I could throw you off? Forget trying to re-enact Act one, Scene five, just tell me the facts.'

Felix looked disappointed. Clearly, he had wanted to relay his story via the words of the Bard. He sighed. 'Very well, take a seat and I will tell you the whole sorry tale.' Felix pointed to two deckchairs leaning up against the west wall.

'I didn't realise King John left some deckchairs.'

'He didn't, I bought these beauties with Green Shield Stamps.' Felix clicked one open and passed it to Oliver. 'Real plastic, none of that heavy wooden rubbish.'

Oliver lowered himself gently into it, and it was surprisingly comfortable.

'There's a drink holder on the end of the arm.'

'Have you brought any drinks?'

Felix shook his head. 'No, I was just pointing it out.'

Felix placed his chair opposite Oliver and sat down. 'You ready?'

'I'm ready, but please just tell me the facts.'

'Philistine,' replied Felix, with a smile. 'The point I was trying to make was that if you were Prince Hamlet, the Old King would have been Richard Jenkins.'

'My father,' said Oliver.

'I didn't explain this in the letter. Like you, your father was a very great actor. He had come from the valleys of South Wales and risen like a phoenix from the coal dust of the Welsh mines.'

'My father never worked down the pit, grandad wouldn't let him.'

'I was being prosaic.'

'Don't be, the scent of morning will be upon us at this rate.'

'When your father came to Stratford, he was a virtual unknown, a spear carrier, but it quickly became apparent that he had a special talent. Morris Oxford took your father under his wing but Richard was becoming famous. Before long, Morris feared that he had a challenge to his crown. He also had the hots for your mother.'

'What!'

Felix nodded sadly. 'I know this is all going to come as a

terrible shock but your mother was having an affair with Morris before your father died.'

'I don't believe you,' said Oliver angrily.

Felix held up a hand. 'Just listen, you can ask questions later.' Felix waited for Oliver to nod his agreement. 'Beatrice was a very beautiful woman.'

'And a great actor,' said Oliver.

Felix shook his head. 'Not really, you were young. The nuances of a performance would have been lost on you. Your mother was gorgeous but she was often out-acted by the scenery.'

'I can't believe you would say that; you were friends with my parents.'

'I was, but that doesn't change the fact that your mother had the stage presence of a brick, does it.'

For once in his life, Oliver was speechless, and Felix used the opportunity to press on with his tale.

'Old Uncle Morris. That's what you called him, wasn't it?'

Oliver nodded. 'Well, he wasn't the lovely uncle you thought he was. In his second year, your father got the lead in Coriolanus and won critical acclaim unheard of for such a new talent. It was then that dear Uncle Morris began to feel threatened.'

'But why would he feel threatened?'

'When you reach the top there is only one way to go. Morris was old school, like Edmund Kean, he attacked the text like an enraged bull. Your father wasn't like that, he found the weakness, the sensitivity of his characters, and painted an emotional canvas. It was a different kind of acting. The public loved it.

I once stood at the side of the stage with Morris while your father was playing Coriolanus. You know the "If any think brave death outweighs bad life" speech?'

Oliver nodded.

'The way your father acted that night was amazing. I turned

to Morris and there were tears streaming down his face. "How does he do that?" he said. "I can't do that." And there were the seeds of your father's doom sown. I saw it in Morris's eyes, he was in awe of your father, he feared his talent. From that moment something changed in Morris and he turned against poor Richard.'

'What could he do, my father was amazing. If he hadn't killed himself, he would have been one of the greats.'

'Have you never wondered why he killed himself?'

There was something in the way that Felix posed the question that made Oliver shiver. 'He drank, he was depressed.'

Felix shook his head. 'But why did he drink?'

Oliver said nothing.

'Lovely Uncle Morris began to plot against your father from that moment onward. Losing the role of Henry V the following season was the final nail in your father's coffin. Morris gathered his cronies in the press, Terry Fibs from the Daily Smear, Gerard Soames from the Review, and they started to write slightly critical reviews. Like a dripping tap, gradually undermining your father's confidence. And then there was Desmond.'

'Desmond Tharpe?'

'The very same. He was Morris's lapdog, still is. A capable actor who would do anything to please the great Morris Oxford.

Morris asked him to start altering the cadence of his lines, he was playing Aufidius to Richard's Coriolanus. Basically, he was trying to throw your father off his timing. I even heard him deliver a false line and then just leave your father hanging. It was horrible to watch and nobody else seemed to notice, the few that did said nothing. Morris Oxford was a powerful chap.'

None of this had been in the letter.

'How can you be so sure?'

'I was there, Oliver, and Richard was my friend. Morris didn't have friends. He used people. If you couldn't help him look good, he wasn't bothered with you. If you were better than him, as your father was, you were a threat. He had one more trick to get to your father.'

'What was that?'

'Morris is an old-fashioned guy, so he decided to make your father a cuckold. He seduced your mother, like Richard III seduced Lady Anne, and then he laid the guilt of their affair at her door and twisted the knife slowly. He made her a shell of the person she once was, advising her to be distant from your father lest she give herself away. Your poor father, his stage confidence now rapidly ebbing, must have wondered why his beautiful wife was becoming so distant, so cold.'

'Can you be sure of this, Felix?' asked Oliver.

'Certainly, I watched it all unfold before me. Morris was clever. To most of the cast he was a ray of generous, revered sunshine, but he and his little coterie were gradually pulling your father's career and life apart. I'm sure he only wanted to end his acting career, like he did with you, but your father spiralled downwards. Near the end, Desmond didn't need to feed him any duff lines, he began to forget. He mumbled and other reviewers mentioned his apparent decline.'

Oliver felt the rage burn within him. 'All of this is true; he did the same to me twenty-one years later.'

Felix nodded. 'But you didn't throw yourself in front of a train.'

Oliver sat there in silence, digesting the story that Felix had told him. He had thought it was bad but this was worse; his own mother had betrayed him and his father. 'I remember standing on that lonely bridge outside Long Marston years later and wondering why my father had jumped. My mother said he was depressed and everyone in the theatre just told me how great he had been, how it was such a terrible loss. And dear old Uncle Morris,' Oliver scowled. 'He told me he would be my new father.'

The words hissed from Oliver's lips, laced with venom. He turned to Felix. 'You know I'm going to kill him?'

Felix nodded. 'You should. I was in the café at the theatre when the news of your father's death came through. Morris was with Desmond Tharpe, Theo Cumberbatch and Terry Fibs. Do you know what he said when they told him?'

Oliver shook his head.

'That's the first line he's hit in months.'

Oliver sprang from his deckchair. 'Bastard! I will see him and his merry band rot in hell for this.' He turned to Felix, the fire of pure hatred burning in his eyes. 'Let slip the dogs of war.'

Felix remained seated and surprisingly calm while he waited for Oliver's rage to subside. You can only be screaming mad for so long and, as Oliver calmed, Felix could see a terrible resolution had descended upon him. For a brief moment he wondered if he had done the right thing.

'Sit down, Oliver, there is so much more I need to tell you.'

'More?' asked Oliver incredulously. 'You have given me just cause to kill the greatest acting Knight of our age, two highly regarded stage and TV actors and two members of the esteemed British press, not forgetting my mother.'

Felix shook the index finger of his right hand. 'Not your mother, Oliver, she was as much a victim as you. Morris wore her down, tormented her until she surrendered.'

'She betrayed my father.'

Felix nodded sadly. 'You could view it that way but I knew your father, he was my friend. A complicated man, not an easy man, and given to huge mood swings. Life for your mother, especially in the last six months as Morris ramped up the campaign to undermine him, must have been hell.'

Oliver didn't look convinced.

'Trust me, don't kill your mum. Kill the rest of them, but not her. When you're done with them, you will be able to see things more clearly.'

Oliver leaned back in his deckchair. The clouds had scudded away to the east and the sword belt of Orion twinkled reassuringly above. He gazed over at Felix, suave and debonair, for all the world looking like he was waiting for someone to bring him a gin and tonic at the Garrick. 'You seem very ambivalent about me committing mass murder.'

Felix shrugged. 'That's because I am. They're a nasty little bunch, responsible for your father's suicide and for ruining your career. Up until now they've got away with it. Yours aren't the only careers they've ended. An evil cabal, a cult of personality, all built around the great Sir Morris Oxford. The world of theatre would be better off without them. We need a cleansing.'

'And I'm the sword of Damocles, am I?'

'If you want to be, Oliver. If you don't, we can just shake hands and forget everything I've said.'

A brooding silence fell between them. For almost a minute, neither spoke, until Oliver broke the silence.

'I will kill them. Sir Morris, Desmond Tharpe, Terry Fibs and Gerard Soames, I'll kill them all. I may even kill Tabitha.'

'Tabitha Tharpe, why would you kill her? She was engaged to you.'

'Even more reason to kill her, given the level of her betrayal. Since you wrote me that letter, I've done little but think back to those last few months of my career. You were right, so many worked against me. Undermined me, turned their backs when I needed them most. There are so many that it will take a whole season to work through them. I have it all planned out; revenge in three acts.'

Felix nodded nervously. 'But Tabitha, you were in love with her.' He leaned forward, his eyes dreamily remembering a moment from the past. 'Do you recall your time performing Romeo and Juliet together?'

'How could I forget, we were young and in love.'

'Yours was the most tender Romeo I ever saw. You weren't

acting, were you?'

A tear welled in the corner of his eye and he stared at Felix with a sad desperation. 'I loved her, she meant the world to me. There was no acting on that stage, I was that poor hopeless love-struck youth, lost in a love that I thought was real but she …' Oliver's words trailed off.

'Loved you?'

Oliver looked at Felix with pity. 'She was acting, it was all an act. She was good, I never saw it coming. She landed me like the prize fish of the season, the pick of that year's crop and then, with just a word from Morris Oxford, dropped me.' Oliver fell silent, his face a mask of sadness. 'She betrayed me, Felix. I don't think I can ever forgive her. What I thought was love was just an act in a play. She was faking it.'

'How can you be so sure of that? It was a long time ago and memory can play tricks on us all, especially when it's coloured by emotion.'

Oliver wasn't so sure. 'Tabitha was a capricious young woman, her moods could change like the passing clouds on a stormy day, but when the sun broke through and she gave you that look … it was like the whole world putting its arms around you. To realise that none of that was real, it was just an act …' He shook his head. 'That's betrayal.'

Felix wasn't sure how to respond. 'Does this mean you are considering adding her to the hit list?'

Oliver considered Felix's question. When he spoke he used the words of Romeo. 'I fear too early, for my mind misgives; Some consequence, yet hanging in the stars. Shall bitterly begin.'

Felix recognised the quote and understood its implication. Tabitha was now a definite maybe.

'That's a lot of deaths. You sure about this?'

Oliver grinned at him. 'There's something you're not telling me, Felix.'

'Is it that obvious?'

'You were never a great actor and you're holding back. What is it?'

Felix rubbed his chin thoughtfully. 'As usual, Oliver, you've seen through my performance. You always could see the join, couldn't you.'

'It was only a crack, most of the public would have missed it.'

'But you didn't, that's what made you special, like your father. You could look into the heart and soul of a character and become him. Me? I just wore the costume.'

'So, what is it that you're not telling me, Felix?'

Felix sighed. He knew what he said next would endanger the lives of many more people; actors, directors, press. He hesitated and tried to picture the faces of those he would condemn but, as he did so, he realised there wasn't one that he liked. There were none who hadn't helped to betray Oliver. Some had betrayed both Oliver and his father.

'The names I have given you are the tip of an iceberg, there are many more. I have the evidence of my own eyes and confirmation from several others. This betrayal ran deep. There is a sickness in the heart of Denmark which only you can cleanse.'

'Tell me.'

Felix shook his head.

'I won't do that, Oliver. It's too much to take in. Deal with these offenders first then see how you feel. Vengeance feels good in principle, but actually taking a life … you may not be able to do it. I don't think I could.'

Oliver laughed, but it was a cold, humourless bark that made Felix shiver.

'You have unleashed a monster, Felix. Fifteen long years I have wasted. That alone deserves a dark reward, but that it was my beloved uncle who led the betrayal … me, my father, my mother … this must end and I will end it. These others, give me their names.'

Felix shook his head once more. 'Too much, too soon. Do this and do it well and then we can move to the next act. For now, you must focus your hate to be successful. If you are caught, the game is up and the guilty will never face their judgement.'

Oliver liked the comparison to a play. Sir Morris and his band of toadies were act one of his revenge. Get through them and the scene would be set for act two. 'Very well, Felix, we'll do it your way. Where shall I begin?'

'Wherever you like but I would leave Sir Morris till last, let the old boy know it's coming. Let him feel the angel of death upon his neck.'

'Desmond, then?'

'A most agreeable point of departure.'

'I will make him sing like a bird, before I clip his wings … forever.'

Felix nodded approvingly. 'You know, Oliver, I do believe you could pull this off. All you have to do is channel your anger. Revenge can make you blind, stop you thinking. You need to be cold and rational if you are to succeed.'

Oliver smiled. 'Listen to you giving me stage direction on committing mass murder. Have you no scruples?'

'Not where this lot are concerned.'

Oliver stood up. 'Then, my good friend, I will take my leave and set out on the task you have set me.'

'I've set you no task, just given you the facts. Act upon them as you will.'

'That the disclaimer?'

Felix smiled. 'Sort of.'

Oliver walked over to Felix and lifted him from his chair. Felix felt the power in Oliver's body.

'Thank you for telling me the truth after all these years, you're a good friend.' He hugged him.

'I hope you still feel the same if you decide to revenge

yourself.'

Oliver smiled at him, turned on his heel and disappeared into the shadows of the tower.

Felix listened to his footsteps scamper down the many steps. They seemed lighter. Had he done the right thing? He had primed Oliver and pointed him at his targets, everything that happened from this moment was his doing. Dark days were coming and he had been their catalyst. He could hear the sound of a pale horse clattering across the moonlit road that headed back to Stratford. That'll be death, he thought.

Chapter 14
The Wages Of Sin

As they pulled up at Stratford HQ, Fred turned to Toby. 'Before we go into the office, just be aware.'

'Of what?' asked Toby.

'Chief Constable Wilson is a political animal; he has eyes and ears everywhere. Let's keep what Whomper told us yesterday to ourselves while we look into it.'

Toby nodded. 'Makes sense. You think there's something in it?'

'Whomper's seldom wrong. Get over to Coventry this afternoon.'

'What's there?'

'It's where Wilson is based.'

'What am I supposed to do there?'

'You're a detective, detect.'

Toby scratched his head. 'And how exactly do you suggest I frame my questions? I've heard the chief has married a big spending dolly bird.'

Fred thought for a moment. 'Yeah, that would do it.'

'Are you serious?'

'You got a better idea?'

Toby hadn't.

'Get yourself into the canteen there. Say you have been over in Leicester, questioning a suspect about a burglary in Stratford. You've just popped in for a cuppa and a sandwich on your way back.'

Toby nodded. 'That's plausible.'

'Wait until you get some uniforms in there, preferably on their own. Once you get into a conversation, just drop in the fact that you heard that the chief has got himself a new dolly bird wife. Then just sit back and see what comes out.'

'How long should I stay?'

Fred thought about this for a moment. 'Forty minutes max, anything more will look like loitering with intent. When we get in, if anyone asks, we've had a tip off and you are going to speak to a bookie in Leicester, that way the two stories sort of tie up.'

'OK. What are you going to do?'

'I'm going to ask Beeching about Wilson's new bride; he's bound to have an opinion given his upstanding membership of the local church.'

'You're not letting on that it's to do with Tommy Vaughan, though?'

Fred looked at Toby like he was an idiot. 'Why would I do that? I've just given you a cover story to interview a bookie in Leicester who may have some information.' Fred paused for a moment. 'Tell you what, let's leave it for today. You head over to Coventry tomorrow but don't come in here first, and don't arrive in the canteen at Coventry HQ before 1 p.m.'

'What am I supposed to do all morning?'

'Do what you're best at, nothing.'

'Funny.'

'I know,' said Fred. 'You have to make it look like you've been to Leicester, so you wouldn't have time to be in the office for most of the morning. Have a lie-in or something, just don't let anyone from the station see you, and don't drive through town on the way to Coventry.'

Toby knew Fred was right but the idea of lazing around the house for most of the morning seemed wrong, especially in his first week. He nodded.

'OK then, let's do it your way.'

'Good lad, Toby. Fancy a cuppa?'

Toby nodded. 'Yeah, I'm parched.'

'Good, two sugars in mine and there's some chocolate

digestives in the left-hand drawer of my desk.' Fred slipped out of the car. For a big man he was light on his feet.

Toby sat and watched his new boss walk briskly across the car park. DS Fred Williams was an enigma wrapped up in a mystery, one he would probably never solve.

By the time Toby had followed Fred into Guild Street Police Station, Fred was already ensconced in Inspector Beeching's office. Fred spotted him and opened the door.

'Make that two teas, white with two, and don't forget the biscuits.' Fred closed the door and resumed his conversation with Beeching.

'How you enjoying working with Fred?' The question came from DC Sam Bernstein.

Toby shook his head. 'He's not like any policeman I've ever known.'

Bernstein chuckled. 'He's not like any human you've ever known, he's a damn good cop though.'

Toby nodded his agreement. 'Can't argue with you there, Sam.'

'My friends call me Kinky.'

'Why?'

'I used to be on the Vice Squad.'

'Why'd you stop?'

'I started taking my work home with me.' Kinky held Toby's gaze for a moment and then winked. 'Tell you about it when I know you better.'

Inside Inspector Beeching's office, the conversation had turned towards Toby.

'How's DC Marlowe working out?'

'Pretty well, for a Brummie he's surprisingly intelligent.'

'You know he has a degree.'

Fred shook his head. 'We can't hold that against him.,

Beeching picked Toby's file up from his desk and opened it. 'Drama.'

'That's a degree?'

'Apparently. Says here he was the best actor in his year group.'

'That'll come in handy when I ask him to play good cop in interviews. I've always thought the force needed more thespians.'

Beeching wrinkled his nose. 'Really.'

'No, of course not, sir, but Toby or not Toby, that's the question.'

'What question?'

Fred was tempted to finish the speech from Hamlet but Beeching clearly wasn't getting it.

'I want to keep him with me. He's clever and he listens. I think he has the makings of a damn fine detective.'

'Good,' nodded Beeching. 'Will he be more orthodox in his methods than you?'

'To start with, sir, but I'm hoping to knock that out of him as soon as I can. Working by the book is all very well if you are chasing criminals that play by the rules.'

Beeching gave Fred a stern smile. 'He's not going to be kicking anyone down the stairs, is he?'

'Oh no, sir, I shall keep him on bungalow and low-rise crime to start with, he can build up to high-rise when he moves to Coventry.'

Fred said this with a straight face.

Inspector Beeching leaned towards him and spoke quietly.

'He can throw them off the top for all I care as long as it's justifiable homicide. I want results. Do what you have to do, Fred, just get me results.'

Fred nodded. 'Talking about results, I have something brewing away that may just tickle your fancy.'

Beeching arched an eyebrow. 'Tell me more.'

Fred held up a hand and pointed to an approaching Toby with a tray carrying tea and chocolate digestives.

'This is for your ears only, sir.' Fred opened the door. 'Come in, Toby, have your ears been burning?'

'No, sir.'

'Put the tray down there, please.' Fred paused while Toby put the tray down on Inspector Beeching's coffee table. 'I've just been telling Inspector Beeching how well you're doing.'

'Thank you, sir.'

'And he's been telling me that you have a degree in drama.' Fred looked playfully at Toby. 'Did you study Stanislavski?'

Toby looked surprised. 'Yes, sir.'

'Given circumstances, too?'

'Yes, sir, how do you know all this, sir?'

'I've trod the boards in my day.'

'Shakespeare?'

'Panto.'

Inspector Beeching shook his head slowly. 'You two are definitely in the right town, just the wrong job.'

'I'm not so sure. When you question a villain, you have to play a part, pretend you believe him. Draw him out.'

'And then what.'

'Then you kick him down the stairs, sir.'

Toby sniggered and Beeching turned to him.

'Are you aware of DS Williams' chequered past.'

'Yes, sir. Apart from the panto bit,' added Toby.

'Panto aside, DS Williams is a damn fine detective, you can learn a lot from him. Just avoid the throwing people downstairs bit.'

'Slipped in the showers, sir, for variety,' added Fred.

'I'd avoid anything that involves a fall if I was you, DC Marlowe.'

'Yes, sir, is there anything else, sir?'

They both shook their heads.

'That's all for now. Thank you, DC Marlowe,' said Beeching.

Toby left Beeching's office and closed the door behind him. As he walked back into the main CID office, Kinky looked up at him.

'What was all that about?'

'Stanislavski, panto and police violence.'

'What?' said Kinky, but Toby was already headed for the toilets to splash some cold water on his face.

Back in Beeching's office, both officers were now seated and drinking tea. 'Chocolate digestive, sir?' asked Fred.

'Does our catering budget extend to the chocolate variety.'

'I took these into custody after a ram raid at the Co-op, sir, just in case they had prints on.'

Beeching smiled knowingly. 'And did they?'

'Not the first eight packets, but before I could go back for some more I caught the thief and the insurance paid up. The Co-op didn't want them back so I said we would destroy them.'

'Burn them?'

'No, eat them, sir. I thought while we were having a cuppa we could destroy some more.'

Beeching chuckled quietly. 'You really are a law until yourself, Fred.'

'Thank you, sir.'

'That wasn't a compliment.'

'I know. Are the biscuits all right?'

Beeching took a big bite out of one and nodded his agreement. 'So, what have you to tell me?'

Fred looked over at the door to make sure it was closed.

'It's the Tommy Vaughan case, sir.'

'What about it.'

'I have an informant, a very reliable one, who tells me that Tommy has been money lending again.'

'Can you prove it?'

'Not yet. I have a lead that I am sending DC Marlowe to check out tomorrow in Leicester.'

'That's a long way to go. Is it worth it?'

'You tell me, sir,' said Fred. 'My informant says that Tommy was lending money to a very senior police officer. Senior, uniformed police officer.'

He had Beeching's attention. 'How senior?'

'Senior to you, sir.'

'Which force?'

'Warwickshire, sir.'

Beeching tried to absorb this information. Warwickshire was a small force, and, unlike the Met, there weren't that many bigwigs above a chief inspector.

'Someone based in Coventry then,' said Beeching.

The Warwickshire and Coventry forces had been amalgamated in 1969 and the major HQ now resided in Coventry.

'You would think so, sir. Apparently, the officer who borrowed the money wasn't keen to pay it back.'

'Well, you can understand that, Fred. Money lending without a licence is illegal and by paying it back he's committing a crime.'

'Isn't he committing a crime by borrowing it in the first place?'

Beeching leaned back in his chair and rubbed his chin thoughtfully. 'If he didn't pay it back, he could claim it was a gift. The second he does, he's admitting it was a loan.'

Fred nodded. 'That's a good point, sir. My informant did give me one really useful clue.'

Beeching leaned forward, sensing blood. 'And what was that?'

'The officer in question has recently married a much younger woman.' Fred waited for Beeching to join the dots; it didn't take long.

'Wilson!' Beeching shook his head incredulously. 'This can't be, he earns a lot of money.'

Fred shrugged. 'Word is that the young lady is quite high maintenance. No fool like an old fool, sir.'

Beeching sat back in his chair trying to imagine all the possible ramifications. 'This has to be very delicately done, Fred.'

'Delicate is my middle name, sir.'

'I've got hospital files that would beg to differ.'

'Fair comment, sir. You want me to make discreet enquiries?'

'Very discreet, just you and I in the loop. If this is true, the ramifications don't bear thinking about.'

'Oh, I think they do, sir. You root out a bad apple discreetly and that's going to be a feather in your cap. Opens up a bigger job up the food chain.'

Beeching shook his head. 'You're very sceptical, Fred.'

'I've been a DS for eighteen years. Never mind a glass ceiling, mine's made of stone.'

'Well, if you will keep putting suspects in traction, it's bound to go against you.'

'But they were all found guilty.'

'Only after a lengthy stay in hospital.' Beeching had raised his voice a little, he took a deep breath and then continued in a quieter tone. 'If this gets to the press, I will be seen as bringing the force into disrepute. We need to build a case that is bullet proof and then pass it up the chain. That's how we get rid of Wilson and we both get to move up.'

Fred was surprised. 'You think I could move up?'

Beeching winked. 'DI Williams has a nice ring, don't you think?'

Fred did think, it also had a hefty pay rise. 'I will get onto it tomorrow, sir … discreetly.' Fred stood up to leave, as he did so he reached for the half-eaten packet of chocolate digestives.

Beeching leaned over, picked them up and put them in his desk drawer. 'I'm going to hold these for questioning.'

'Fair enough, sir.' Fred opened the door of the office and walked back into CID. Detective Inspector Williams, it certainly did have a nice ring to it. As he made his way towards his desk, he made a mental promise that he wouldn't throw anyone down the stairs for a while.

It was a promise he would be unable to keep.

Chapter 15
Don't You Know Who I Am?

Oliver had taken the opportunity to have a lie-in. It had been nearly 2.30 p.m. when he got back to his house in Old Town. He had tried to sleep but everything that Felix had told him just confirmed the allegations in his letter. He wasn't lying; he had been there and seen what had been done to his father. He had witnessed history repeat itself over twenty years later. Felix was angry at the injustice that had been enacted upon Oliver's family, and his anger had passed to Oliver.

The news about his mother had come as a terrible shock but, for now, he would follow Felix's advice and leave his mother alone. He needed time to process the level of her guilt. For Desmond Tharpe, the case was proven. Oliver finished his cup of tea and pulled on his jacket. Today Desmond was performing in Julius Caesar. Time for a walk around Stratford. It was approaching lunchtime and Desmond needed to eat. He would try the Dirty Duck first.

As he strolled down Southern Lane, he watched as a rower powered along the Avon towards the weir. The river was wide here, with a gentle curve which allowed the rowers from the Stratford Club to get a good pace on. He sculled along smoothly, the rhythmic fluid movement of the oars against the water belied his speed.

Oliver, walking briskly, was soon left behind. He would be like that. Moving swiftly, but unhurriedly, he would move through his enemies with deadly precision. Removing them one by one until the stage, once more, was his.

He checked himself, had he really just thought that? Did he really want to stand once more upon that famous stage? He shut out the thought. In his heart there was no room for hope, only vengeance. He took a deep breath, let it slowly out and then smiled. One thing at a time, he thought. Desmond Tharpe, wherefore art thou? With a little skip in his step, he walked on towards the Dirty Duck. He heard a cry from the river as the sculler cocked up his turn and disappeared over the weir.

Dick Mayrick was behind the bar, he looked up and recognised Oliver. 'Back again.'

'Couldn't stay away.'

'What can I get you?'

'Pint of bitter please, Dick.' Oliver realised his mistake the moment he said it.

'Did I tell you my name?'

Oliver thought quickly. 'I heard one of the locals speaking to you.'

'Ah, I guess that comes with being a part of the fixtures and fittings,' Dick stepped up to the bar and offered his hand. 'Dick Mayrick.'

Oliver hesitated as he realised, he hadn't thought of a cover name. 'Francis,' he spluttered.

'Francis what,' pressed Dick.

'Er, Bacon.' Oliver made a mental note to slam his head against the wall when he got home. A wry grin spread across his face.

'Unfortunate. I do hope you will be using a pen name on your TV interpretations of the Bard.'

'Count on it,' said Oliver.

They shook hands and Dick leaned conspiratorially towards him. 'Let's just call you Frank.'

Oliver nodded. When he got back to the house, he would need to invent a whole back story for himself under the name of … Francis Bacon. 'Had any actors in today?'

Dick shook his head. 'It's only midday, got a couple of late lunch bookings though.'

'Anyone famous?'

Again Dick leaned forward. 'Desmond Tharpe and Theo Cumberbatch, coming in at two p.m.'

'Impressive,' said Oliver, trying to hide his excitement.

'Not every day you get Mark Antony and Brutus in for lunch.'

'Hope they don't fall out.'

'Not those two. They star in that TV show together,' said Dick, missing the joke. 'Can I tempt you to a pie?'

Thoughts of unspecified mince crossed Oliver's mind and he declined. 'Maybe later, just a ham sandwich for now, please.'

'Righto, pint of bitter and a ham sandwich, that'll be fifty-eight pence, please.'

That sounded a bit pricey, but Oliver passed over a pound note without comment. 'I'll be sitting outside.' He grabbed his pint and a copy of the Stratford Herald, and headed for an outside table.

The patio at the Dirty Duck was raised several feet above the pavement. He would be able to watch passers-by, searching for familiar faces while he waited for Desmond and Theo. He sat down, the sun on his face, a pint in his hand in the town he loved most. Life was good and, to top it all, his first victim was being delivered to him on a plate, a dinner plate. He couldn't kill him here though, too risky. Best just to follow him to the theatre, maybe even watch the performance and then wait.

At some point, Desmond would emerge from the stage door and he could just follow him down the quiet, dark streets of late-night Stratford and await his opportunity. How would he kill him? He realised that he really hadn't put much, if any, thought into this aspect of his revenge. As a potential serial killer, he really did need to plan better.

The lunch hour wore on. A handful of locals and several tourists had been in but, as two p.m. approached, he heard Desmond before he saw him.

'Of course, the man's a fool. Been directing those kitchen sink dramas in the north. Shoving a ferret down your trousers and getting your girlfriend pregnant while you're on the dole doesn't really qualify you to direct Shakespeare.'

Oliver turned discreetly to watch Desmond and Theo approach. Neither seemed to have aged a day.

'He did a really good job with Cathy Bugger Off,' said Theo.

Desmond scowled. 'Cathy, You Have No Home would have been a better title. Kitchen sink dramas, who cares? There's a big world out there, I don't want to spend half a play in a kitchen.'

'I think you're being a bit unfair, Desmond.'

'Course I am, I just don't like all these angry young men who seem to be writing all the plays today. Commies, the lot of them.'

Oliver smiled. Desmond hadn't changed, still a hanger and flogger. With any luck, he would soon be tasting some of the medicine he so approved of.

Desmond swept up the steps from the street and surveyed the diners already seated on the patio, keen to be recognised.

'Over here,' said Theo, pointing to the empty table next to Oliver. Oliver hadn't noticed the reserved sign.

Desmond squeezed past him. 'Good afternoon.'

Oliver looked up into the face of the man he intended to kill.

'Good afternoon, lovely day.' Oliver gave them both a warm smile and then returned to his paper, pretending not to know who they were. He knew this would infuriate Desmond.

'You're not from round here then?' asked Desmond.

'Yes, I live in Old Town.'

This seemed to irk Desmond. 'Do you not go to the theatre?'

'Yes, I do, regularly.'

Desmond brushed his hair back from his face with his left hand and gave Oliver his most winning smile. 'Then you would surely recognise me.'

Oliver pretended to scrutinise Desmond's features. After a few moments, he slowly shook his head. 'No, sorry, are you an actor?'

A sound like compressed air being shot through a punctured inner tube issued from somewhere within Desmond. 'Am I an actor? I am Desmond Tharpe!'

Oliver nodded. 'Oh, that's nice.'

He pointed at Theo Cumberbatch. 'I recognise you, though, you're that Sergeant Coffee off that TV show.'

The hissing of pressurised air from Desmond's direction grew louder.

'Yes, Coffee and Cream,' said Theo, desperately trying to hide his amusement.

'I play Inspector Colin Cream in that.'

'Do you, that's nice.' Oliver was having more fun than he had anticipated.

'I'm his boss!' Desmond's voice was now tinged with indignation.

'If you say so,' Oliver turned to Theo. 'I thought you were very good in it. You should play Othello.'

'What, just because he's black.' said Desmond, indignantly.

'Well, he is the Moor of Venice, he would be perfect casting.'

'Nonsense, man. That's a leading role, I've played it myself. Bit of boot polish and I was good to go.'

'I'm sure you were very good.'

'I was wonderful. When I wrung old Desdemona's neck there was sobbing in the audience.'

'Hold on, I've just pictured you blacked up.'

Desmond brightened. 'You recognise me now?'

'Yes, you were in the Black and White Minstrels on TV.'

'Good God, man, you need to get your eyes tested.' Desmond turned his back on Oliver and, as he did so, Theo looked over at him.

Oliver winked and Theo snorted with laughter.

An irritated Desmond turned on him. 'What do you find so funny?'

'I can't believe that anyone in this town could confuse you with a Black and White Minstrel.'

'The man's clearly suffering from a mental problem.'

A large grin spread across Oliver's face. That was the most fun he had had in ages.

Oliver lingered over his lunch and left when Desmond and Theo were having their final coffees. During the last hour, several tourists had recognised Desmond and Theo and asked for autographs. Two Americans had praised Desmond's Mark Antony.

'That bit where you wanted to borrow their ears, it was amazing.'

Desmond grinned distastefully. 'Friends, Romans, countrymen, lend me your ears?'

'That's it, borrowing their ears.'

Desmond turned away and caught Oliver's gaze. 'Good God, you see what I have to put up with?'

Oliver nodded sympathetically. 'We are all but actors upon a stage.' Oliver spoke the line as he would have delivered it on stage. A vague look of recognition crossed Desmond's face.

'Do I know you?'

'I shouldn't think so.'

'You have a wonderful voice, there was something very familiar about it.'

'Do you act?' asked Theo.

Oliver shook his head. 'Not any more. I prefer to write these days.'

'I don't blame you; the hours are a lot better. We'll be working until 10.30 tonight. You coming?'

'I don't have a ticket.'

Desmond smiled. 'Well now you do. Come to the box office at seven this evening, I'll leave a ticket for you, give you chance to see some proper acting.'

'I'd like that,' said Oliver.

'What's your name?'

Oliver leaned forward. 'You're not going to believe this. Francis Bacon.'

Desmond looked at Theo and they both roared with laughter.

'No wonder you don't act any more. Tell you what, I'll just put Frank on it.'

Oliver thanked Desmond and bade them both farewell.

As he walked towards Sheep Street, he felt happier than he had in years. He was back where he belonged, none of his old colleagues seemed to recognise him, which was very helpful when he was planning on killing them.

Chapter 16
Get Thee To A Nunnery

There were still four hours until the performance started, so Oliver decided to check out some of his favourite haunts. He turned left from Waterside and headed up Chapel Street. Near the top there were tourists wandering around what had once been William Shakespeare's back garden.

New Place was long gone now, pulled down by the Reverend Gastrell, the last owner. He had bought the house without thinking about the many visitors to Stratford, even back in 1759.

There was a Mulberry tree which had grown from a cutting that Shakespeare had planted; there was always somebody hopping over the wall to pinch a twig from the famous tree. The Reverend Gastrell did not display a very Christian attitude to this and cut the tree down.

This did not go down well with the good residents of Stratford and, when a punitive Tax of £2 was levied against him, he flew into a rage and ordered his own servants to gather some helpers and demolish the place.

Oliver smiled. Reverend Gastrell had clearly been an overly emotional man. It was like chopping off your foot because you didn't like your new shoes.

Legend had it that since that day, anyone called Gastrell was banned from living in Stratford.

He paused and looked at the tourists gazing upon the site of where Shakespeare had once lived and wondered how many of them had actually heard of the Reverend Francis Gastrell.

Oliver turned right onto Chapel Street and strolled into town. After about a hundred yards he turned left into Ely St and headed towards the antiques store he was seeking. He noted with delight it was still there.

As he crossed the road, he noticed a beautiful woman moving towards him, he was about to smile until, with an awful, gut-wrenching certainty, he realised who she was. Tabitha Tharpe.

He dove into the entrance of the small, brick-built gents that was just by the alleyway leading to the entrance of the antique shop. He pushed himself back against the wall and watched her walk by. His heart was pounding like a drum.

'You all right, mate?'

Oliver looked at the old man coming out of the gents. He was still repackaging his family jewels. Oliver made rapid eye contact.

'Yes, fine now, thanks.'

'Looks like you've just seen a ghost.'

Oliver smiled weakly; a ghost from his past. 'I did, sort of.' The man gave Oliver a confused glance and then hurried on his way. Oliver gave him a moment and then peeked around the corner of the entrance; he caught sight of Tabitha walking down Sheep Street. The words of the old man rang in his ears. 'You looked like you've seen a ghost.' An idea occurred to him, maybe he should be the ghost.

He hurried out of the toilets, crossed Church Road and began to follow Tabitha. Halfway down the street she paused to look into a clothes shop and Oliver knew what he must do. She had once played Ophelia to his Hamlet; it was time to let her hear the voice of a ghost from her past. As she gazed through the window, he eased past her and spoke. 'If thou wilt marry, marry a fool.'

Tabitha spun around looking for the source of the voice but Oliver had drifted past a group of foreign students and lost himself in their midst. He stepped into another shop doorway and glanced back up the street to where Tabitha was standing, gazing up and down the street in search of the mysterious but oh so familiar voice. Oliver smiled to himself. He had certainly disturbed the calm of Tabitha's morning.

At the corner of Sheep Street and Waterside there was a café with tables on the wide pavement. Tabitha sat down and ordered a coffee. Behind her was a table of workmen who had been working on the bridge. They laughed and spoke loudly, nudging each other and nodding towards Tabitha. She was indeed a beautiful woman. Oliver smiled and sat down at a table with the workmen's table between him and Tabitha. He waited for a lull in their conversation, when it came he picked up where he had left off.

'For wise men know well enough what monsters you make of them.'

Tabitha spun round only to be confronted by the leering faces of the four workmen.

'Who said that?'

They grinned back stupidly at her, assuming that she had overheard their lewd conversation about her attributes.

'We didn't say anything love.'

Tabitha shook her head. 'You did, I heard you. One of you was quoting from Hamlet.'

They looked at her like she was mad. 'Ham who,' said the fat one at the front.

'Hamlet,' said his mate. 'He's from round here.'

Tabitha stood up to confront them. 'Who spoke those lines?'

They looked at her blankly.

'Search me love, there was a bloke behind us but he's gone,' said the fat one.

'What did he look like?' she demanded.

'How would we know, like I said, he was behind us.'

Tabitha glanced anxiously up and down Waterside. She knew that voice but just couldn't place it. When she'd heard it for the second time, a cold shiver had run down her spine, like someone was walking on her grave. She turned away from the workmen who were looking at her like she was a little touched in the head. She sat back down and waited for her coffee to arrive

Oliver stood on the steps to the theatre, chuckling at Tabitha's discomfort. One more for the road he thought. He waited for her to finish her coffee and then followed her as she walked down towards High Street. She turned right off Waterside and started up High Street. The pavements were full of tourists enjoying the early summer sunshine. Here would be a good place, there was a crowd of Japanese tourists between them. They were in high spirits and he inserted himself behind them. Tabitha was walking directly in front of them, now was his chance.

'Get thee to a nunnery, go. Farewell.'

Tabitha let out a nervous scream and spun around to face the Japanese tourists. They looked blankly back at her.

'Who's there, who are you?'

The tourists looked uncomfortably back at her, none of them had enough English to answer her question.

As Tabitha stared desperately amongst them, Oliver had crouched down and walked around them and behind Tabitha. There was another group of students coming down the path towards them, when the two groups met his chance would come for a final word. He waited until Tabitha was trapped between the two groups moving in opposite directions.

'Wise men know well enough what monsters you make of them.'

With a frightened squeal, Tabitha turned and ran back towards the theatre. Oliver's work here was done. The once love of his life was now thoroughly spooked. Somewhere, deep in her subconscious memory, Tabitha recognised his voice and it terrified her.

As he emerged back onto Waterside, Oliver watched Tabitha hurrying towards the theatre and a thought struck him. If

Tabitha was his Ophelia, then Desmond must be Polonius. Cruel, sadistic, self-centred, Polonius. He knew now how he would kill Desmond. Like Polonius, he would run him through with a blade.

Chapter 17
Iced Buns
And Lost Romance

Toby pulled into the car park at Coventry HQ. It was a lot bigger than Stratford Police Station. He made his way into the reception and flashed his warrant card.

'Any chance I can use your canteen? I'm just on my way back from Leicester.'

The sergeant glanced at the clock. 'You should be able to get an iced bun and a cuppa, Mavis doesn't go until five. If you're lucky, you might even get a sandwich out of her.'

'Thanks, where do I go?'

'Through those doors over there then third turn on the left, might see you in there myself.'

Toby nodded. 'Thanks, I'll get you a cuppa and a bun then.'

'That's decent of you, you really don't need to.'

Toby smiled. 'My pleasure.' It was going to be a lot easier getting the sergeant to open up about his boss if he was eating tea and cake provided by Toby. He made his way into the canteen. It was unlike anything they had at Guild Street.

'You all right, love. What can I get you?'

This must be Mavis, he thought. 'Could I have two iced buns and two teas, please.'

Mavis looked him up and down, like a wolf assessing her prey. 'They all for you or are you looking for some company.' She smiled alluringly at him through a mouth that retained most of its teeth.

'The sarge is going to be joining me.'

Mavis nodded. 'You're not from round here, are you?'

'No, I'm based in Stratford.'

Mavis sighed. 'Oh, I do love Stratford, such a beautiful place, so romantic.'

'It is. Do you get over there often?'

Mavis smiled coyly over the tea urn. 'Not for years, my love. The blokes in Cov don't go in for that Shakespeare lark. No romance, see.'

Oliver did see. 'I'm sure you could find plenty of romantic types in Stratford.'

'I did the last time I was there. He quoted some Shakespeare sonnet at me while we were getting a leg over at the back of the boat house.'

Toby nodded. 'That was romantic, can you remember which sonnet?'

Mavis thought for a moment, an action that clearly pained her. 'Something about going into a breach.'

Toby tried hard not to smile as Mavis remembered that tender moment from years ago.

'Then he was stiffening his sinews ... it was all very romantic.'

'It sounds it. Stratford is full of artistic types.'

'You know the sonnet?'

'Yes, it's from Henry V.'

Mavis poured two mugs of tea. 'Henry V, you say? Sounded very romantic.'

'Not if you're French.'

'Well, luckily I'm not.' Mavis then grabbed two side plates and placed an iced bun on each. 'There you go, my love, that'll be fifty pence.'

Toby paid up and placed his items onto a tray. 'Thanks, Mavis, my name is Toby.'

'That's a nice name. You married?'

'Only to my work.'

Mavis shook her head. 'Ambitious boy. You remind me of Chief Constable Wilson, he's very ambitious.'

Toby's ears pricked up and he sat down at the nearest table. 'Oh, I've heard of him. Hasn't he just got married?'

Mavis's eyebrows climbed up her forehead. 'Hasn't he just. Married a woman young enough to be his daughter.'

'That is ambitious,' said Toby.

'Bloody stupid more like. She's a real handful from what I've heard. If she doesn't kill him in the bedroom, she's going to bankrupt him. I dunno how he does it on police pay. Took her to Monte Carlo last month.'

This was all music to Toby's ears. 'Is she a police woman? Is that how they met?'

'Have you met her?' asked Mavis.

Toby shook his head.

'You need to be able to read and write to join the police, she struggles with a shopping list.'

'So, he's not married her for her brains then.'

'Not unless she keeps them in her bra.' Mavis winked knowingly at Toby.

Toby turned his attention to his iced bun. As he munched down and relished the first surge of the sugar hit, he realised that Mavis had already given him enough information to cast doubt on Chief Constable Wilson's good character.

A man in his late fifties with a much younger, spendthrift wife. It was a situation almost guaranteed to end badly. As he drained his cuppa, Toby eyed the second iced bun, maybe the sarge wasn't coming.

Before he could succumb to temptation, the canteen door swung open and the desk sergeant barrelled in. He saw Toby and the unattended bun and made a beeline for him. 'That for me?'

'It certainly is. Cup of tea as well, milk two sugars.'

The sarge nodded. 'How did you know?'

'I'm a detective.'

The sarge looked at Toby, a smile playing around the edge of his mouth.

'Good guess, more like.'

Toby shrugged. 'It's a fair cop.'

'You want another cuppa, love?' asked Mavis.

'Yes, please.' He turned back to the sarge and held out his hand. 'Toby Marlowe, Stratford CID.'

The sarge reluctantly put down his iced bun and shook Toby's hand. 'Frank Godiva.'

Toby paused. 'As in Lady Godiva?'

Frank nodded. 'It's a very old Coventry name, hardly any of us left.'

'Killed off by Pneumonia.'

Frank looked puzzled.

'All that riding horses naked, catch your death,' explained Toby.

'Yeah, very funny. I've had that shit for twenty-five years, son.'

'I'm sorry, sarge, I couldn't resist, bit like your chief constable.'

Frank looked hard at Toby. 'What does that mean?'

'I heard that the chief couldn't resist a young wife.'

For a moment Toby thought he had overplayed his hand, gone in too hard too soon. Frank took a big bite of his bun and chewed it thoughtfully for a full twenty seconds before responding.

'The chief has done very well for himself. Imagine a cross between Marilyn Monroe and Diana Dors, but without the brains.'

Toby found he could. 'That'll keep him on his toes.'

'On his back more like. If she doesn't kill him in bed, she'll bankrupt him with her shopping.' The sarge winked at Toby.

'Took on more than he can chew, I reckon.'

'Maybe they're in love.'

Just then, Mavis placed a tray with two iced buns and two more teas down in front of Toby. 'Lust more like. Chief Wilson is the same age as me,' said Mavis. She turned and looked into Toby's eyes. 'I'm still sexually active, maybe I should try someone young enough to be my son.'

Toby swallowed hard and turned to the sarge. 'How old are you, sarge?'

Sergeant Godiva took another mouthful of iced bun and refused to be drawn. Mavis laid a hand on Toby's arm.

'Got you boys two more buns and teas on the house, had an over delivery today and I don't want them going stale.' She squeezed Toby's arm. 'You've got to keep your strength up.'

Yes, thought Toby, I'll need it to fight you off. 'Thanks, Mavis, that's very kind.'

Mavis gave him her lopsided smile and the sun glinted upon her remaining teeth which gave the image of a vandalised graveyard at sunset. 'I'll be just over there if you need me.'

He watched her walk back to her counter. She tried to sway provocatively but unfortunately it looked more like she had an arthritic hip.

'Buns are on you then, son.'

'Looks like they are.' Toby got stuck into his second bun and tried to ignore the hunger in Mavis's eyes as she stared longingly at him over the urn.

Chapter 18
Final Curtain

Oliver lurked in the shadows of the gardens behind The Swan Theatre. The play had finished fifteen minutes ago, and most of the audience had melted away to their cars and homes. The tourists were back inside their hotels and he was alone, waiting in the moonlight for Desmond Tharpe. If all went well, tonight would be Desmond's final curtain.

Oliver had watched the performance from the stalls at the rear of the theatre. He had been thrilled to be back in the place he loved once more, but the performance had left a lot to be desired. Both Desmond and Sir Morris had seemed to be quoting the lines instead of becoming the characters. The stentorian vocals were full of theatricality but, to Toby, it felt more like a pantomime. He could see the acting and he wasn't convinced.

The audience seemed to have lapped it up, which no doubt explained why Sir Morris and Desmond were still going strong. Ken Tynan would have ripped them to shreds if he had been asked to review it but most of the press wouldn't dare go after a national treasure like Sir Morris.

Being one of Sir Morris's close circle also protected Desmond. If this was the pinnacle, Oliver knew he could still, despite the lost fifteen years, regain his place on the stage. If he managed to settle old scores there would be a lot less competition.

Ten minutes later, Oliver heard the unmistakable sound of Desmond Tharpe addressing two fans who had been waiting at the stage door.

'Oh, Mister Tharpe, we loved your Mark Antony.'

'Of course you did,' he modestly proclaimed.

'Especially that bit about the ears.'

Desmond frowned but bowed theatrically. 'T'was my pleasure, dear madam. Are you American?'

'Yes, sir, we're from Gary, Indiana.'

Desmond smiled. 'That would explain the ears.'

The ladies looked confused. 'What's wrong with our ears?'

'Nothing, your ears are lovely.' He signed the programme and headed off towards the Dirty Duck.

Oliver slipped out of the gardens and followed him. He had planned to wait until Desmond emerged from the pub but if he met some fellow actors in there, it would make things tricky. Oliver looked up Southern Street and past the theatre where it ran into Waterside; there was nobody headed this way. He glanced back down Southern Street past the Dirty Duck … the street was empty. Now was his chance. Swiftly he crossed to the pavement and walked briskly up to Desmond.

'Evening, Desmond, long time no see.'

Desmond turned to him, and peered hard at his face in the shadows of the night. 'I'm sorry, do I know you?'

Oliver nodded and felt his hand tighten on the bayonet he had purchased in the antique shop on Ely Street just a few hours before.

'Yes, many years ago, we actually acted here at Stratford together.'

Desmond stopped and turned to Oliver. 'We did? Who are you?'

'A ghost from your past, come back to haunt you.'

Desmond gave a nervous chuckle. 'Very funny, now who the hell are you?'

'I could have been your son in law.' Oliver watched his words sink in.

'I don't think so. Tabitha was only ever engaged once and he is dead.'

'Are you sure about that?' asked Oliver.

Desmond looked closely at him. 'You do look familiar and you remind me of someone, I just can't think who.'

'Shall I give you a clue?'

Desmond shook his head but Oliver began to speak.

'Though this be madness, yet there is method in't.'

Desmond stood perfectly still; he recognised that voice.

'Hamlet, Act Two, Scene Two. Who are you?' There was uncertainty in his voice now.

'You remember me, Desmond, last time we stood upon that stage …' Oliver pointed towards the theatre, 'you were Polonius and I was Prince Hamlet.'

Slowly realisation began to spread across Desmond Tharpe's features. 'But you can't be, you're dead.'

Oliver thumped his hand into his chest. 'Apparently not.'

'But … I thought …'

'"There's nothing either good or bad but thinking makes it so." Do you remember now?'

'Oliver!' His name fell from Desmond's lips like a long-forgotten secret. 'Is that you?'

Oliver nodded. 'Could we speak privately?'

Desmond was clearly in a state of shock and agreed. 'There is a bench by the river in the cemetery.'

Oliver took Desmond by the arm and steered him rapidly back into the shadows of the gardens. As they got further from the street lights, he felt a little resistance.

'I need to speak with you in private. Nobody else knows I'm back and you're the only one I can trust.' He felt the resistance lessen.

'Of course, dear boy, you can always confide in me.'

Oliver smiled to himself. With just a little flattery he persuaded Desmond deep into the long shadows of the gardens.

He guided Desmond down towards the river and then into the clearing that lay at the side of the graveyard wall. In the moonlight, the huge trees stood like cathedral walls. Ahead of them a wall ran along the top of a bank, at the end, nearest to the river, there was a small gateway through the wall and the metal gate was open.

'It's just through here, Desmond.' Oliver pushed Desmond through the small opening and into the graveyard of Holy Trinity. They reached the bench overlooking the river and sat down.

Desmond shook his head. 'Bit creepy in here, couldn't we talk in the pub?'

'No, I need your help.'

'Where have you been? We all thought you were dead. I didn't recognise you until you spoke those lines.'

'I still have it then.'

'Of course you do. I always said you would go far.'

'I did. Morocco.'

'Why?' Clearly Desmond had failed to remember why. Oliver reminded him.

'Because my lovely Uncle Morris decided that I was getting too big for my boots. Like my father.'

Desmond looked confused. 'What, surely you're not suggesting …'

Oliver cut him short. 'Not suggesting, stating. Morris Oxford decided that I was a threat and he got his cronies, people like you, to take against me. To give me bad reviews. To feed me faulty lines.'

There was an edge to Oliver's voice now and, for the first time, Desmond's voice betrayed fear.

'Why would I do that?'

'Because Morris told you to. You did it to my father and you did it to me.'

Desmond shook his head. 'Now listen here, Oliver, I don't

know where you got this idea from but ...'

'Felix Richards, he told me everything.'

The mention of his name was like a dagger going into Desmond's portrayal of innocence. The lies that had been held for so long began to leak out.

'It wasn't like that; you know I always liked you but ...'

'But what?' Oliver was standing now, looking down on Desmond.

'You know Morris, he has to be the top dog, the king of kings. We didn't want to finish you, just take you down a peg or two. You have to earn the right to play the big roles.'

'I agree, but you earn them through ability not by long service. You helped to take all that away from me. I lost fifteen years; my father lost his life.'

'But now you are back, let me help you.'

'Too late for that. Do you remember my last words to you upon that stage?'

Desmond did and now he started to tremble with fear, he tried to stand but was pushed back down.

Oliver reached into his pocket and withdrew the bayonet; it glinted in the moonlight as he pulled it back.

'No, Oliver, please.' Oliver held his finger to Desmond's trembling lips.

'How now rat. Dead for a ducat, dead.' He swung the knife into Desmond's chest with the force of hatred borne of fifteen lost years and the death of a father he had never properly known.

The bayonet went straight into Desmond's heart, he barely made a sound.

Oliver watched the light of life dim and fade in his eyes and then, like a deflating balloon, Desmond slowly slid off the bench and onto the pathway.

Oliver took a step backwards and watched the dark viscous

essence shimmer in the moonlight as it drained from Desmond's body. The deed was done and his revenge was begun. He leaned towards Desmond's inert form.

'Thou wretched, rash, intruding fool, farewell.' Oliver straightened up and looked at the bloody dagger clasped in his hand. He hurled it into the middle of the river where the dark waters swallowed it and washed the evidence of his guilt from it.

Chapter 19
Careful What You Wish For

The next morning as Toby pulled up on the car park at the back of Guild Street Station, he knew something was wrong. There were press waiting outside; not just the papers but TV and Radio too. What the hell was going on? As he climbed out of the car, a microphone was pushed into his face.

'Are you working on the murder?'

'What murder?'

'The murder at the theatre.'

Toby was confused. 'I don't know of any murder at the theatre.'

More questions were fired at him as he locked his car and, as he tried to get through the mass of press and into the station, he heard a familiar voice.

'Could you all please be quiet,' barked Fred Williams. 'We will be making a statement in fifteen minutes; we ask that you wait here until we make that statement.' Fred pushed through the assembled journalists and grabbed Toby's arm. 'Come on, there's a briefing in CID now.'

Toby put his head down and pushed through the crowd behind Fred. Kinky Bernstein opened the back door and let them in, before quickly closing and locking it behind them.

'Bit crazy out there. Inspector Beeching is waiting in CID.'

Fred nodded. 'Righto.'

'Who's been murdered, boss?' asked Toby.

Fred smiled. 'All in good time, young Toby. Now we've

really got something to get our teeth into.'

Fred seemed pleased and, when they entered CID, they were greeted by a positively beaming Inspector Beeching. Toby scanned the room. DS Ken White and DS Tony Parsons were there, along with DCs Kinky and Ginger Dalton. The whole of CID.

'Shut the door, DC Marlowe,' ordered Beeching. He waited for Toby to do so and then his smile turned to a frown. 'We have a murder.'

'At last,' sighed Fred.

Beeching nodded. 'Exactly, and whilst it's regrettable ...'

'Especially for the victim,' said Toby.

'Quite,' bristled Beeching, 'As I was saying, this is our chance to show what we can do.'

Beeching had been waiting for an opportunity like this; his chance to grab some headlines, to smooth his path to promotion and a job in the Met.

'Do we know who the victim is yet, sir?'

Beeching nodded at Fred. 'His body was found in the graveyard at Holy Trinity. Apparently he's a well-known actor.'

'Do we have a name?' asked Fred.

Beeching looked at his notes. 'It's not been corroborated yet but the dog walker who found him says it was Desmond Tharpe.'

'Wow,' said Toby. 'He's a regular here at Stratford and he plays Inspector Cream in that TV series.'

This was music to Beeching's ears. 'I know that series, Coffee and Cream, my wife likes it.'

'The actor who plays Coffee is also at Stratford this year. You want me to get him to identify the body if we can't get a next of kin?'

Beeching nodded. 'In the short term, just to be sure we know who we are dealing with.' Beeching looked seriously at his assembled task force. 'This is the biggest murder in Stratford for a long time, the eyes of the nation will be upon us. Everything by the book; I want this wrapped up quickly. It's our chance to shine. Fred.'

'Yes, sir.'

'I'm putting you in charge. DSs White and Parsons will act as your assistants and DCs Marlowe, Bernstein and Dalton will be at your disposal. SOCO are already at the scene.'

'Has it been secured?' asked Fred.

'Yes, Sergeant Whittle is down there with some uniforms. Get yourself down there, Fred, and report back to me at lunchtime. I'm going to go and make a statement to the press.'

Fred smiled; he knew Beeching would grab the limelight, but by putting Fred in charge he knew that the price of failure would end up firmly at his door. Beeching had played this game before.

'What are you going to tell them, sir?'

Beeching grinned. 'Nothing, but I'm going to do it in a very informative way.' He clicked his heels together and nodded to his assembled detectives. 'Very well, gents, let's get to work.'

Fred waited until he had left the room. 'Shut the door, Kinky.'

Bernstein closed the door behind his departing boss.

'Right. I want an operations room set up here. Ken, you and Tony will be in charge. Start doing a door-to-door and see if anyone in the neighbourhood saw anything last night. Get the press to ask if any tourists or theatregoers saw Tharpe after the show, you know the drill. Use Kinky and Ginger as your runners and they can use uniform for door-to-door. I want information flowing into this place. Like the boss said, the eyes of the nation will be on us.'

Everyone proceeded to follow Fred's instructions, and Fred tapped Toby on the shoulder. 'You come with me.'

'To the crime scene?'

'You got any better ideas.'

It had been a stupid question. Toby shook his head.

'Good, let's get moving. I've left my car out front to avoid the press.'

They headed out through the front door and, sure enough, parked on the double yellow lines was Fred's Cortina. They jumped in and Fred fired it up and shot off towards Clopton Bridge with no regard for speed limits.

At the back of the station, Inspector Beeching approached the waiting press corps. Voices began to call at him from the crowd.

'Can you tell us who the victim is, inspector?'

Beeching held up his hand and waited for silence. It took nearly twenty seconds. 'I am Inspector Beeching and I will be in charge of this operation. I can confirm that we have a body and that the circumstances are suspicious.'

'We heard it was a stabbing. Can you confirm that, inspector?'

'DS Fred Williams is on his way to the scene as we speak and he will liaise with the Scenes of Crime Officers to ascertain the exact cause of death. Once I have that report in my hands, I will share it with you at the press conference.'

'There's been a rumour that it's Desmond Tharpe. Can you confirm this?'

'I cannot confirm a rumour; there is no place for speculation. As soon as a formal identification has been made and next of kin have been informed, I will release that information.'

The next question came from Patrick Fryer. Beeching knew him well, his paper, The Daily Smear, had gone after him when he was an inspector in Northamptonshire.

'Do you think that the Stratford force can handle a big murder investigation?'

'I'm confident that we can.'

Fryer smirked. 'You were confident about solving the Man in the Water murders but, to my knowledge, you have three dead bodies and still no charges.'

Beeching tried hard to show no reaction. 'I think you are referring to the Angler Murders in Northamptonshire. Those investigations are with our colleagues in the Northamptonshire force and, as such, I cannot comment.'

'But you were in charge of that investigation, weren't you, and you had to call the Met in?'

Fryer's questioning was starting to gather interest among the gathered press who could suddenly smell blood.

'Will you be calling in the Met, inspector?'

Beeching shook his head. 'It's far too early to say. Once we have assessed the crime scene, identified the victim and gathered statements from witnesses, we will be in a far better position to make a judgement. Until then, everything else is speculation. We would ask that you allow us to get on with our job and we will keep you updated with regular press conferences, the next of which will be here at twelve noon. Thank you.'

Thirty questions were shouted at Beeching as he folded his notes and headed back into the station. His face was set in a determined stare right up until the moment he got inside. Sergeant Frank Hodges slammed the door shut behind him.

'Did you hear that smarmy little git!'

'I did, sir, you want me to check if his vehicle has up-to-date tax?'

'Yeah, do that Frank. And pull him over tomorrow morning, he's bound to be over the limit.'

Beeching stormed back into his office, slamming the door behind him. He needed to get a lid on this. He had only led one murder case and that had developed into a triple murder. That had been a year ago, when he left Northamptonshire. It was still unsolved. It didn't look good; it didn't look good at all. He needed to nip this in the bud. Fryer was a nasty piece of work. He'd built his career on tearing people in power down; people like him. Fryer had implied that Beeching wasn't up to the job and, by not being able to catch the killer, it had left him exposed. He wasn't going to let that happen again.

Chapter 20
And By A Sleep
To Say We End

Fred Williams pulled up outside Holy Trinity Church. The churchyard had been cordoned off and the young WPC on duty recognised Fred.

'Straight down there, sir. SOCO are just by the river.'

'Thanks, PC Kettles. Do you know which team?'

'Fellows and Allen, sir.'

Fred nodded approvingly. They were a good team which gave him one less thing to worry about. As he and Toby walked briskly down the path towards the river, Fred glanced at Toby. 'You ever worked on a murder?'

'I was based in Birmingham, sir.'

'I know, but did you ever work on a murder?'

Toby pursed his lips then shook his head. 'No, sir.'

'Didn't think so. The secret of scenes like this is to keep an open mind. There are so many ways for a murder to happen, and most aren't planned. Take everything in, make notes and don't jump to conclusions.'

'Yes, sir.'

As they walked towards the scene, Toby could make out the body at the foot of the bench. There was a woman taking photos and she looked up as they approached.

'Morning, Fred.'

'Morning, Christine, lovely day for it.'

She smiled. 'Yeah, no rain and warm. Nice clean crime scene.'

'Not a suicide then.'

'Not unless he managed to stab himself and then get rid of the weapon. Simon reckons that the wound was directly into the heart. Be lights out almost instantly.'

'So, definitely a murder then.'

'Looks like it. Pathologist will have to confirm it though.'

'You know who we've got?'

'Butcher, I think.'

Fred nodded his approval. Alf Butcher was the best pathologist in Warwickshire, very thorough but approachable. The other SOCO turned round.

'Morning, Fred, who's this.' He nodded towards Toby.

'This is DC Toby Marlowe, he's new on the force from Birmingham.'

'Never mind.' Simon Allen glanced at Toby. 'You want to take a look?'

Toby turned to Fred. 'Take a look, just don't touch anything.'

Toby walked around the bench and looked down at the motionless form lying on the gravel path. His skin had become as white as marble. He recognised him. 'It's Desmond Tharpe, the actor.'

'Are you sure?'

'Hundred per cent, I've seen him here in about twenty productions. It's definitely him.'

Fred and Simon exchanged glances.

'Oh, bugger,' said Simon.

'Indeed,' said Fred. 'A famous victim means lots of press. We'd better not cock this one up.'

Fred turned to Toby. 'What's he doing at the moment?'

'He's playing Mark Antony in Julius Caesar.'

'Hope they've got an understudy.' Simon snorted. 'Maybe you should interview him. With this guy dead, a big role has just opened up.'

Fred scratched his chin thoughtfully. 'I've known folks

murdered for less.'

Toby stood up and looked down the pathway towards the entrance to the graveyard. 'Why did he come down to this bench in the dark?'

'Either someone lured him down here or he was forced.' Fred looked back down the gravel path. There were no signs of a disturbance to the surface. 'Doesn't look like he was dragged.'

'I don't think he was. He was sitting on the bench,' said Toby.

'What makes you say that?' asked Simon.

Toby pointed to the blood on the bench. 'He was sitting on the bench when he was stabbed, look at the blood trail.'

Fred saw it too. 'Well spotted, young Toby. So, maybe he was lured here by someone he knew. Why else would you leave a nice, lamp lit road to walk into the darkness of a graveyard? Not normal behaviour, is it.'

Christine Fellows came up to the bench and took more pictures.

'Any sign of a weapon?' asked Fred.'

'No. I've followed the path back to the road and been into all the bushes along the way, nothing.'

Fred turned to Toby. 'What do you think?'

'I reckon the weapon's in the river, that's what I'd do.'

This made sense to Fred. 'Better get the frogmen in then.'

'Be a waste of time,' said Simon. 'All the blood will be washed off and there won't be any prints.'

'I know but we might be able to trace where the weapon came from.'

Simon shrugged. 'Better than nothing, I suppose.'

Just then there was a commotion from the road and a burly figure wearing a tweed jacket and moleskin waistcoat came bounding down the path.

'Bloody hell, who put you in charge of a murder, Williams? Is it April the first.'

'Get lost, Alf.'

Alf Butcher smiled as he glanced down at the victim. 'What happened here then, Fred. Did he fall down some stairs?'

Simon and Christine sniggered, Fred Williams reputation for throwing folks downstairs was clearly not confined to Guild Street.

'You're the pathologist, you tell me.'

Alf bent down and inspected Desmond's wound. 'Single stab wound direct to the heart by the look of it, death would have been almost instantaneous.'

'Time of death?' asked Fred.

Alf Butcher felt around the victim's chest and back. 'Well, he's cold and stiff, so at least eight hours. I'll do a temperature reading but my guess would be about ten or eleven hours.'

'That would put it at about eleven last night, forty minutes after the play finished,' said Toby.

'He was probably going to get one in at the Dirty Duck before he got side-tracked down here.' Fred looked back up the path and then towards the theatre through the riverside park. 'The murderer was probably waiting in the park for him to come out of the stage door and head towards the Duck.'

'You want me to check for footprints?' asked Toby.

Fred shook his head. 'Nah, it's been too dry and there are hundreds of footprints on a daily basis in here.'

Alf looked up from the victim. 'Looking at the wound, I'd say we're looking for something like a bayonet, long and thin.'

'Thanks, Alf. When do you think you can get me a full report?'

Alf looked up at Fred. 'I'm guessing it's urgent, given the celebrity status.'

'Afraid so.'

'OK, I'll have it ready for six p.m. latest. I'll have it couriered over.'

'Thanks, Alf,'

Fred turned back to Simon and Christine. 'I can get you some uniforms for a fingertip search of the area and park. How many do you want?'

Simon surveyed the crime scene. 'Christine and I will concentrate around here and get me four PCs to comb the graveyard and park for the weapon or anything else that might be useful. Be a waste of time, though. I think Toby's right, that blade is in the river.'

'Better get your trunks on then, Simon.'

'Or Christine could get her bikini on,' said Alf, looking lasciviously across to where she was taking pictures.'

Fred shook his head. 'You just concentrate on the dead ones; you'll have more luck with them.'

Toby had stepped back a few paces to try and take in the scene. In the clearing by the river bank, with the dappled sunlight streaming through the trees and glittering across the surface of the river, Desmond Tharpe's inert body seemed strangely out of place. He lay at the foot of the bench like Waterhouse's painting of the Lady of Shalott.

What had drawn him into this place in the dead of night and who had a motive to kill one of the great stage actors of his generation? Maybe someone who had watched Coffee and Cream, the terrible TV show that Desmond starred in with Theo Cumberbatch. Maybe a critic, he thought.

'Penny for them, Toby.'

He looked up to see Fred Williams was looking directly at him.

'Sorry, sir, I just keep wondering why Tharpe would have come down here at night. Someone must have drawn him here.'

'Do you think he was meeting someone?'

'Like who?' asked Toby.

Fred winked. 'You know, another actor. They're all a bit … you know.'

Toby shook his head. 'Not all actors are that way inclined.'

'Really? I thought it was compulsory.'

'Tharpe was a well-known womaniser.'

'He could have been meeting a woman.'

'Why would he come down here? His wife died years back. He could take her back to his hotel, no questions asked. Who would want to make love in a graveyard?'

'Who hasn't,' observed Alf Butcher.

'I'm sure that's where you find most of your girlfriends, Alf, but for most people it's not regarded as normal.'

'Define normal.'

'Not you.'

Fred's remark drew a chuckle from Simon. 'He spends too much time with dead bodies, can't be good for him.'

'They're better company than you lot.'

Toby tried to block the conversation out, he wanted to build a picture of what could have happened.

'If it is a bayonet, it must be premeditated. Who carries a bayonet around with them?'

Fred looked impressed. 'That's a very good point, Toby.'

'It's probably a man too, I can't see a woman using a bayonet. It's got to be awkward to hold, you'd need to have strong hands to hold it without a handle.'

'So, you reckon we are looking for someone he knows, who has a reason to kill him, probably a man.'

Toby nodded. 'We just need to establish a motive.'

'Any thoughts?'

Toby looked at Fred. 'Be worth talking to Theo Cumberbatch, he plays second fiddle to Tharpe in the TV series.'

'Is he Coffee or Cream?'

'He's mixed-race,' said Toby. 'Who do you think?'

'Fair point. Is he any good?'

'Much better than Tharpe, but he's always been in his

shadow.'

Fred nodded slowly. 'Sounds like a possible motive. Is he understudying Tharpe in Julius Cesar?'

'No, he's playing Cassius.'

Alfred Butcher packed up his kit. 'I'll leave you to discuss the works of Shakespeare and await the arrival of Mark Antony on my slab.'

'Thanks, Alf, I'll probably call you when I've read your findings.'

He nodded and tapped Fred on the shoulder. 'I'll do my best, Fred, but this one looks a bit tricky.'

'Why?'

Butcher scratched his head. 'I don't think I'm going to find anything significant. One stab wound straight to the heart, pretty damn clinical. Thin blade that went straight between the ribs and virtually no splatter on the clothes.'

Fred sighed. 'Yeah, I see what you mean. No struggle, nothing.'

Butcher nodded to Toby and the SOCOs and headed for his car. Toby and Fred watched him go.

'He any good?' asked Toby.

'The best,' said Fred.

'That doesn't bode well.'

'No, it doesn't, does it,' agreed Fred.

Chapter 21
A Crack In The Glass Ceiling?

As they drove up Chestnut Walk and turned right onto Rother Street, Fred Williams looked pensive. 'This case could make us look bad.'

'I agree,' said Toby. 'Whoever killed Desmond Tharpe had planned it.'

'It was pretty clinical. Why Tharpe though? We need to find a motive. You think this Cumberbatch character has one?'

Toby shrugged.

'Who knows, he was pretty close to him so maybe he knows something.'

'You sure he will be at the White Swan?'

Toby nodded. 'It's Sir Morris Oxford's favourite hotel, he always books in when he's doing a season up here. It's a block booking for the major players in his company.'

'Cumberbatch is one of them?'

'Oh, yes, if you ask me, he's the most talented of the lot.'

'So, why isn't he the star then?'

'He's mixed-race, you do the maths.'

Fred knew that Toby had a point. Even in these modern, enlightened times the colour of someone's skin could still form a glass ceiling.

'You do the interview, Toby. I'll just back you up.'

Toby was surprised. 'Why, sir?'

'You know who he is, you've seen him act. Be easier for you to get him to open up, maybe you can butter him up a bit first.'

Toby could understand his bosses reasoning but it was still a big responsibility on his first murder case.

'What if I get it wrong?'

'That's how you learn. If you do, I'm going to be there to get you back on track. OK?'

'Thanks, sir.'

The inside of the White Swan Hotel was all old oak beams and history. Built in 1450, it was one of the oldest buildings in Stratford. History leached from every wall. Fred looked around the foyer. 'If these walls could talk.'

Toby knew what Fred meant. In a town so full of history, buildings like this were a living connection to the past.

'Can I help you?'

A smartly dressed young lady had appeared at the reception desk from an office behind it. Toby pulled out his warrant card.

'DC Toby Marlowe and DS Fred Williams, we'd like to speak to Theo Cumberbatch? Is he in?'

For a brief moment she looked flustered and then, without a beat, she resumed her cool professional demeanour.

'I think so, let me just check.' She looked at a log in front of her and dialled a number. It rang out twice before it was answered.

'Hello, Mister Cumberbatch, I have two visitors for you in reception.' She listened briefly and then continued. 'Two police officers, sir.' She nodded as she listened. 'Yes, they definitely asked for you.' She nodded several times more before handing Toby the phone. 'Mister Cumberbatch would like to speak to you.'

Toby reached for the outstretched receiver but a meaty hand came from behind him and took it.

'DS Fred Williams here, Mister Cumberbatch. Just get down to reception now before I come and get you.' Fred handed the phone back with a smile. 'I think that's cleared up the misunderstanding that he has a choice.'

The receptionist took it from him. 'Do you want to sit over there while you wait?' She pointed to a Chesterfield settee against the wall.

'No, thanks,' said Fred. 'We will sit in a quiet corner of the lounge and have a pot of tea for two and some biscuits, please.'

The receptionist swallowed hard. 'Of course. Something for Mister Cumberbatch?'

Fred shook his head. 'He can order his own.' Fred turned and headed for the lounge, the conversation over.

For a moment Toby stood awkwardly looking at the receptionist. 'Er, thanks.'

She smiled weakly. 'No problem,' She then turned and hurried back into the office, no doubt to inform her superior that there were two detectives after one of their famous clients.

Fred sat down and made himself comfortable. 'This is more like it.'

'I thought I was doing the talking.'

'You are, the interview is all yours, but don't ever let anyone fob you off. You're the police. If you tell someone that you want to speak to them, it's not open for debate. You have to assert yourself, you understand?'

'Yes, sir.'

'We have him on the back foot now he's been summoned, not asked. We are in control.'

Toby understood exactly what Fred meant and a couple of moments later, when Theo Cumberbatch appeared, it was clear that he did too. He looked nervous. Toby stood up to greet him.

'Thanks for coming down, sir.'

'Did I have a choice?'

Toby ignored the comment. 'I'm DC Marlowe and this is DS Williams. We wanted a word with you about one of your colleagues.' Toby pointed to an armchair. 'I think you'd better sit down, sir.'

Cumberbatch nervously took a seat. 'What's all this about, officer?'

'I understand you know Desmond Tharpe.'

'Of course, we've worked together for years.'

Toby tried to work out how to word his next sentence. 'I'm afraid we have some bad news about Mister Tharpe.'

Cumberbatch looked genuinely concerned. 'Is he OK?'

Toby shook his head. 'I'm afraid not, there's been an incident.'

'Is it serious?'

'Serious enough to kill him,' said Fred.

Cumberbatch looked stunned. 'Is this a joke?'

'I'm afraid not,' continued Toby. 'Mister Tharpe was found dead by the river at the edge of Holy Trinity graveyard this morning.'

Cumberbatch's mouth fell open but no sound came out. Toby watched him closely. If he was acting, he was doing it very well but Toby knew he was a great actor. He said nothing and waited for Cumberbatch to say something, anything, that could betray him. When he did it was short and concise.

'How?'

Toby glanced at Fred, who gave the slightest nod to indicate that he should continue.

'He was murdered.'

'My God, that's terrible.' He looked from Toby to Fred and back. 'Do you know how?'

'He was stabbed through the heart with a blade of some sort.'

Theo Cumberbatch dropped his head into his hands in shock. 'Who did it?'

'We were hoping you could shed some light on that, sir.'

Theo Cumberbatch did not understand the question. 'How would I know?'

'You would if you had killed him,' interrupted Fred.

'I didn't kill Desmond; he was my friend.' There was resentment in his voice.

'I never said you did,' said Fred. 'I was just putting it out there for discussion.'

'As I was saying, Mister Cumberbatch,' said Toby, trying to wrestle the interview back under his control. 'As my colleague was implying, we have an open mind on the events leading up to Mister Tharpe's murder. Any background that you can give us would be very helpful.'

'Like what?'

'Did he have any enemies that you know of?'

Theo shook his head. 'Desmond was well liked by everyone; he's been with Sir Morris for nearly forty years.'

'And how long have you known him?'

'Probably twenty years. We met on one of Sir Morris's productions, The Tempest, I think.'

'Was that your first performance with Sir Morris's company?'

'Yes, it was a dream come true for a young actor. If Sir Morris hired you and then kept you in his company, you were almost guaranteed to get to Stratford and the Old Vic to do Shakespeare.'

'You like Shakespeare?'

Theo looked surprised. 'It's the reason I took up acting. For a black kid from Birmingham it was an impossible dream, being in Sir Morris's company made it possible.'

'But you're not really black, are you,' said Fred pointedly.

Toby squirmed uncomfortably at Fred's heavy-handed comment. 'I think what DS Williams is trying to say …'

'I know what he's trying to say,' interrupted Theo, smiling. 'I'm guessing you've never been black, DS Williams?'

'Not recently. Never been mixed-race either.'

Theo shook his head, an ironic smile playing on his lips. 'There is no mixed-race in this country; if you're not white you're black.' There was a vehemence in his words that surprised

Toby.

'Have you experienced racism in this country? It's hardly South Africa.'

'How would two white boys from Stratford know anything about that?'

There was an uncomfortable silence.

'I'm from Birmingham, actually,' said Toby.

'What part?'

'Hollywood, near Wythall.'

'Hardly the front line, is it.'

'It is surrounded by countryside to be fair but I did work out of Kings Heath station, so I know a bit about inner city Birmingham.'

'No, you don't,' sighed Theo. 'I was brought up in Highgate, it may have only been four miles from Hollywood but it might as well have been another country.'

'Turned out all right though, didn't it. Look at you now, big star on the stage and a hit TV show. Coffee and Cream, isn't it?'

Theo nodded. 'Yes, it is.'

'And who do you play?'

Theo stared at Fred and then looked at Toby. 'Is he for real.'

Toby nodded. 'He was a farmer before he became a police officer.'

Theo smiled. 'I was Coffee, Winston Coffee.'

'And Tharpe was Cream because …' Fred hesitated. 'Ah, now I see, quite clever actually.'

'You think.'

Toby could feel the interview getting away from him but, before he could get it back on track, Fred dived in again.

'I suppose it would come in handy if you wanted to play Othello.'

Theo Cumberbatch smiled at Fred and slowly shook his head. 'Either you are incredibly stupid or you are deliberately trying to wind me up. Which is it?'

'Probably the second one. You see, Mister Cumberbatch, I do understand that there is plenty of racism in this country but we need to understand how your relationship with Desmond Tharpe worked. He's been murdered and you were very close to him. You've been DS Coffee to his Inspector Cream for nearly ten years but he doesn't treat you very well, does he.'

'It's just a TV show, it's make believe.'

'Maybe, but you always seemed to be playing second fiddle to him.'

Both Toby and Theo were now staring at Fred, surprised at his knowledge of the TV show and the way that he seemed to be implying that Theo had been badly treated.

'I don't know what you mean.'

'Really? I think you do. Last year the company performed a short run of Othello. Now, excuse me, but I think you would make a perfect Othello, but for some reason Tharpe got the part, why do you think that was?'

'Perhaps I wasn't black enough.'

'Oh, I think you are. Not one of the boys though, are you, Theo. Nice bit of window dressing for Sir Morris's liberal credentials but you're never going to be one of the gang.'

Toby sat silently watching as Fred slid the knife into the open wound of Theo Cumberbatch's past and waited for the truth to ooze out.

'Not as thick as you look, are you,' said Theo.

'No, and you haven't answered my question.'

'I didn't kill Desmond; I may not have liked him much but I didn't kill him.'

Fred nodded thoughtfully. 'Fair enough,' he paused for a moment. 'What's it like being the only black actor in Sir Morris's company?'

The question took him by surprise. 'How is that relevant?'

'Because somebody just killed Desmond Tharpe. He was probably the second biggest star in the company, so we need to establish if anyone within that group would have a motive to kill him.'

Toby understood where Fred was headed and joined in. 'I have to tell you, Theo, I've seen a lot of Sir Morris's productions and you can act the pants off Sir Morris and Desmond, so why do you never get the major roles?'

Theo shrugged. 'Why do you think. Morris and Desmond are the stars. There's a pecking order in the theatre and you have to wait your turn. It's his company and I get well paid and plenty of work, that's not often the case for an actor.'

'Must be frustrating though, knowing that you're better but having this glass ceiling holding you back.'

'Talent isn't enough, never has been, but I'm one of the lucky ones. I have worked non-stop for twenty years on both TV and Stage. Not many actors get that.'

'You know your place then, the faithful retainer.'

Theo laughed. 'I'm no Uncle Tom, if that's what you're suggesting.'

Toby blushed. 'I'm not saying that.'

'Aren't you?'

'No, we just need to understand who, within Sir Morris's company, would have a motive to kill Desmond.'

'None of us. Desmond was the manager of the company and without that company none of us would have any work.'

'So, what's going to happen to Coffee and Cream?' asked Fred.

Theo shook his head. 'I really don't know.'

'Could be a promotion in it for you, maybe it could be Inspector Coffee investigates.'

'I doubt it. The series is based on the novels of Donna Muffet and she didn't write Inspector Cream out. I've a nasty feeling my TV career is about to hit a quiet patch.'

Toby could see in his eyes that the implications of Desmond's murder were just beginning to hit home with Theo.

'I think that will be all for now, Mister Cumberbatch. We just need you to come down to the station to make a statement. We'll take you down when we've finished here.'

Fred leaned forward. 'Could you tell us where you were last night after the performance?'

'Yes, I walked down to the Dirty Duck with Suzy Tench.'

'Dame Suzy?'

Theo nodded. 'Yes, we're friends.'

'But she's not in anything here this season, is she?' asked Toby.

'No, but she is doing her one woman show for four nights at the Swan. I'm doing some readings with her.'

'Not really a one woman show then, is it,' said Fred.

'Well, I'm not a woman, so I guess it is.'

Toby smiled. 'Will Dame Suzy be able to confirm this?'

'Yes, we didn't leave until gone midnight and then we walked back to the White Swan together.'

'Oh, is Dame Suzy stopping here too?'

'Yes.'

'Separate rooms?' asked Fred.

Theo glared at him. 'Dame Suzy is a married woman.'

'So are millions of women who commit adultery every year.'

'Not Dame Suzy, our relationship is professional. She's just offered me a part in a film her husband is producing. I'm not going to risk that now, am I.'

'That's convenient. Desmond is barely cold and you have already replaced the work you would have lost on Coffee and Cream. Don't hang around, do you?'

Theo stood up and looked down at Fred angrily. 'How dare you! I didn't even know Desmond was dead until you told me.'

Toby stood up and tried to placate Theo. 'DS Williams is just making a point, Mister Cumberbatch. The timing is unfortunate but, if it's any comfort, I believe you. Once we have talked to Dame Suzy, we will be able to eliminate you from our inquiries.'

'As long as she confirms your story,' added Fred.

Both officers made for the door.

'Thanks for your co-operation. If you'd like to come with us, we'll drop you at the station.'

Theo Cumberbatch nodded and reluctantly followed them through the open door.

Chapter 22
No More Fibs
From Terry

Oliver wasn't sure how he felt. He'd never killed anyone before and, he had to admit, he was rather good at it. Sticking the bayonet into old Desmond had been very satisfying, like scratching an itch he hadn't been able to reach for a long time. Vengeance, as the old saying goes, is a dish best served cold. Fifteen years down the line, it tasted very good indeed.

He leaned back in his armchair, cup of tea in hand, and played back the events of the previous night. The way he had approached Desmond, persuaded him into the riverside woods and then calmly despatched him had been so simple. He had particularly enjoyed quoting the lines from Hamlet to him.

'Thou wretched, rash, intruding fool, farewell.'

If it had been a play, that would have made a perfect final scene, but it wasn't the final scene. This was just the beginning. Oliver had not been sure that he could go through with his plan; last night had shown him that he could. Worryingly, he had to admit that he had enjoyed it. Did that make him a monster?

It didn't matter. His course was now set and there would be no going back. The only question was, who next? The answer lay in the array of papers spread out on his coffee table. The Daily Smear was on top. He picked it up and found the arts section; there it was.

Terry Fibs' review page. One of the most acerbic wits of theatrical criticism, Terry Fibs could close a show with one review. Many years before, at the behest of Sir Morris, he had produced a review that had mortally wounded Oliver's career. All these years later, he could still remember every word.

'I had the misfortune of watching Oliver Lawrence play Henry V last night. Seldom have I wished more fervently for a French Victory, if only an English archer's arrow could have found my heart and silenced the misery. Lawrence's Henry was more like a rabble-rousing union leader heading a wild cat strike, than a noble King leading his troops into battle. "We few, we happy few." From where I sat, very few were happy and most who remained wished they were, "now a-bed." Those of us that had not left, "shall think themselves accursed that we were here." His acting was so wooden it cast more splinters about the stage than the archer's arrows. What has happened to the huge talent that burst onto the Stratford stage just a few short years ago? The crown sits uneasy on his head. Maybe abdication is in order and a spell in pantomime, which would surely be more fitting for his current delivery, is in order. On the evidence of this performance … Oh no it won't!'

It was brutal. When Oliver had read it, he had nearly fainted, it was an absolute hatchet job. He hadn't been good that night but the review that Fibs had posted sent a shockwave through the theatre world. The next morning when Oliver arrived at the theatre nobody would look at him, they turned away, embarrassed but also frightened of getting too close and being contaminated by the stench of failure that seemed to surround him.

Oliver had tried to confront Fibs but he had avoided him and never returned his calls, all the time adding new snide and acerbic comments about the dimming of a once bright star. His confidence now shaken, Oliver had begun to fluff lines and then started to earn the bad reviews he was getting.

Desmond Tharpe had been complicit, altering his cadences in scenes with him to throw off his timing and deliberately misquoting a line and then staring at him as if it was Oliver who had missed a line. As he remembered the events, it was all very clear. There had been a concerted effort to break him and it had succeeded. Terry Fibs would be next.

Chapter 23
Light The Blue Touch Paper

Felix Richards was listening to the news on Radio Four.

'Distinguished star of stage and screen was found dead near Shakespeare's grave in Stratford. Police suspect foul play. Inspector Sidney Beeching gave a press conference ten minutes ago.

'We can confirm that the body found near the river Avon this morning was that of Desmond Tharpe. He had been stabbed and we are looking at what we believe is a first-degree murder. Anyone who saw Mister Tharpe after the performance of Julius Cesar last night is asked to come forward and give us any information they can relating to sightings of Mister Tharpe. On behalf of the officers of the Stratford-upon-Avon police force, we would like to extend our sympathies to Mister Tharpe's family at this difficult time. Furthermore, we would like to reassure everyone that we are doing everything possible to apprehend the perpetrator of this terrible crime as soon as possible.'

Felix turned off his radio. That was it, Oliver's revenge had begun. He had set in place a chain of events and lit the blue touch paper. Everything that happened from this point on was his fault. He had primed Oliver like a heat seeking missile and set him on the targets he had selected. Although he had not wielded the knife, he was just as guilty. He had created an avenging angel, an angel of death. He reached for the marmalade. This was going to get interesting.

Chapter 24
Report On
A Murder

The phone in the corner of Oliver's little kitchen in Trinity Street rang, making him jump. Only one person knew he was here; if it wasn't a wrong number, it had to be Felix.

He picked up the phone. 'Hello.'

There was a short pause. 'You didn't hang around.' It was Felix.

'You heard.'

'Everyone's heard. It's the lead story on the BBC. How'd you do it?'

'I ran him through, just like Polonius.'

Felix nodded approvingly. 'Thou wretched, rash, intruding fool, farewell.'

'That's exactly what I said as I ran him through. It would have made a great scene.'

'I'm sure it did. Did Desmond say anything?'

'"Urrrgh," and a bit of gurgling.'

'Before you stabbed him,' said Felix pointedly.

'He begged a bit and told me it was all at Morris's instigation.'

'Well, we knew that already.'

Felix hesitated for a moment. 'How do you feel?'

'What, about killing him?'

'Of course. Any regrets?'

Oliver thought for a moment. He looked out into the sunlit garden and realised he was happy.

'No regrets at all. What Morris and his little gang did to my father and then did to me was terrible. I'm glad I did it, it feels like a great weight has started to lift from my shoulders.'

Felix picked up on Oliver's comment. 'Started? The plan is going to proceed. I wasn't sure you would be able to go through with it.' He heard Oliver chuckle down the line.

'This is just the beginning, Felix. Everyone you told me about is going to pay. I will have justice for my father and me.'

Felix nodded to himself. 'Seems I really have let slip a dog of war. Who's next?'

Oliver's answer came without hesitation. 'Terry Fibs.'

Felix had suspected it would be. 'Good choice and very fortuitous.'

'How so?'

'Mr Terry Fibs arrived in Stratford last night, he's reviewing Julius Cesar.'

Oliver gave a cold laugh. 'With his old mate Sir Morris in it, that'll be a toadying, rubber stamp job.'

'Course it will. More interestingly, he's going to review Dame Suzy's one woman show.'

'She's a mate of Morris's, isn't she?'

'God, no!' exclaimed Felix. 'She hates the lot of them, never liked Morris or his little band of arse lickers.'

Oliver was surprised. 'I assumed she was.'

'Un-assume it,' said Felix vehemently. 'Dame Suzy is one of the good guys, you definitely do not want to be killing her.'

'Well, she wasn't on the list but ...'

'No buts, Oliver. Just stick to the names I have given you. They are all guilty, I don't want you killing anyone that doesn't need killing.'

'You're enjoying this, aren't you?'

Felix thought about Oliver's question. 'I know it sounds terrible, but I am. They are all such horrible people, killing them would be in the public interest.'

'Interesting defence.'

Felix smiled. 'There's no defence if you get caught. Morris and his merry band are all National treasures.'

Oliver knew that Felix was right but he had no intention of getting caught. 'I realised something last night.'

'What's that?'

'I'm good at this, after all those years on the stage. I just plan it out like playing a part. Set the scene, block it out and then just play it. Only difference is that this time I'm not acting. When I killed him, it was …' Oliver searched for the right word, '… brilliant.'

At the other end of the phone line, a cold shiver ran down Felix's spine. What had he started?

'Keep to the script, Oliver. You have your targets and your reasons. Don't get carried away.'

'Don't worry, Felix. I'm not a maniac, I just want my revenge and then I'm done.'

'Do it without getting caught and you may even get your career back.'

The thought had crossed Oliver's mind, but he didn't want to think about it until he had completed his task. Hope would distract him, make him vulnerable. 'Do you know where Terry Fibs is stopping?'

'The Falcon, I think.'

The line went dead. Felix held the receiver; with just four words he had condemned a man he had known for twenty-five years to death.

Chapter 25
I've Got
A Bad Feeling

Fred Williams sat with his feet on his desk. He had the pathology report from Alf Butcher. 'Single wound, straight into the heart. Death would have been almost instantaneous, according to Alf.'

Toby nodded. 'Any sign of a struggle?'

Fred shook his head. 'Nope, no cuts or scratches. Nothing under his nails. Seems like murder came as a big surprise to our Desmond.'

'Must have been someone he knew.'

Fred winked at Toby. 'Well spotted, that's exactly what I was thinking. Went to his death like a lamb to the slaughter.'

'Do we know what kind of knife?'

Fred looked at the report. 'According to Alf, it's a bayonet of some type.'

'Not a lady's weapon.'

'True, but let's not rule them out. There's a lot of young ladies working on farms round here. Solid girls, if you know what I mean. They could clap a bayonet in a gloved hand and shove it in deep. Could be a crime of passion.'

Toby wasn't convinced. 'Nah, this is a bloke. Desmond wouldn't be seeing a young lady after a performance. He had an ego like a bad back; constantly needed to be massaged. He would much rather have been in the Dirty Duck taking the plaudits of the fans. I know a bit about the late Desmond Tharpe.'

'OK, I'll bow to your superior knowledge of theatre. If it is a bloke, and someone he knew, who? And what was the motive?'

Toby looked at Fred. 'I can't think of a reason.'

Fred took a long sip of his tea and then stared out of the window. 'Does there have to be a reason? What if we just have a killer out there.'

'Without a motive?' asked Toby.

'Does he have to have one? What if he just likes killing.'

'Sounds a bit far-fetched.'

'Does it? Jack the Ripper killed five women that we know of. They were all prostitutes but there was no apparent motive.'

'You think we have a serial killer on our hands?' said Toby sceptically.

'Could be.'

'But we only have one body.'

'Got to start somewhere.'

'I'm not sure, sir, still sounds a bit far-fetched.'

Fred took his feet off his desk and leaned close to Toby. He spoke quietly, as if he didn't want to be overheard. 'I've got a bad feeling about this one. It was cold, clinical. Tharpe was lured there by someone he knew. No signs of struggle, and killed with a single thrust. Whoever killed him knew he would be leaving the theatre and going down Southern Street. It's almost as if the whole thing was planned and our murderer was just playing a part.

'I've seen a lot of murders and, for most of them, I knew who the killer was within minutes. Murder is usually done in the heat of the moment by someone you are close to. A husband, a wife, a business partner, a friend. Anger and hatred make you careless, in that moment the blood is pumping with murderous intent. That kind of passion stops you thinking, you leave evidence, you panic and flee the scene.

'Tharpe's crime scene was as if they had just walked down to the riverside, sat on the bench like old friends and then the murderer had just stabbed him. The killer wasn't acting in hot blood, he despatched Tharpe like a vet putting down a sick dog.'

'You think this could be the start of something?' asked Toby.

Fred nodded. 'I've got a bad feeling about this one.'

Chapter 26
Felixstein's Monster

In Trinity Street, Oliver was about to go in search of Terry Fibs but his phone rang again. He picked it up. 'Hello.'

'You better sit down,' said Felix.

'What's wrong?'

'Tabitha Tharpe is in Stratford.'

'I know, I nearly bumped into her yesterday in Ely Street.'

'Did she recognise you?' Felix sounded concerned.

'I don't think so. Why?'

'Her father has just been murdered and you used to go out with her. If she saw you, don't you think it would raise suspicions?'

'She never saw me, but she did hear me.'

'What do you mean by that?'

'I followed her.'

'Are you mad, what if she saw you?'

'She didn't. I always put people between us and I only spoke when her back was turned.' At the other end of the line Felix sounded incredulous.

'What the hell did you say to her?'

'I quoted some line from Hamlet, the lines that he spoke to Ophelia. We did it once.' Oliver paused, grinning at the memory. 'She recognised my voice, you should have seen the way she reacted. She screamed when I told her to "Get thee to a nunnery." Took off down Waterside like her arse was on fire.'

'For God's sake, Oliver, it's almost as if you want to be caught. You need to lay low for a while, let the dust settle before you go after Terry.'

'I've been lying low for fifteen years, Felix. If you think I'm going to do it again you can forget it. Tabitha didn't recognise me, trust me. She recognised something in my voice though. Her reaction … it was like she had heard a ghost. She feels guilty about something.'

'Forget Tabitha, the police are bound to interview her. What if your name comes up?'

'It won't, everyone thinks I'm dead.' Oliver thought for a moment. 'Maybe I should kill her too.'

Felix couldn't believe what he had just heard. 'Are you mad?'

'Course I am, I just killed a man in cold blood.'

Felix ignored the comment. 'Never mind that, Tabitha is not on the list. She did nothing to harm you, her only crime was falling in love with you and you ditched her because you didn't think she could act.'

'She couldn't, but I did love her. She dumped me because her father told her to. Maybe I'd be doing the theatre a kindness if I did for her too.'

Felix tried to stay calm. Oliver was starting to frighten him. 'Tabitha never did anything to harm you, you can't put the sins of the father onto the daughter. Maybe you don't love her any more …'

'I don't but …' Oliver hesitated, as a wonderful idea occurred to him. 'You know I stabbed Desmond as if he were Polonius?'

'Yes,' said Felix, unsure of where this was headed.

'She's Desmond's daughter. What if I send her mad, just like Ophelia?' Oliver really liked the idea.

Felix didn't. 'This isn't a play, Oliver, it's real life with real people.'

'That just makes it more fun, don't you see?'

Felix didn't see. He had set Oliver on a course for revenge but, after just one murder, Oliver was starting to write a new script.

'Keep to the plan, I can't help you if you don't.' There was silence on the end of the line. 'Oliver? Oliver?' There was no reply.

Oliver pulled on his jacket and opened the door, he was going into town to find Tabitha. He had a pretty good idea where she would be staying; the same place as Terry Fibs. Two birds with one stone.

Felix put his phone back on the receiver. Oliver was out of control. What would he do if he couldn't get him back on script? He had created a killer. How could he stop him? More importantly, how could he stop him without implicating himself?

Chapter 27
What Dreams May Come

As Oliver walked up Sheep Street, he whistled happily to himself. It was suddenly all very clear to him. Tabitha was Ophelia; she must be sent mad. It all made perfect sense. If Desmond had been Polonius, then Tabitha must be Ophelia.

This was Hamlet. It had all come to him in a moment of perfect clarity. His father had been betrayed by Sir Morris and now he was here to avenge him. Sir Morris had stolen his mother's affections from his father, now he would revenge his father. Terry Fibs and Gerard Soames, the two Fleet Street hacks who had colluded with Sir Morris to bring him down, would both have to go, but who were they? It was obvious … Rosencrantz and Guildenstern!

He burst out laughing and a startled dog walker crossed the street thinking him mad. Maybe he was but now he understood, and he remembered what his Uncle Morris had once said to him.

'The play's the thing, Oliver, the play's the thing.'

His old uncle had been right all along. As he reached the top of Sheep Street, he looked left towards the Falcon. As he had feared there was a mob of journalists outside all hoping for a glance or a word from the grieving daughter. He would go down Scholar's Lane and slip in the back way, pretending to be a member of staff. He was a trained actor; how hard could it be?

He walked casually past the waiting journalists, with nobody giving him a second glance. There must have been twenty or more. To think that he had created all of this. The killing of Desmond had started a snowball rolling down a mountain, and now that snowball was about to turn into a full-blown avalanche. Newton had been right, for every action there is an equal and opposite reaction. He walked down the lane some fifty yards and then turned right into the busy delivery yard. There were two workers chatting at the side of the open lorry.

'Can I help you, mate?'

The other wasn't so helpful. 'Press out the front, mate.'

'I'm not press. I'm the new sous chef.' Oliver smiled and, without breaking stride, pushed on into the back of the hotel via the kitchens.

There were a couple of kitchen staff tidying up and starting the prep for lunch. Oliver strode through like he belonged and went unchallenged. He came out of the kitchens at the base of a staircase. As he reached the first floor, there was a tray outside a room with a pot of coffee. He looked up and down the corridor and, seeing nobody, he bent down and picked it up. The pot was warm.

He smiled. Someone was having too much fun to get their coffee, that or they could have fallen asleep. Oliver preferred to think the former. He walked down the corridor and headed up the next flight of stairs. The rooms up there were more expensive and that was where he would find Tabitha.

As he turned into the next corridor, he froze. There in front of him, not fifteen yards away, stood Terry Fibs. He stopped for a moment and then continued to walk towards him, pretending he was looking for a room number.

'Excuse me, I have an order here for Tabitha Tharpe. Is this her room?'

Fibs gave him a condescending stare. 'You're the waiter, you tell me.'

Oliver curbed the desire to smash the coffee pot into his weaselly face. 'You're right, sir, it's just that with everything going on today I clean forgot. I don't know how I'm going to look her in the face after what happened to her father last night.'

Terry Fibs did something he rarely did; he showed compassion. 'I know. It's terrible, isn't it. I'm an old friend of the family and I've come to comfort her.'

Get an exclusive, more like, thought Oliver. 'So, this is her room then?'

Fibs nodded. 'Yes, I've been standing outside trying to get up the courage to knock. What do you say to a daughter who's just been told her father was murdered?'

'That's not going to be easy.' Oliver looked over Fibs' shoulder. The room next door was open and the key was in the door.

'I've got an idea, sir. Perhaps we could help each other.'

'How do you mean?'

'Why don't you give Miss Tharpe her coffee, be something to break the ice with.'

Fibs nodded. 'Get you off the hook too, wouldn't it?'

'Yes, it would, sir.'

Fibs sighed. 'Go on then,' he reached for the tray, but Oliver pulled away from him.

'No, sir, it's too hot. Let's just pop into this room. I can put it down on the table and give you the napkin so you don't burn yourself.'

Before Fibs could disagree, Oliver leaned on the open door and entered. He glanced around. The bed was unmade, the guest had gone. He placed the tray down on the table and turned to offer the serviette to Fibs.

Fibs had followed him into the room and reached out for the proffered serviette. Oliver dropped it and, as Fibs stooped to grab it, Oliver met his face with a vicious upper cut. Fibs fell forward like a felled tree. Oliver let him fall.

He rushed to the door, took the key from the outside and then locked it from the inside, leaving the key twisted in the lock so no maid could enter. As he turned back into the room, Terry Fibs was trying to lift himself up on his elbows. Oliver took four paces towards him and kicked him in the head; not too hard, he only wanted him stunned for now, not dead.

He glanced around the room and saw what he needed. There was a writing desk with a solid looking chair. He grabbed the chair and dragged it into the middle of the room. On the bed he could see one of the hotel bathrobes. He pulled the towelling belt out, this would do to tie Fibs' hands.

He went into the bathroom and there on the door was another unused bathrobe. Perfect. He pulled that one out and headed back into the room.

Fibs was conscious and moaning quietly, which in Oliver's book was the best kind of moaning for a victim. He bent down and lifted Fibs onto the chair. He was heavier than he looked but Oliver was strong. He had worked out a lot in Morocco, fifteen years of push ups, pull ups and sit ups had made him stronger than he had ever been in his acting days.

When Terry Fibs opened his eyes, Oliver was standing before him, and there was blood on his shirt. Oliver watched dispassionately as Terry tried to move but his hands and feet were tied to the chair. He tried to speak but Oliver held a finger to his lips.

'Not now, Terry. Let me tell you a story first. You can ask questions later.'

'But …'

He was silenced with a vicious slap across his face, and he cried with pain. As he tried to recover, Oliver shoved a serviette into his mouth. Terry recoiled and attempted to scream, but it was too late. The serviette, which had been on the floor, was now jammed in his mouth. He gagged.

'Don't try to fight it, Terry, you can breathe, just don't try and talk. All you need to do is listen. Can you do that, Terry?'

Terry stared at him; he was terrified.

'Do you understand?' repeated Oliver.

Terry nodded.

'Good.'

There was another chair in front of the dressing table. Oliver grabbed it, brought it over and placed it in front of Terry.

Oliver flashed a smile. 'I want you to look at me, Terry, can you do that?'

Fibs nodded.

'Good. Now look at me really hard, do you recognise me?'

Fibs shook his head.

'Let's try and give you a clue. I'm going to recite something. It was something you wrote over fifteen years ago, let's see if it jogs your memory. Are you ready?'

Fibs nodded, his eyes wild with fear.

Oliver smiled contentedly. 'Then I shall begin. "I had the misfortune of watching Oliver Lawrence play Henry V last night. Seldom have I wished more fervently for a French victory, if only an English archer's arrow could have found my heart and silenced the misery."' Oliver paused and looked questioningly at Fibs. 'Sound familiar?'

Fibs shook his head but, in his eyes, Oliver could see recognition beginning to dawn. Oliver stood up and continued as if he were a character in a play.

'Lawrence's Henry was more akin to a rabble-rousing union leader heading a wild cat strike, than a noble King leading his troops into battle. From where I sat, very few were happy and those that remained wished they were now a-bed. Those of us that had not left, shall think themselves accursed that we were here.

'I see what you did there, Terry, mixing the St Crispin's Day speech in with your review. Very clever, but not very kind, or true. Nobody had left. Would you like to add anything?'

Fibs shook his head, his terror now abject. He clearly knew who his captor was and he recognised his own words.

Oliver continued. 'His acting was so wooden it cast more splinters about the stage than the archer's arrows. What has happened to the huge talent that burst upon the Stratford stage just a few short years ago? The crown sits uneasy on his head, maybe abdication is in order and a spell in pantomime, which would certainly be more suited to his current style of delivery. On the evidence of last night … Oh no it won't!'

Oliver smiled, gazed about the room and then took three deep bows. 'An actor is only as good as the text he is given. Your words were lyrical, acerbic, maybe a little cruel.' Oliver leaned close to Fibs. 'And untrue.' Oliver turned away and walked over to the open window and closed it. 'Now, I think you and I need to have a little chat, don't you, Terry?'

Fibs shook his head vigorously. It was obvious he wanted no part in this.

Oliver smiled wistfully. 'Unfortunately, as you're tied to a chair, you really don't have much say in the matter, do you?'

Fibs shook his head.

Oliver sat down opposite Fibs; he was calm. Before I remove your gag, I want you to know something. I killed Desmond Tharpe last night, I ran the wretched, rash, intruding fool through. A bayonet to the heart.'

Fibs was trembling in terror; he clearly didn't want to hear Oliver's confession.

'I know what you're thinking, Terry. If I confess to you, I can't let you live. And you'd be right.'

A muted howl came from behind Fibs' gag.

Oliver raised his hand to silence him. 'I am going to kill you, Terry, but you have a choice. I can make it easy or hard. We are going to have a little chat now and if you make one sound that isn't part of our conversation, I will do to you what Regan had done to Gloucester.'

Fibs pushed back on his chair, trying to get away from

Oliver, but the chair was up against the settee.

Oliver looked over to the abandoned tray of coffee that the previous guest had left and picked up a teaspoon. He turned back to Fibs. Holding the spoon between the thumb and index finger in his right hand, he tapped it gently against the palm of his left hand.

'Now, where were we? Oh yes, the blinding of Gloucester.'

A muted howl came from behind the gag in Fibs' mouth and he writhed against his bonds. Oliver simply stood and watched; he had time to savour Fibs' terror. He realised that he was enjoying it. Oliver took his seat in front of Fibs once more.

'Look, Terry, I've got a bit of a problem here and I'm going to need your help with it. Would you do that?'

For a moment, Fibs looked hopeful and nodded vigorously.

Oliver smiled. 'Thanks, Terry, I appreciate that. You see, Tabitha's in the room next door. If Desmond was my Polonius, then Tabitha should surely be my Ophelia, and we all know what happened to Ophelia, don't we.'

Fibs nodded.

'Of course we do, she went mad. I think I've gone a bit mad, Terry. When I found out how you and the rest of Sir Morris's little gang had plotted against me and my father, I only had one thought ... revenge. You can understand that, can't you?'

Terry Fibs reaction showed that he understood only too well. He jerked violently against his bonds in a hopeless attempt to get away but Oliver had bound him tightly. Once again, the chair bumped back against the sofa. There was no escape. He tried to speak but his words were just a series of grunts and mumbles from behind the gag.

Oliver waited patiently for him to finish. When he did, he spoke. 'Would you like to say something, Terry?'

Terry nodded.

'Be warned; if you cry out, I will cut out your tongue.' Oliver produced a Stanley knife from his pocket. 'Do we understand each other?'

Fibs nodded.

'Very well.' He leaned forward and pulled the serviette from Fibs' mouth. 'What have you got to say for yourself?'

Fibs' mouth worked and, in a horse croak, he spoke. 'Water.'

Oliver nodded, there was an undrunk glass on the tray. He grabbed it and held it up to Fibs' mouth. Fibs took two trembling gulps before Oliver pulled it away.

'OK, so what is it you want to say?'

'I'm sorry.'

'That's it. You're sorry?'

'Yeah, it got out of hand.'

'Didn't it. You and Morris's little gang caused my father to kill himself, then, a few years later, you treated me the same way.'

'None of us thought that your father would kill himself. Morris just wanted to take him down a peg or two.'

'Oh, you did that all right.' Oliver leaned back on his chair. 'So, tell me something, Terry. After you and Gerard Soames wrote those terrible reviews about my father, did you feel guilty? Especially when he killed himself.'

There was a tear in Fibs' eye now. 'Of course we did.'

'And yet, just a few years later, you were quite happy to repeat the process with me.'

Fibs sighed and the fear on his face was momentarily replaced by regret. 'I know, what we did was terrible but ...' He trailed off.

'Go on.'

'When you're in Sir Morris's group, it's like being on a train.'

'A big fat gravy train?'

Fibs nodded shamefully. 'Yes, he can make or break anyone in the group and once you're in, you can't get out. He's a powerful man.'

Oliver nodded. 'I understand that, Terry, but was it worth

the price? The death of my father, the ending of my career with a nervous breakdown. Can you live with that?'

'No.'

'Well, lucky for you that you won't have to.'

Fibs looked back at Oliver's smiling face and the terror returned.

Before he could cry out, Oliver swiftly jammed the gag back in his mouth. He struggled but it was hopeless. He shook his head, his eyes pleading for mercy. There would be none, he knew that.

Oliver leaned in close. 'Now you've admitted your guilt, we can move on. I'm back in Stratford to kill every one of you. Morris Oxford's little nest of vipers, who did for my father and nearly did for me. Desmond was first and you are going to be next, but I need your help. In my version of Hamlet, you and Gerard are Rosencrantz and Guildenstern, the two little toadies doing the King's bidding. You have a preference?' Oliver asked the question matter-of-factly.

Fibs didn't respond, his whole body seemed to be vibrating in sheer terror. 'In that case you can be Rosencrantz. Now, I know I'm taking liberties with Shakespeare's plot here, but Rosencrantz and Guildenstern were told by the King, that's Morris, to take Hamlet away, that's me, and have him killed. You both metaphorically stabbed me, so that's close enough.'

'Mees non … mees.'

Oliver slapped Fibs hard across the face. 'No begging, Terry, it's not an option.' Oliver sat perfectly still, staring into Terry Fibs' eyes.

The terror was still there, and something else. Acceptance. He'd stopped struggling and just sat waiting for his sentence to be carried out.

Oliver nodded. 'Thanks, Terry, no need to make this harder than it has to be.' Oliver picked up the teaspoon again.

He watched as Fibs' eyes followed it and he started to shake again.

'Now, as I was saying, Tabitha is in the room next door.'

'Nooo, nooo.' The muffled cry came from behind Terry Fibs' gag.

Oliver leaned forward and gently ruffled his hair. 'Don't worry, Terry. I'm not going to touch her, I just want her to go a little mad. Poor girl has had a terrible morning and it's just about to get a lot worse. Being told her dad's been murdered and then finding dear old Uncle Terry dead in the room next door. That should be enough to push her over the edge.' He winked at Fibs. 'Give her a touch of the Ophelias.'

'Murstaa.'

'Were you trying to say bastard, Terry?'

Fibs nodded defiantly.

Oliver shrugged. 'You're probably right. Still, you can't please everyone now, can you.'

Oliver walked round behind Fibs and locked his left arm around his neck tightly, not so tight that he couldn't breathe, but tight enough. He whispered in Fibs' ear. 'Tabitha wasn't in on the plan to ruin my career but she knew what went on and said nothing. I loved her once, you know. Turned out she was empty, no love and no empathy. A cold, over privileged brat who only wanted me when I was on the way up. As my star waned, so did her love. She probably never wanted me.' Oliver paused for a moment and chuckled. 'I sound a bit sorry for myself, don't I. Don't worry, Terry, I'll soon snap out of it.'

Oliver tightened his grip around Terry Fibs' neck. 'Before you go, Terry, I just want to thank you for your help. You see, to drive Tabitha mad I'm going to have to go a bit King Lear on you. You see that adjoining door?'

With his right hand, he pointed with the spoon towards the door that linked the room they were in to Tabitha's room. 'I didn't plan this, just lucky, I guess. When Tabitha comes through the door the first thing she will see is your dead body.

No eyes, no tongue.' Fibs started to struggle again but Oliver held him firm. 'There's going to be a nice little message written in your blood too. You think that will be enough to send her over the edge?'

'Noooo!'

Oliver tapped Fibs on the forehead with the spoon. 'Quiet, Terry, soon be over and because you've been so helpful, I'll make it easy.' Oliver began to squeeze his arm tightly around Terry Fibs neck choking off his air. As he did, he spoke quietly into his ear. 'Goodbye, Terry. "To die, to sleep, to sleep perchance to dream, ay, there's the rub, for in this dream of death what dreams may come."'

Chapter 28
Though This Be Madness

Toby and Fred stood in the doorway of the bedroom. From the bathroom, they could hear someone being violently sick.

'Jesus Christ,' whispered Toby.

Fred just shook his head. 'I told you I had a bad feeling about this.'

Neither of them moved into the room, they just stood there taking in the full horror of the scene. The body of a man was tied to a chair, his eyes had been gouged out and were lying on a bloodied white pillow in front of him, below the eyes was a tongue and below that, written in blood, was a message.

'Though this be madness, yet, there is method in't.'

'Shakespeare,' said Fred.

'Hamlet, Act Two, Scene Two,' whispered Toby.

Fred turned to him. 'You sure?'

Toby nodded. 'Positive, did it in the school play.'

'Where'd you go to school, RADA?'

'Woodrush Secondary Mod.'

Fred looked back at the gruesome scene. 'Thoughts?'

'I think you're right, sir. We've got a serial killer on our hands. He's telling us that this isn't just a random butchering, it's part of a plan.'

Fred nodded. 'I agree. Even more disturbing, he's quoting Shakespeare, which means he's probably a clever bugger.'

Fred stepped gingerly into the room. As he did so, PC Green emerged from the bathroom. Fred looked him up and down. There were flecks of vomit down his jacket and on his boots.

'Morning, PC Green.'

Green nodded weakly. 'Morning, sir, terrible business.'

'Especially for the laundry lady.' Fred scanned the room. 'You touched anything?'

'No, sir, I came in here and saw ...' he nodded towards the corpse, 'that, and I, er ...'

'Headed for the toilet.'

'Yes, sir.'

Fred turned and looked at the young constable, he was clearly in shock.

'This your first murder?'

He nodded.

Fred smiled weakly. 'Well, it won't be your last. Console yourself with the thought that we are going to catch the maniac that did this. Who found him?'

'Another guest, sir, she was in the adjoining room.'

Fred glanced at the open door that led to the next room. 'Do we know how that door was opened?'

PC Green hesitated. 'No, sir. I haven't had chance to check it out yet.'

'Too busy being sick.'

'Yes, sir.'

Fred smiled. 'Very well, do you know the name of the guest?'

'Tabitha Tharpe, sir.'

Fred turned to Toby. 'The daughter of last night's victim.'

Toby nodded. 'That can't be a coincidence.'

'Where is she?'

'They've taken her to Warwick Hospital, sir. One of the staff heard her screams and when they came into the room, she was standing in front of the victim screaming uncontrollably. They sedated her and took her away.'

'Poor girl,' said Toby. 'Her father was killed last night.'

'I want this room sealed. Have SOCO been called?'

'On their way, sir.'

'Good, get down to reception and get a call in to Alf Butcher. I want him here.'

PC Green nodded and hurried from the room, clearly glad to be leaving the scene.

Fred turned to Toby. 'Thoughts?'

'These murders are linked.'

'Obviously. By what though?'

'Tharpe was a Shakespearian actor and this victim had a Shakespearian quote written in his blood.'

Fred nodded and looked back at the corpse. 'What else?'

'His eyes have been gouged out.'

'Like Gloucester, you mean.'

'Yes,'

Fred looked at Toby and then back to the bloody pillow. 'Though this be madness, there is method in't.' He turned towards the open door to the next room. 'Look at the victim. The killer turned the chair so he is facing that door. The first thing that Tabitha sees when she walks in is that. There's no coincidence here, it's all part of a plan.'

'You think there's going to be more?' asked Toby.

'I'm sure of it. Whoever is responsible for this,' he looked distastefully at the horribly mutilated corpse sitting in the chair. 'This wasn't just about killing; he's sending a message. He wanted Miss Tharpe to see this, read the message and understand.'

'Understand what, sir?'

'This is just the beginning.' Fred Williams looked slowly about the room. 'Why remove the eyes and the tongue? It must have been a terrible death.'

Toby walked over to where the body sat and peered closely at the mutilated features. He felt the bile rise in his throat but swallowed it back. 'I think he was dead before the eyes and tongue were removed.'

'Go on,' said Fred.

'Look at the blood. There's a fair bit but, if his heart was still beating, there would have been a lot more than this.'

Fred came closer and looked into the bloody caverns in the victim's face, where his eyes had once been. 'Good point, a little blood goes a long way. There's not that much.'

'And his tongue, sir, look how clean and straight that cut is. If the victim was still alive, he would have screamed the place down. It would have been impossible to make a clean cut. The killer would have had to hack it out.'

Fred bent down and looked at the bloody tongue. 'It is a nice clean cut.' As he looked around the room, Fred began to think that Toby was right. There was no comfort in the thought. 'We need to know who this poor sod was.'

'You think there will be a connection to last night's victim?'

'I'd bet my pension on it.'

'There's a jacket over there on the sofa.'

Fred raised his hand. 'Leave it, Toby, we've already disturbed the scene too much, lets back out and leave the rest for SOCO.' He took a long look around the room trying to imprint the scene on his memory. He needed to think. 'Come on, let's wait outside so we can brief SOCO when they get here.'

As they stepped into the corridor Fred pulled the door to behind them.

'What about the adjoining room, sir, we don't want anyone going in there do we?'

'No, we don't. Whoever that was,' Fred nodded his head towards the room, 'was mutilated to send a message to Tabitha Tharpe. If we can find out what that message means, we can crack the case.'

'I think you could be right, sir. If the victim was already dead, it would make sense to leave the scene quickly but the killer didn't do that. He gouged out the eyes, cut out the tongue and then displayed them on a pillow with a cryptic verse from Shakespeare. That must have taken him five or six minutes. Why would he take the risk?'

'Exactly.'

There was a commotion at the end of the corridor, the fire doors swung backwards and Inspector Beeching came bursting through. He didn't look happy.

'Morning, Fred, this is a bad business. Two murders in twelve hours. We need to get a hold of this. HQ will want to bring in Coventry. We don't want that, do we.'

Fred knew that Beeching didn't. He wanted the glory of solving these murders to come to his force, raise his profile and get him the promotion with the Met that he so craved. 'SOCO are on the way and I've called in Alf Butcher, he's the best pathologist for a job like this.'

Beeching nodded his approval. 'Good, Butcher's a good man, he won't leave any stone unturned.' He pointed to the door. 'Victim still in there?'

Fred nodded and Beeching turned to go in.

'I wouldn't if I was you, sir.'

Beeching turned sternly to Fred. 'And why wouldn't I?'

'It's pretty gruesome, sir.'

Beeching gave him a condescending smile. 'I've been to more murders than you've had hot dinners, detective, there is nothing in that room that I haven't seen before.' He turned the handle and entered the room. After two steps he stopped dead in his tracks. He stifled a yelp and then, under his breath, he whispered, 'My God!' The only other sound he made was the thump of his body as it landed on the floor.

Toby hurried into the room. Beeching was lying on the floor of the apartment but thankfully clear of all the areas that they wanted to forensically investigate.

'Give me a hand to get him up.'

Fred shook his head. 'Let's leave him there for now, Toby, we've got enough on our plate. If Beeching is kind enough to knock himself out for a while the very least we can do is to not interrupt his slumbers.'

Toby put him in the recovery position.

'He still breathing?'

'Yes, sir.'

'Let's let him take a nap why we try to figure out what's going on here. He's going to be unbearable when he comes round.'

'You don't seem very concerned about him, sir.'

Fred shrugged. 'I'm not. The mans a career copper, he's not interested in solving crime, he just wants to play the game and climb the promotion ladder. His type makes me sick. "Seen more murders than I've had hot dinners," has he? I heard he only had one murder case in Northampton and he didn't solve it! He's been praying for a big case to bring him to the attention of the Met but he's got more than he bargained for here. This isn't a career maker, it's a career breaker. The bodies are going to pile up and we are going to look like fools.'

Toby was shocked by Fred's assessment.

'You think it's that bad?'

'It's worse. This guy's clever but he's also insane. None of this is done in the heat of the moment and yet the things he does …'

Fred trailed off and they gazed at the eyeless corpse, staring forever and seeing nothing. His tongue lolled out beneath his vacant, staring eyes.

'See no evil, speak no evil. Is there a message for us there?'

'Of course there is, young Toby. "Though this be madness, there is method in't." He's saying to us that this looks a bit crazy, tearing out eyes and tongues.'

'It does, sir.'

'Clearly, but there is a reason behind it. This guy isn't a random victim, he's been selected and then he has been displayed deliberately to Tabitha Tharpe. A young lady who had her father murdered last night on the way home from performing a Shakespeare play. This is all linked, we need to know who this guy is to discover what those links are.'

Fred pointed to a satchel on the sofa. 'That could be the victims. You think you could walk round behind the sofa without disturbing the crime scene?'

'Yeah, I'm sure I could.'

Toby moved carefully over to the couch and picked it up. He brought it back to Fred. He opened it carefully and looked inside.

'Anything interesting,' asked Toby.

Fred pulled out a wallet from the satchel. He opened it and started to riffle through. 'He's a journalist, or was.'

'What's his name?'

'Terry Fibs.'

The name sounded vaguely familiar. 'He writes for one of the big weeklies. Daily Smear, I think.'

Toby looked hard at the accreditation card. 'The Daily Smear is right, sir. There's a ticket for last night's performance of Julius Cesar.'

'There's our connection, right there. He saw the play last night and he's a journalist who writes about the theatre. Go and find out everything you can about him, he's the key to understanding what's going on here.'

'Yes, sir.' Toby left the room without looking at Fibs, the memory of the eyeless corpse would live with him for a long time. He glanced back over his shoulder and Fred was just standing there taking in the whole, horrific scene, desperately trying to make sense of something that, on the surface, made no sense.

It was at times like these that being a detective felt like the loneliest job in the world. Trying to make sense of the nonsensical. In the margins where insanity meets the normal world. Somehow, they needed to find a way to navigate in this margin and understand the motivations of a killer who was guilty of a monstrosity like this. Toby knew he was out of his depth. He would have to lean on Fred's experience, it was the only thing that could help them now.

'What the hell's happened here?'

Fred turned around and there was Simon Allen.

He looked at the eyeless corpse. 'Jesus, what kind of a maniac would do that?'

'The kind that enjoyed it. He's mad but he's clever. Get me anything you can.' There was a hint of desperation in Fred's voice which Simon Allen had never heard before.

A groan came from a body lying by the bed. The both looked over in its direction.

Simon nodded. 'Is that Beeching?'

'Yep.'

'What happened?'

'Took a look at our dead friend's face and fainted.'

'Is he OK?'

Fred shrugged. 'Well, he's groaning so I'm guessing he's still alive.'

'Shouldn't we do something?'

Fred nodded towards the victim. 'Don't know if you've noticed but I'm a bit busy.'

'But what if he dies?'

'We can frame him for the murder and be back at the station in time for lunch.'

Simon smiled. 'You're a sick bastard, Fred Williams.'

'Thanks, it's one of my strong points.' They both grinned.

'Bugger me.' They both looked up and, in the doorway, stood Christine Fellows, her camera already in hand, ready to record the scene. The sight had stopped her in her tracks. 'What madness is this.'

'Well, that's what we've got to find out, Christine. You've seen the quotation on the pillow. I'm sure this is linked to last night's murder. His name is Terry Fibs.'

'What, the hack that writes for the Daily Smear?'

'Not a fan?'

Christine shook her head. 'The guys a hatchet man for Rupert Fox. Gutter press.' She looked disdainfully at Terry Fibs' butchered remains. 'Looks like one of his victims finally caught up with him.'

Fred nodded. 'Would a bad review lead to this?'

Christine shrugged. 'Maybe. Actors' egos are fragile.'

Fred didn't look convinced. 'It's not a bad theory but …' He frowned and shook his head.

Beeching groaned again.

'Is that Inspector Beeching?'

Fred nodded at Christine. 'Yeah.'

'What's he doing down there?'

'Dying, hopefully.'

'Fred's going to stitch him up for the murder if he does,' said Simon.

Christine smiled. 'Seems fair. What happened, did he faint?'

'Yeah. I told him not to go in but he barged past me, took one look at the late lamented Terry Fibs and hit the deck.'

'Can't say I blame him, not a sight for the faint-hearted.'

'True.'

Fred was interrupted by another groan and, this time, Beeching raised his head from the floor. He rubbed his neck and opened his eyes, unfortunately he was facing towards Terry Fibs. He took one look and promptly fainted again. His head thumped pleasingly on the floor.

'That should keep him quiet for another few minutes. Do me a favour, Christine, make sure you get Beeching in as many shots as you can. I can use it against him in the future.'

Christine smiled. 'You cunning old bastard.'

'Never look a gift horse in the mouth. If we don't get these murders solved pronto, Beeching will be all over us. Be nice to have something to take the wind out of his sails.'

Simon and Christine got on with their work, minutely covering every inch of the apartment around the body. Apart from the spot where Beeching lay, snoring gently. From down the corridor, Fred heard the approach of Alf Butcher, who was humming Beethoven's Ode to Joy from the 9th Symphony. As he entered the room, the joy swiftly left him.

'Bloody hell, better not tell the tourist board about this.'

Fred couldn't help but smile. Alf Butcher was unshockable.

'See Stratford and die,' said Fred.

Alf looked at the eyes displayed on the bloody pillow. 'These buggers aren't going to be seeing anything.' As he moved towards Terry Fibs' mutilated body, he stepped carefully over the sleeping Beeching. 'Fainted again?'

'Yep, hit the deck like a felled oak.'

Alf glanced briefly as he dropped his bag next to Beeching's inert form. 'He going to live?'

'Unless he turns up on your slab, he should be fine.'

'Pity, death becomes him.' Alf turned his attention to the mortal remains of Terry Fibs. 'Messy, not too much blood.' He peered closer. 'I'm not saying this definitively but if you asked my opinion, I reckon he was dead before the eyes and the tongue were removed. If his heart was still beating there would be far more blood.'

'That's what DC Marlowe thought.'

'Clever lad. Hang on to him, Fred.'

Fred smiled. 'I intend to. Cause of death?'

Alf lifted Terry Fibs' head and felt around his throat. 'I'd say he was choked to death. The tongue would normally be distended.' He glanced across to the bloody lump on the pillow. 'But not usually that far.

Fred and Simon grinned.

'You're a sick git, Alf.'

'Goes with the territory, old son.' Alf began to inspect the fingers on Fibs' left hand and then moved on to his right. 'This bugger's never done a hard day's work in his life.'

'He's a writer. Has a column in the Daily Smear.'

Alf looked distastefully at Fibs' mortal remains. 'I wouldn't call working for the Smear writing. A monkey with some crayons could do better.'

'Be hard to disagree but something he wrote got him killed.'

Alf turned to Fred. 'You think?'

Fred nodded. 'I've got a prominent actor starring in a Shakespeare play, dead. His daughter has been driven half out of her mind by his death and seeing this. She's also a Shakespearian actor, and our victim was a theatre critic who watched last night's play and was a close family friend. It's all connected.'

Alf pulled a thermometer out of his bag and turned to Fred. 'Sounds like you have a serial killer on your hands. Better get him caught quick, Fred, I'm off on my holidays in ten days' time. The south of France waits for no man.'

Chapter 29
The Law's Delay

Two hours later, Fred Williams sat at his desk in Guild Street eating an ox tongue sandwich.

Toby shuddered. 'How can you eat that after what we just saw?'

'If I want to catch the killer I need to eat, I can't think when I'm hungry.'

'But tongue.'

'It was on special offer at the Co-op. Besides, I made my sandwich before I knew what had happened. Could have been worse.'

'How.'

'I could have had some pickled onions with it.' Fred winked and took a huge bite. Before he got anywhere near swallowing, he continued, 'I still reckon we have a serial killer on our hands. What do you say, young Toby?'

Toby nodded gravely, looking down so as not to see the death throes of the sandwich as it made its final journey to Fred Williams' stomach. 'I agree, sir, I think both victims are linked and Tharpe's daughter was set up so that she saw Fibs.'

'How is she?'

'In shock, she's been sedated and she has been moved to the White Swan on Rother Street. Sir Morris Oxford has organised it, apparently, he's her godfather.'

'Isn't that where her father was staying?'

'Yes, sir, moved into her father's old room.'

'Makes sense. Probably been paid for before he got the chop.'

Toby winced. 'I would think it was for comfort, to feel closer to her father.'

'Yeah, but that suits us. We need to have a word with Sir Morris. Both the victims and Miss Tharpe are part of his little group. If they were targets, maybe he is too.'

Toby hadn't thought of that. 'Bloody hell, shall I get a uniform over there?'

Fred shrugged. 'No need, we are going there ourselves as soon as I've finished my sandwich.'

As he took another bite, the door swung open and Kinky Bernstein and Ginger Dalton entered. Fred had sent them to find out everything they could about the connections between Terry Fibs and Desmond Tharpe.

'Here they are, Batman and Robin. What've you got for me, boys?'

Bernstein sat down on the edge of Fred's desk. 'I spoke to the editor at the Daily Smear and he told me that almost every actor in Britain could have a reason for stabbing Fibs. His reviews are real hatchet jobs but, interestingly, he's never gone after Tharpe or his boss.'

'Sir Morris?'

Bernstein nodded. 'He only said good things about both of them.'

Fred looked at Dalton. 'What did you get from the Herald?'

'About the same, boss. Fibs was a nasty little sod, tore everyone to pieces but never Tharpe or Sir Morris.'

'Was he close to the victims?'

'Yeah, almost like family. They all seem to be in a little gang, known each other for years.'

Toby nodded. 'Someone's targeting their group, maybe someone with a grudge.'

'Makes sense,' said Fred.

Toby went over to a blackboard in the corner of the room and started writing down names.

'Desmond Tharpe was in Sir Morris Oxford's players, so was

Tabitha Tharpe. Terry Fibs was a lifelong friend of all of them and, despite being known for his cutting reviews, never seems to have given any of them a bad review.'

Toby drew a line down the middle of the board. On the left were the names of the two victims. On the other side he wrote 'Sir Morris Oxford' and then turned to the other detectives. 'We need to find out everyone who is in Oxford's little group, they could all be under threat.'

Fred nodded approvingly. 'I like it. Kinky and Ginger, you can find out the names of everyone in that group, anyone in town now is considered under threat, Toby and I can start looking into who has had the chop from the group. Bound to be actors who didn't make the cut, Sir Morris is a ruthless old git. I'm sure he's made plenty of enemies over the years.'

'And one of them turned killer?'

'You got a better idea.'

Toby shook his head. 'No, sir.'

'Let's work on that basis then until events prove us wrong.'

Just then the door to CID swung open and in walked Inspector Beeching. Amused looks passed between the team.

'Feeling better, sir?'

Beeching looked cautiously at Fred Williams. 'Yes, took a blow to the head, but it's all in the line of duty.'

Fred nodded gravely. 'Sight like that is enough to cause anyone to fall flat on their face.'

Beeching blushed. 'I tripped on the carpet, DS Williams, must have been rucked up during the murder.'

'Course it was, sir.'

'Where are we with the investigation?'

'We're looking at the links between the victims and they all seem to be in Sir Morris Oxford's little gang. We reckon that it could be someone who has left the company under a cloud.'

Beeching looked dubious. 'Being sacked from a theatre group is hardly grounds for murder.'

'It is if it's Sir Morris Oxford's group. They never stop working, do big tours of the world and once you're in it's virtually a job for life. That's almost unheard of for an actor.'

'That it? Seems a bit thin.'

'While you were sleeping, sir, we all did a bit of digging.'

There was some sniggering from the detectives.

Beeching blushed angrily. 'I was not sleeping.'

'No, sir, you were unconscious, but while you were, that's what we came up with. It's the only apparent motive we have at the moment so we are going to run with it unless something comes up to prove us wrong.'

'Very well, Fred, but the eyes of the country are on us. Two gruesome murders in Stratford in less than twenty-four hours. We need to solve this quickly.'

'We do, sir. Do you have any thoughts?'

The question stumped Beeching. Fred suspected his only thought was how these murders would affect his promotion to the Met if he didn't solve them quickly.

'Er, yes.'

'Care to share, sir?'

Beeching blushed once more. 'Catch the killer, Fred, catch the killer.' With that, he spun on his heel and left the office.

Fred watched him go. 'Thanks, sir, that's very helpful.'

Chapter 30
Cruel To Be Kind

In Trinity Street, Oliver Lawrence was soaking in a warm bath. The morning's events had gone better than even he could have hoped for. In his search for Tabitha, Terry Fibs had fallen right into his lap. The fact that the room next to Tabitha's had been empty and had an adjoining door was more than he could have dreamed of.

Killing Terry had been easier than he'd thought. Seeing the fear in his eyes when he told him who he was, then the terror when he explained what he was going to do to him. The memory of it made him smile. He thought about that for a moment; in the last twenty-four hours he had killed Desmond Tharpe and Terry Fibs, and driven Tabitha out of her mind. This was not normal behaviour; Felix would have something to say about this.

Oliver held up his hands before him, the hands of a killer. He stretched out the fingers of both. He had long fingers and curved artistic thumbs, these were the hands of a musician or an artist, and yet …

His years in Morocco had made him strong. He had worked in a warehouse in Fez for a period and built muscle from the arduous work, he had liked the way it felt. The power, the way his muscles rippled when he moved. He was not the same broken man that had fled from the shame of failure, the man he had become was strong and driven by a desire that even he recognised he could not control.

This thing, whatever it was, would not be over until all the names on the list that Felix had given him had paid the price for betraying his father. Somehow, it made it easier to imagine he was revenging his father, it wasn't just about him. He knew he was lying to himself but, if it made the task easier, so be it. He leaned forward and turned the hot tap on again, he felt like luxuriating in the warm soapy waters for a little longer. He was clean but he could never wash away his guilt; luckily for him, he didn't feel any. He caught his reflection in the full length mirror, and turned to face it. 'I must be cruel, only to be kind.' His reflection smiled back at him in agreement.

Chapter 31
A Touch Of The Gloucesters

In his room at the Alveston Manor, Felix had listened to the news on Radio 4. Oliver was working a lot faster than he had anticipated. His avenging angel was on a roll. First Desmond and now Fibs. All the news had said was that Desmond had been stabbed, there was no mention of how Fibs had died. Felix was guessing that it must have been pretty gruesome or the police would have said something. He needed to speak to Oliver soon. He decided to pop round to Trinity Street for a little chat.

Forty minutes later he was knocking on the door. He heard Oliver's footsteps come cautiously down the corridor. He knew that Oliver wouldn't open it, so he bent down and called through the letterbox. 'Oliver, it's Felix, let me in.'

He heard the footsteps move rapidly towards the door and then the bolt being shot. It swung open and Oliver's smiling face ushered him in.

'Come in quick, we don't want anyone seeing you here.'

Felix slipped inside and Oliver rapidly locked and bolted the door. When he turned around, Felix had already made his way into the kitchen.

'You want a cup of tea?'

Felix nodded. 'Someone's been a busy boy.'

'Can't look a gift horse in the mouth, they both just fell into my lap.'

'So you killed Fibs and drove Tabitha crazy.'

'Be rude not to.'

Felix smiled weakly. 'Are you sure about this? You could stop now. Two of the culprits behind your father's demise and your career being ruined, are dead, isn't that enough?'

Oliver shook his head. 'It will never be enough. It won't bring back my father and it can never make up for all those lost years. I realised, as I killed Desmond, that it was the right thing to do. I told you, I ran him through like Polonius. I even quoted the text to him as I did it.' Oliver mimed plunging the bayonet into Desmond.

'And you call me a luvvie,' sighed Felix.

'It just felt right. It's like doing a Shakespeare play for real. When people are killed, they really die.'

Felix looked at the spark in Oliver's eyes as he talked, he was enjoying this. 'Did they say how Fibs died?'

'No, just said he had been murdered too.'

'I found him outside Tabitha's room at the Falcon.'

'What were you doing there? Tabitha's not on the list.' There was a note of alarm in Felix's voice.

'Not to kill, no, but she knew what they were doing to me, and she said nothing.'

'You can't kill Tabitha, that's not right.'

Oliver held up his hand. 'Relax, I wasn't going to. I just wanted to give her a terrible scare. Drive her round the bend so she could be my Ophelia to her father's Polonius. She was already in a state of shock after they told her that her father had been killed. I found Fibs outside her door trying to build up the courage to knock, the room next door was open so I persuaded him to come in on the pretext of taking the coffee to her room.' Felix looked confused. 'I was pretending to be a waiter, I had a tray with coffee. I told him I was dreading knocking, and so was he, so I suggested he deliver the coffee to break the ice. Once I got him in there, I knocked him out and trussed him to a chair. I told him who I was and what I was going to do to him.'

'Did he scream?'

'He tried to but I had already gagged him.'

'How did you kill him?'

'I strangled him.'

Felix winced. 'That's a bit hands on.'

'He was tied to the chair so it was pretty easy, I choked him out from behind.'

Felix looked unimpressed. 'Not very Shakespearian, was it.'

Oliver grinned. 'That's where you're wrong, Felix. I went full Gloucester on his ass. Gouged out his eyes with a spoon and stuck them on a pillow in front of him.'

'Jesus,' whispered Felix.

'Then I cut out his tongue. Slippery little bugger but it was no match for my Stanley knife. I laid it out below the eyes and then, using his eye socket as an inkwell, I left a message for Tabitha. I scrawled it on the pillow below the tongue.'

Felix went very pale.

'If this be madness, there is method in't.'

Oliver stood smiling at Felix; he didn't smile back.

'When I gave you the truth behind what happened to you, I didn't expect this.'

'Dead is dead Felix, he never felt a thing when I did it, he knew it was coming though, because I told him. There was a connecting door between the room I killed him in, and Tabitha's. I lined him up with the door and then unlocked it and called to Tabitha. It took a while for her to answer but eventually I heard her.

'Who's there?' she said.

'You didn't tell her.'

'Course not, I was a bit more creative than that. I was always able to do a passing imitation of Desmond so I leaned close to the door and called her. 'Tabitha, it is I, your father. Open the door and let me live.'

'That was cruel. Why do that?'

'Ophelia went mad. When she opened that door and saw Terry she screamed like a wounded hound. Totally lost it. I slipped down the back stairs and out into the street. I could still hear her at the bottom of Church Road.'

Felix didn't know what to say. Tabitha had never been part of the plan. Oliver seemed to playing out his own play and it involved scenes he had never envisioned. 'You've gone too far, Oliver; I can't allow it.'

Oliver stared at him and the look sent a cold shiver down his spine. Oliver was no longer his to command.

'I didn't kill her; I just gave her a fright. If it sends her over the edge then so be it, she had it coming. Left me hanging when her father and his cronies turned on me.'

'I understand but we agreed the list. Can we just stick to it?'

Oliver stood and stared at Felix again. It took only a few seconds, but it felt like hours. 'Very well, but I still don't regret it.'

'Who's next?'

'Soames.'

Felix nodded approvingly. 'Good. I never liked him.'

Chapter 32
A National Treasure

Sir Morris Oxford was still an impressive figure. He was a big man with rosy cheeks coloured by many years of robust drinking, and a round stomach from a very healthy appetite. Moderation was not in his vocabulary. But at over six feet and with a booming voice, like chocolate forged on an anvil, he hypnotised you when he spoke.

'This is a terrible business. Desmond and Terry, within twenty-four hours, in Stratford!' He was in shock. 'Do you have any idea who is behind this?'

Fred shook his head. 'No, Sir Morris, I'm afraid we don't. We are working on a theory that it is someone with a grudge against the Oxford Players.'

Sir Morris looked aghast. 'Who could possibly hold a grudge against me? I'm a national treasure, the Daily Mail said so.' Righteous indignation flowed from him. 'Tynan said I was the jewel in the English theatrical crown, even that northern upstart Bragg said my Richard III was a classic. I have stridden the stages of the world like a colossus, reinterpreted Shakespeare and, some would say, made it better. I was knighted by the Queen for my services to the theatre. I'm loved, admired even. Who could possibly want to harm me?' He slumped back down in his armchair; his declamations had left him breathless.

Fred and Toby sat passively listening to his self-important speech. It had been like one of his speeches on stage, overblown and theatrical. The voice was superb but there was no nuance. Toby wondered how he had got away with it for so long.

'We don't think it's personal against you, Sir Morris, we think it's about your company. It's a very prestigious one.'

'It is,' agreed Sir Morris. 'Probably the greatest collection of Shakespearian actors the world has ever known. You can keep Henry Irving and Edmund Keane. Forget about Larry Olivier and Richard Burton, they are more interested in film these days. My company is the one true bearer of the torch; we keep the flame of Shakespeare alive. Anyone else is just following in our footsteps.'

'We agree,' lied Fred. 'That's exactly why anyone who got sacked from your company would feel aggrieved. Have you sacked anyone recently?'

Sir Morris thought for a moment. 'Not for five years, we have a very settled company. My players love me.'

'What about Hugh Pitt, he didn't like you much.'

Sir Morris turned his angry gaze on Toby. 'And who might you be?'

'DC Marlowe, sir.'

A sneer spread across Sir Morris's face. 'Marlowe … Marlowe! I should have known. The pretender to Shakespeare's crown, only a Marlowe could suggest something like that.'

Toby was not intimidated; he had long thought that Sir Morris Oxford's posturing on stage were more suited to vaudeville than Shakespeare. 'He did say in an interview that your Henry V was more pantomime dame than warrior king.'

Oxford sprung back onto his feet and exploded with anger. 'How dare you! Do you know who I am? My Henry is still talked about in hushed whispers. I held the audience in the palm of my hand. The St Crispin's day speech lives on in the annuls of history. Long after Larry Olivier and Johnny Gielgud have shuffled off their mortal coils, people who were there will say, did you see Oxford's Henry? Were you there?' His eyes looked upward and he extended his arms. 'We were there, they will say. No Henry will ever compare. That night we were truly on the field at Agincourt and Sir Morris was Henry. He inhabited the heart and soul of the young King and took us with him to the battlefield. He was magnificent.' Sir Morris trembled as he finished the quote.

'That's wonderful, sir, but it doesn't alter the fact that Hugh Pitt was sacked from your company and clearly held a grudge.'

'He had no talent for the stage.'

'But he has gone on to be a big star in Hollywood.'

'Hollywood,' scoffed Sir Morris dismissively, 'is just a place for those that can't do it on stage.'

'Four Dates and a Christening turned over $200 million at the box office. Pitt was on a percentage and walked away with a couple of million.'

The resentment played across Oxford's face Despite being an actor, he couldn't conceal his anger.

'I did him a favour then, didn't I. He should be thanking me.'

'But he didn't, did he. How bad was your relationship?'

Fred looked at Toby, surprised at how aggressive he was being. 'We are trying to stop another murder here, Sir Morris, so your co-operation would be appreciated.'

'He is on location in Hollywood, shooting the sequel to that ghastly Four Dates and a Christening, so he couldn't have done it.'

'Are you sure about that?'

'How could I not be; the wretched boy has been crowing about it in the press. Reckons being sacked by me was the best thing that ever happened to him.'

Toby looked over at Fred. 'I guess we can remove him from our list then.'

Fred nodded. 'Seems like it.' He turned back to Sir Morris. 'I'd like you to sit down with DC Marlowe and go through every employee that you have let go in the last ten years. We need to trace all of these people so that we can eliminate them from our enquiries. Could you do that for me, Sir Morris?'

'Do I have a choice?'

'Not if you want to avoid being murdered. We think the killer is linked to you in some way. He has already killed two of your colleagues and given poor Miss Tharpe the fright of her life.'

For a moment Sir Morris looked concerned. 'Poor Tabitha, I heard what happened. A sight like that, so soon after the news of her father, must have been enough to drive her insane.'

'She's in shock, sir. I believe you have arranged for her to have her father's room. Is she under sedation?'

The talk of Tabitha seemed to bring Sir Morris to his senses. He sadly shook his head. 'I think you are wrong, sergeant, but I will co-operate if there's even a slim chance of avoiding a repeat of the events of last night.'

'Thank you, sir. We are going to speak to the theatre and ask them to cancel tonight's show, given the events of the last twenty-four hours.'

The indignation returned once more to Sir Morris Oxford's features. 'You cannot cancel; the show must go on. It's what Desmond would have wanted. Tabitha too.'

'And what about Terry Fibs?' added Toby.

'What about him?' asked Sir Morris.

'He was a close friend of yours, wasn't he? As a mark of respect.'

Sir Morris laughed. 'Respect for a critic? You're having a laugh. Terry Fibs was a hanger on but a very useful one.' He winked at both of the detectives. 'Best having the likes of Terry in the tent pissing out, if you get my drift.'

They did. 'Could you excuse us for a second, Sir Morris.'

'Yes, of course.'

Fred went out into the corridor and Toby followed. 'What do you think?'

'The man's a buffoon, totally in love with himself.'

'That much is obvious. What he said about Hugh Pitt, do you believe him?'

'I do, sir. I heard Pitt on Radio 4 the other day talking about the current film he is making on location in Hollywood. His alibi is sound, but I'll get Ginger to double check to make sure he hasn't flipped back over on Concorde to do a spot of murder.'

'Dig as deep as the old boy can remember, then find out who does his accounts and dig into those.'

'How far back should I go?'

Fred thought for a moment. 'Ten years should do it.'

At that moment Oliver Lawrence was granted a stay of execution. He had been forced out over fifteen years before. The net that should have been closing was going to miss him completely.

Chapter 33
A Conflict Of Interest

When Fred Williams got back to Guild Street, he was greeted by the sight of Chief Constable Wilson in Beeching's office. Beeching didn't look happy. The events of the last two days had put his investigation into the chief's lifestyle, and how he paid for it, firmly on the back burner. Fred tried to sneak to his desk but Beeching spotted him. The door to his office swung open.

'Get in here, DS Williams, the chief and I need an update.'

Like a condemned man, Fred made his way slowly into the office.

The chief nodded sombrely at him. 'This is a bad business, Williams. I may need to get some of my boys in to help you out. Any leads?'

'Yes, sir. We are working on the basis that it could be one of Sir Morris Oxford's ex-employees. Everyone that's been targeted seems to have Sir Morris as the connection. DC Marlowe is going through a list of possible candidates with Sir Morris as we speak.'

'Hardly seems like grounds for murder.'

'This killer is clever, sir. Leaves no evidence and is in and out without being seen. He left Shakespearian quotes at the scene of the second murder, which is another link to Sir Morris.'

'Well, if you're sure this is the best avenue. I'll send over DI Townsend and her team to help.'

Fred's heart sank. Melanie Townsend, the Blonde Bombshell. They had once been close, more than close. He didn't need old wounds opened at a time like this but there was no choice in the matter. This was becoming a major incident and the small Stratford force was going to get help whether they wanted it or not.'

'Will she be working under me, sir?'

'She outranks you, Williams, but she can take direction from you until you are otherwise advised.'

Fred knew that was the best he could hope for and smiled weakly at the chief.

'Inspector Beeching has been bringing me up to date on the second murder, pretty gruesome stuff. We've got a maniac on our hands here.'

Fred nodded. 'I think so, but he's clever. Takes his time, never too long. Nobody sees him come or go and he leaves no weapon or trace. It's all done very calmly, no sign of a struggle which makes me think he knows the victims and they know him.'

'Tabitha Tharpe is still alive.'

Fred nodded. 'She is, sir, but she is in no state to be questioned. One of our uniformed officers managed to question her briefly before she was taken to hospital. She was in shock but she did confirm she never saw the killer's face. Another reason why we think he is known to them. If he wasn't going to kill her, he couldn't afford for her to see his face.'

'I suppose this has taken your attention away from the racecourse robbery.'

Wilson's comment took Fred by surprise and he tried hard not to show it. Why, at a time like this, would he even be thinking about a simple robbery? It made no sense, unless … Fred Williams knew in that moment that Chief Wilson had something to hide and he would find it, just as soon as he caught his serial killer.

'Yes, sir, that will have to wait until we can put some resources to it. We have bigger fish to fry.'

Wilson smiled happily. Given the situation, it really wasn't appropriate. He nodded towards Inspector Beeching who was sporting a nasty black eye. 'I believe our inspector here got injured in the line of duty.'

Fred blinked at the description of Beeching's faint, now wasn't the time to throw his boss under the bus. 'Yes, sir, he was running to the aid of the victim and he tripped on a piece of carpet that must have been rucked up during the incident.'

Wilson nodded approvingly. 'Not so sure I could have run towards a sight like that.'

'All in the line of duty,' said Beeching, grateful to his sergeant for saving his blushes. 'I think DS Williams is on the right track with this one. He's getting some protection for Sir Morris, and other senior members of his company. We believe that they are all potential targets.'

Wilson nodded again. 'Very well. I will have DI Townsend over here tomorrow morning. I'll get her to report direct to you at nine, Williams.'

'Thank you, sir.'

The chief nodded to Beeching and Fred and turned to go. 'Let's catch this maniac as soon as we can or we'll have the tourist board on our backs.'

Fred and Beeching watched him go. Beeching waited until he had left the CID office and turned to Fred.

'Very keen to put the racecourse robbery to bed, wasn't he.'

Fred nodded. 'Surprisingly keen, sir.'

'Let's keep this on the back boiler for now, Fred, but let's make sure we don't let it go. I've got a feeling that Chief Constable Wilson has secrets.'

Fred looked forward to discovering what they were but that would have to wait. He had two unsolved murders, a half-crazed actress and his ex to deal with.

Chapter 34
Return Of The Prodigal Son

Sir Morris finished dialling and waited. On the eighth ring, it was answered.

'Hello.'

'Beatrice, it's me.'

'Morris?' There was surprise in her voice. 'What are you doing ringing, shouldn't you be at the theatre?'

'Haven't you seen the news, my dear?'

'What news? You know I never listen to the news, far too depressing.'

'It's Desmond.'

'What about Desmond. Is everything all right?'

'I'm afraid not …' Sir Morris paused, unsure how to break the news.

'What's wrong, darling? You sound terrible.'

'Desmond is dead.'

His words landed like a blow from a hammer. For a moment, Lady Beatrice Morris was stunned into silence. She gathered herself quickly.

'How?'

'He was murdered, my dear. Stabbed through the heart in the graveyard of Holy Trinity last night.'

'Oh, my God, that's awful.'

'It gets worse, I'm afraid.'

'How could it get worse?'

'Terry Fibs has been murdered too.'

The line fell silent as Lady Beatrice tried to comprehend the terrible news.

'Are you still there, darling?'

'Yes, sorry, Morris. I can't believe it. Who would do such a thing?'

'The police have a theory that it's someone who has a grudge against me and my company.'

'Terry wasn't an actor, he was a critic.'

'But he was a friend and supporter. He died a terrible death.'

'What happened?'

Sir Morris could hear the rising anxiety in his wife's voice. 'I'd rather not say, darling, it's too awful.'

'Tell me.' Her voice had hardened, there was no mistaking that tone. He had to tell her.

'He was tied to a chair and strangled. The killer removed his eyes and cut out his tongue.' He paused for a moment unsure if he should share the full horror.

'What else? I know you're not telling me everything.'

The hard tone was still there. 'The killer laid them on a pillow in front of him and wrote a message in his blood beneath them.'

'What did it say?'

'Beatrice, dear, do you really need to hear this?'

'Tell me.'

Reluctantly Sir Morris continued. 'Though this be madness, yet there is method in't.'

The line fell silent again as Lady Beatrice tried to place the quote.

'It's Hamlet, Act 2 Scene 2.'

'It is, my dear. The police believe they were killed by the same man. Whoever did it knew that poor Tabitha was in the next room. There was an adjoining door. He displayed Terry so that when she opened the door, she would see the awful scene spread out before her. He knocked on her door and called for her by name. The poor girl is half demented with shock and grief. First her father and then this.'

Lady Beatrice did not answer; she was desperately trying to make sense of what she was hearing. 'The eyes, that's Gloucester from Lear. It's a message, Morris. See no evil, speak no evil.'

'Don't try to read too much into this, dear, you're in shock, we all are. The police are going back through the list of everyone who has been fired from the company over the last ten years to try and find a suspect.'

Beatrice shook her head. 'They need to go back further.'

'Sorry?'

'You heard me, Morris, they need to go back further.'

'How far?'

'Fifteen years. Fifteen long, hard years.' There was a deadness to the tone of Lady Oxford's voice. Or was it fear?

'Why fifteen, dear.'

'You don't need to ask me that. You know too, don't you.'

'Know what?'

'It's Oliver, you stupid man. He's back!'

Sir Morris held the phone away from his ear and stared at it, like it was a cobra dancing before him. He blinked hard and put it back to his ear. 'Oliver's dead.'

'Just like his father. You wish that were so, Morris, but it's not. Oliver is back and the sins of the past are returned to find us.'

Morris sat silently, her words washing over him like the final waves that would drown him. There was resignation in his wife's voice. Almost as if she had known this day would come.

'You can't believe that, dear. If Oliver was alive, he would have come back.'

'He has, you fool. Can't you see? The proof is laid out before you. Desmond is stabbed through the heart and his daughter is driven mad. Polonius and Ophelia. Oliver is playing with us.'

'But what about Terry …'

'Rosencrantz or Guildenstern, don't you see it?'

Sir Morris did not. 'Listen, darling, try and get some rest. You've had some terrible news. I'm going to sit down with the detective and draw up this list.'

'Forget the bloody list,' snapped Lady Oxford. 'There is only one name on it; Oliver Lawrence, my son! Tell the police that.'

'Listen, darling, I can't tell them that. Oliver left in unfortunate circumstances. If it ever came out the company would look bad, I would look bad. I think we should just let certain ghosts from the past lie unmolested.'

Lady Oxford shook her head in despair. When she spoke again, it was in a whisper. 'You stupid, stupid man. Can you not see the truth for wishing it were not so? Oliver has returned with hatred in his heart.' She replaced the receiver and walked slowly to the kitchen. She ran the hot water until it was warm and then began to wash and wash her hands.

Chapter 35
What Light Through Yonder Window Breaks?

Toby Marlowe walked down the riverside path at the back of the Swan Theatre, towards the spot where Desmond Tharpe had been murdered. He walked up the steps that led to the small doorway in the graveyard wall. It was a peaceful place, but a lonely place to die. In the heart of the town and yet so isolated.

SOCO had gone, and only the flattened grass and the broken stems of wild flowers bore evidence to the tragedy that had been played out the night before. Beneath the bench there was a discolouration on the worn pathway. Desmond Tharpe's blood had soaked deep into the ground, the same ground in which he would soon be buried. Toby looked down at the dark stain that had so recently run through Desmond Tharpe's veins. Life was so fleeting and easily ended.

Toby looked through the doorway and down the pathway that led back towards the Dirty Duck. Who or what had drawn Desmond away from the street lights and into the dark seclusion of the trees and onward into the graveyard? It had to be someone he knew; nobody would come here at night with a stranger. It was the only explanation that made any sense and, if that was true, it meant that Terry Fibs must have also known his killer.

The two murders were linked; it was no coincidence that Terry Fibs' mutilated body was put on display in the adjoining room for Tabitha Tharpe to witness. All of these victims were linked to the theatre; a Shakespearian quote had been left written in blood on the pillow for Tabitha to see. Something or someone linked all of these events, he just needed to find out what that link was. The clock was ticking and his killer wasn't done, of that, he was sure.

Fred Williams had left the station and headed back towards the scene of Desmond Tharpe's murder; he wasn't surprised to see Toby there. 'Found anything?'

Toby looked up. 'Hello, sir, how'd you find me?'

'I'm a detective.'

Toby nodded.

'Well?'

'No, sir, but I have a theory.'

'Go on.'

'Whoever did this is known to both the deceased and to Tabitha. Sir Morris Oxford and his theatre company are the key that will unlock this puzzle.'

'Isn't that the theory we already agreed,' said Fred.

'It is, sir, but I've just realised something. They must know this person, they weren't frightened of them. We were looking for someone who has been fired by Oxford recently, someone with a grudge, but if you were Desmond Tharpe and that person stopped you in the street late at night, would you walk into the graveyard of Holy Trinity with them?'

Fred thought for a moment. 'I would if I was at knifepoint.'

It was a good point. Toby considered it for a moment.

'From right outside the Dirty Duck? I don't think so, sir. We need to find out who was drinking at the Duck last night. It was dry and warm, somebody must have been out front.'

'OK, Toby, I'll get the Herald and the local radio to put out a request for witnesses. Ginger can get in there and have a word with Dick Mayrick, see if he can shed some light on who was in last night.'

'Thanks, sir. I'm guessing that if we do find a witness, they are going to tell us that Desmond was just chatting to someone and wandered off in the direction of the graveyard without a struggle.'

'Meaning he knew the person and he wasn't frightened. Whoever the killer is, they weren't expecting him and either they didn't recognise him or weren't afraid of him.'

Fred stood there rubbing his chin.

'Think I'm wrong, sir?'

'No, Toby, I'm afraid I agree with you.'

'That's a relief.'

'No, it's a pain in the arse because now we aren't looking for an obvious grudge but something far more subtle. I reckon that we are going to need to track the records of every actor that has ever worked with Sir Morris and his merry band all the way back to the very beginning.'

'More than ten years?'

'All the way, Toby, I'll get Kinky on it.'

Toby nodded and gazed once more at the scene of the murder. He pointed to the river. 'You know our murder weapon is in there, don't you.'

'That's where I would have thrown it.'

'We need to get a diver in there.'

'Already done, Coventry are sending over two frogmen this afternoon, there won't be any prints on it though.'

'Probably not but at least there will be something tangible we could try and trace.'

Fred looked at the bloodstain on the pathway and then gazed slowly about the graveyard. 'Not much of an epitaph. Soon be washed away by the next rains and then poor old Desmond Tharpe will be confined to memory.

'It's a lonely place to die, Toby.' Fred turned and started to walk back towards the road. 'Come on, we've got an interview booked with Sir Morris in twenty minutes.'

'Where?'

Fred pointed at the Swan. 'Right there, son. He's meeting us backstage before rehearsal.'

'I thought the show would be cancelled.'

Fred laughed. 'It has been, but the old boy thinks he can browbeat us to let it go ahead. You're our resident luvvie, Toby, why don't you convince him that the show can't go on.'

Toby watched his boss stride back towards the road. A sound to his left made him look towards the graveyard and there, just next to the boundary wall, was a gravedigger. He watched for a moment as the shovel dug down into the soil in a steady rhythmical flow, slowly digging the grave in which so many secrets would be buried. He couldn't help thinking that the gravedigger was going to be busy. When they arrived at the Swan Theatre, Sir Morris Oxford was waiting for them. He stood at the entrance; he was a big man who was further blown up by his own pomposity.

'Walk with me, gentlemen, we must make haste.'

'Must we,' said Fred, looking entirely unimpressed.

'We must, sir. Time and tide wait for no man.'

'Well, it's lucky you're not in a boat then.'

Toby stifled a laugh and Sir Morris turned indignantly on Fred. 'I don't care for your attitude, constable.'

'Detective sergeant,' said Fred tersely.

Sir Morris turned back towards him and fixed him with a steely glare. 'Whatever your rank,' he declared, 'I am Sir Morris Oxford and I will be treated with the respect due to my position.'

Toby watched Fred's hands bunch into fists and prepared to dive between them to prevent a career ending brawl. Luckily, he didn't have to.

A broad smile broke across Fred's features. 'Very well, Sir Morris, I will allow you to exercise your right to be brutally murdered in the next twenty-four hours. I'm sure you will be granted a massive amount of respect at your funeral.'

Some of the confidence seemed to drain from Oxford's countenance. 'You think there is a chance of that?'

'I'm certain of it, Sir Morris. There is a killer out there, and we think he is targeting you and your company.'

Oxford looked from Fred to Toby. 'Do you think the same, constable?'

'Yes, I do. There is someone from your past who, for some reason, feels that you did him wrong.'

'Or her,' added Oxford, remembering his many conquests of young actresses.

'You think that's likely, given the nature of the murders?'

Sir Morris smirked. 'Hell hath no fury like a woman scorned, detective.'

For a horrible moment, Toby thought he was going to wink. The man really was a terrible old letch as well as an ego maniac. 'We don't think that's likely, sir, given the nature of the deaths.'

'Some of the farm lasses around here are pretty strong, don't rule them out.'

'I wouldn't rule anyone out from wanting to kill you, Sir Morris.'

'Are you trying to be funny, officer?'

Fred shook his head. 'No, Sir Morris. I'm just making an observation.' Fred pointed down the corridor. 'Is there a cafe where we can continue this conversation?'

'Out of the question, we have a play to put on tonight, we need to rehearse.'

'Play's been cancelled, sir,' said Toby helpfully.

Sir Morris looked aghast and drew himself up to his full height and thrust out his impressive girth. 'Out of the question! My public expects me to rise above this little difficulty and put on the show.'

Fred could contain himself no longer. 'There are two of your friends and colleagues in my morgue, and young Tabitha Tharpe is in a state of deep shock. You really have to take this seriously,

Sir Morris.'

'As this country's greatest Shakespearian actor, I am expected to appear.'

'And I have a duty to your public, and posterity, to ensure that you do survive to tread those hallowed boards once more,' said Toby.

Fred turned to Toby and whispered, 'Pass the sick bucket.'

Toby's fawning words had done the trick.

Sir Morris nodded sagely. 'You make a good point, DC Marlowe. As a national treasure I have a duty to preserve myself for the nation.'

'Yes, Sir Morris, you are a mighty oak in a forest of saplings.'

Sir Morris liked Toby's analogy and smiled. 'Lay on, young Marlowe, let us to the lounge for a small libation whilst we consider this problem.' Sir Morris swept down the corridor in the direction of the café.

Fred followed. 'Does he always talk like this?'

'He's a Shakespearian actor.'

'More like a pantomime dame if you ask me,' muttered Fred.'

In the lounge, Sir Morris headed for a leather armchair and slumped down, indicating the chairs opposite to Fred and Toby. 'Shall I order some tea and biscuits?'

'That would be nice,' said Fred.

Sir Morris clapped his hands and, within a few seconds, one of the ladies came hurrying over.

'What can I get you, Sir Morris?'

'Tea for three please, Mrs Franklin. Are there any of chef's homemade shortbread cookies left?'

'I do believe there are, Sir Morris.'

'Excellent, we'll have a plate of those too.'

'Yes, Sir Morris, right away.'

Sir Morris looked at Fred. 'I trust that Stratford police will be paying for these refreshments.'

'Don't you have an account here?' asked Fred.

'Of course I do, but I'm not paying for your interview refreshments.'

'It would be our pleasure,' said Toby. 'I think we better bring you up to speed with what we know.'

'Very well, you have my undivided attention.'

Toby looked at Fred, who nodded at him to continue. He pulled out his notebook. 'Last night Desmond Tharpe was murdered on the banks of the Avon, as he was on his way home from the theatre. We believe he was headed towards the Dirty Duck when somebody intercepted him and persuaded him to go into the graveyard of Holy Trinity.'

'Terrible business,' muttered Sir Morris.

'Indeed. There was no sign of a struggle so we are assuming that Desmond knew his killer and wasn't afraid of them. All the evidence points to the fact that he went there without a struggle. There are no bruises or contusions on his body, apart from the single stab wound to the heart. It's almost as if they were sitting on the bench for a chat and then his assailant just ran him through.'

'So sad, I've worked with dear Desmond for over thirty years, nobody could have a reason to kill him.'

'Well, somebody did,' said Fred.

'True,' said Sir Morris. 'It has been a terrible shock for all of us, especially Tabitha, poor girl; she has been driven half-crazy by events. I'm not sure she will be available for the matinee tomorrow.'

'There won't be a matinee tomorrow or any performance until we have caught the killer. We believe we are dealing with a serial killer who won't stop until he has killed you.'

'And why would you think that? Maybe Desmond had somebody after him. He was a bit of a ladies' man, after all.'

Toby scribbled in his note book. 'Any ladies in Stratford?'

Sir Morris smiled. 'You're going to need a bigger notebook.'

'That's interesting, we heard that you were the lothario of the group.'

Sir Morris allowed himself a smile. 'I do have something of a reputation with the ladies.'

'And what reputation would that be?' asked Fred pointedly.

Sir Morris was too occupied with his own image to notice. 'When you're a star, the usual rules don't apply. They are like putty in my hands. I may speak a soliloquy from, say, Romeo and Juliet. Imagine you are a fair maiden DS Williams.'

'I'll give it a go,' sighed Fred.

Sir Morris laid a hand upon his shoulder and gestured towards the window in the lounge. 'What light through yonder window breaks? It is the East and you, Frederica, are the sun. Arise fair sun and kill the envious moon.' A slow creepy smile spread across Sir Morris's face. 'Do you see, DS Williams? Are you not swept up in the passion of the words? Captured in the moment, putty in my hands.'

'I don't think I'm the demographic you're targeting.'

Sir Morris waved his comment away. 'Clearly, but you can see how a star-struck young lady would be affected.'

'Yes, if she was looking for a father figure, maybe that would work.'

Sir Morris looked darkly at Fred, the realisation that Fred was taking the micky was clearly starting to dawn on him.

Toby moved to prevent it. 'We certainly can, Sir Morris. With the sheer majesty of your delivery, you had me at light. What female could resist their own soliloquy delivered by the great Sir Morris Oxford.'

Sir Morris beamed. 'Indeed, DC Marlowe. I am like catnip to female theatregoers. The life of an actor is a hard one but if you make it, the fringe benefits are rather appealing.'

Fred wanted to vomit listening to the old letch, but he needed to know all the secrets that Sir Morris held, one of them could unlock the case.

Sir Morris continued. 'All the fair maidens that have fallen under my spell would never harm me or my company.'

'So, you don't think it's a female attacker?' asked Toby.

'Doubtful. I usually get the pick of the totty and Desmond and the others have to fight over the leftovers.'

'Charming,' said Toby, his face wrinkled up in disgust. 'Was Desmond as depraved as you?'

Sir Morris looked at Toby with mild surprise. 'Depraved? I am not depraved. I am a creative genius and that artistic outpouring creates an energy which needs an outlet.'

'Maybe we could plug you into the mains,' suggested Fred.

'Not a female then,' added Toby, keen to avoid a confrontation between his boss and the self-proclaimed, greatest living Shakespearian actor.'

'No, I think not.'

'In that case, who would hate Desmond and Terry Fibs enough to brutally slay them, and do it in such a way as to send poor Tabitha Tharpe into a deep shock? As you said, the poor girl has been driven half out of her mind.'

For a moment, Sir Morris looked genuinely sad.

'It's a terrible situation, there is a monster afoot. Walking the streets of Stratford with a black heart, intent on avenging some perceived wrong. I cannot think of anyone who could have such animosity towards my company.'

Fred could. 'All we can ask, Sir Morris, is that you draw up a list of everyone that's worked for you and been sacked in the last twenty years. Can you do that?'

'Twenty years? I thought you said ten.'

'We think we need to go back to the very beginning of the company.'

'That won't be easy to do. There are no written records for the early years.'

'I realise it won't be easy, Sir Morris, but we have no choice. We need to eliminate everyone we can from our enquiries, and quickly. This person is ruthless and will kill again. I'm going to send DC Bernstein here so you can draw up a list, and it needs to go back twenty years.'

Sir Morris nodded gravely. 'Very well, DS Williams, I will co-operate. Should I wait for DC Bernstein here?'

'I think it best, Sir Morris. I will post two uniformed police officers at the front and rear entrances. Please do not leave the theatre unless you are with either me or DC Marlowe.'

'Very well but do try to catch this rogue quickly. The season here is short and I have a reputation to maintain.'

Fred nodded to Sir Morris and then, as if leaving royalty, reversed out of the room. Toby followed.

As they emerged from the theatre back onto Waterside, Fred turned angrily to him. 'Any chance we can leave his bedroom window open tonight to give the killer a chance?'

'I know, sir, he's a bit of a nightmare.'

'A bit! He's an ego on legs, a molester of women. A total sleazebag.'

Toby nodded. 'But apart from that, did you like him?'

A slow smile spread across Fred's face.'

'Yes, I did, especially when I pictured him in a body bag.'

Chapter 36
To The Ramparts

The phone rang in Oliver's lounge. He stared at it for a moment before picking it up, he didn't speak.

'Hello, Oliver, we need to meet tonight.'

'Do we have to? I was hoping to kill Gerard Soames tonight.'

'Guildenstern?'

'Of course.'

'No, not tonight, Oliver. There will be police everywhere. Meet me on the battlements at midnight.'

'Kenilworth Castle again? Can't we just meet in the Dirty Duck.'

'No, we can't, there are eyes everywhere. This is front page news on every national newspaper. Meet me at twelve.'

There was silence at the other end of the line and then Oliver spoke. 'OK, twelve at the battlements, but if it's raining, I'm not coming.'

The phone went dead and Felix listened to the buzzing of the empty line as he held the receiver in his hand. What had he done? Oliver was no longer who he had once been and that metamorphosis had been his doing. Somehow Felix had to try and defuse the bomb he had planted and stop this runaway train before it ran them all down.

Chapter 37
Farewell, Ophelia

Oliver had waited until eleven p.m. before heading out to meet Felix. He had left his car by the old boathouse on the other side of the bridge, to avoid the traffic earlier in the day. He would take a stroll along Waterside and revisit the scene of his crime.

As he turned the corner from Holy Trinity, he saw her; Tabitha. She walked slowly down towards the entrance of the graveyard and then followed the tree lined path that led towards the river and the bench where he had murdered her father.

Was this a trap? He scanned behind him; nothing. He looked down the road towards the theatre and all was quiet. Tonight's performance had been cancelled.

He fell in behind her some forty yards back. She walked slowly; he could hear her sobs but he felt no sympathy. Tabitha was one of them. She had known what they were doing to him and had said nothing. Just watched as his career, his whole life, was washed away. There was a time when he had loved her but not any more. That moment was long since passed.

She reached the bench and slumped down upon it. The sobs became louder. He looked around him again, frightened that her crying would attract someone, but they were alone. As he walked slowly towards her, he wondered whether he would kill her. It wasn't in his plan. She was his Ophelia; he couldn't kill her.

A wicked thought occurred to him. He couldn't kill her but he could persuade her to kill herself. He drifted silently to the bench.

'Hello, Tabitha.'

She looked up with a start. 'Who are you?'

'Don't you recognise me?'

She looked at him through tear-stained eyes. 'No. Should I?'

Oliver shrugged. 'I don't know, if you had loved me you would.'

Her tears had stopped now and; she shook her head. Who are you?'

'You and I were lovers once.'

She peered closer, the dark shadows that spilled moonlight through the tree-filled graveyard concealed the stranger's face. 'Should I know you?'

Oliver sighed. 'You were once my Juliet. Call me but love and, I'll be new baptised.'

Tabitha looked at him, her face a mask of curious confusion. 'You seem familiar. I have heard you speak those words before.'

'There was a time when you were my world, that time has long since passed. Romeo no more.'

Tabitha stood slowly up and moved towards him; he stepped back into the shadows.

'There is something about you. I feel I should remember you.'

'Many years ago, we played upon that stage,' he pointed through the trees towards the theatre. I was your Romeo.'

'Who are you?'

'I know not how to tell you who I am. My name, dear saint is …'

'Oliver …' the words fell from her lips with a sigh. 'Is it really you?'

'It was, but no longer. I died fifteen years ago when Sir Morris, your father, and his gang ended my career.'

Tears began to fall down her face once more. 'I thought you were dead.'

'I am. You and your accursed family and friends are to blame.'

'But I see you.'

Oliver slowly shook his head. 'You see a ghost. A memory of

what once was, destroyed by you and your kind. Condemned to walk the shadows, but I shall haunt thee until your dying day.'

'No, I see you, Oliver.'

'You see a dream, an image of what once was. Your father is dead, dear Uncle Terry is dead. The past has come to collect the unpaid bill and you, dear Ophelia, must pay it.'

The words hissed from Oliver's mouth, venomous and cold.

'But I am Tabitha.' She clutched her head in her hands and began to rock.

Oliver moved behind her and whispered. 'You are my Ophelia; you are quite mad. The death of your father, Polonius, weighs heavily on you.'

'My father was Desmond, Desmond ...' her words trailed off.

'No, he was Polonius and I was your Hamlet and you betrayed me. There is a bill to be paid and the date is now due.'

Tabitha fell to the ground. 'Stop it, stop it. I am Tabitha and you are Oliver.'

Oliver laughed. 'Oliver is dead, they are all dead, and you ...' he pointed an accusing finger at her, 'it is you that are dead, inside. This world has no place for you now. All those you loved are dead. You are cursed.' Oliver's voice rose to a howl. 'The creatures of the night will walk with you until your days are ended, reminding you of your sins.'

Tabitha rose from the bench and looked at the mask of hatred that Oliver's face displayed. 'Please stop, make it stop.'

Oliver pointed towards the river. 'There is peace in those dark waters, a place where you can be free of your crimes.'

She shook her head in despair, crazed with sadness and horror at the death of her father and the sight of Terry Fibs' mutilated body, her mind balanced on the knife edge of sanity. The tranquilisers the doctor had given her were now mixed with the brandy she had drunk. Her reason was deserting her.

'Get thee to a nunnery. Why wouldst thou be a breeder of

sinners.'

'I am not Ophelia.'

'I am myself indifferent, I care not who you are, but I know of your guilt and that will haunt you for ever.'

Tabitha began to shake uncontrollably. 'Make it stop, please … let it stop.'

Oliver leaned towards her. 'There is peace in those dark waters. No voices of accusation. Your father will be waiting.' Oliver pointed once more towards the river. 'Go now and let this be an end to all suffering.'

Tabitha let out a wretched wail, strode towards the water and threw herself in. She never struggled, and sank gently beneath the bible black waters of the Avon.

Oliver just stood there. What a performance he had given. He had talked Tabitha Tharpe into drowning herself. He walked happily from the riverside and back towards the theatre. 'Still got it,' he chuckled.

Chapter 38
Good Night, Sweet Prince

As he walked onto the battlements at Kenilworth, Felix could distinctly see a spring in Oliver's step.

'This murdering clearly agrees with you.'

Oliver bowed theatrically. 'It does indeed.' He sat down in the empty deckchair that Felix had thoughtfully put out for him. 'What an evening I have had.'

'Never mind the bloody evening, what about the last two days. Desmond by the river and that wretch Fibs in the Falcon. Can't you slow it down a bit. Two bodies in two days is pushing it a bit, don't you think?'

'Three.'

Felix felt a chill run down his spine. 'Three?'

'Yep, just helped Tabitha drown herself.'

'My God, man, you weren't supposed to kill Tabitha!'

'I didn't, she threw herself into the Avon. I just helped her make up her mind. Oh, I wished you could have been there, Felix, I was brilliant. She was already half out of her mind. I pretended to be a ghost.'

'Of whom?'

Oliver laughed. 'Me. Can you believe it? I convinced her that I was the ghost of me. It was a bravura performance. Admittedly she was half crazed with grief over the death of her father, and seeing old Terry with his eyes and tongue gouged out can't have helped. I could smell the brandy on her, coupled with those tranquillisers the doctor had probably given her. Well, she was putty in my hands.'

Felix listened, horrified, to Oliver's description.

'I reminded her that I had once been her Romeo, I even quoted some lines at her. Then, as she realised it was me, I pretended to be Hamlet. We did it a few times at the Swan together. I told her that Desmond had been Polonius and that she was my Ophelia. I wish you could have been there.'

Felix sat there quietly listening, barely knowing what to say. 'Ophelia, you say. That must have been some performance.'

'Oh, it was. Poor girl was quite mad. I drove her over the edge of sanity, and then ...'

'She drowned herself,' whispered Felix.

'Exactly. I even told her to get herself to a nunnery at one point. I tell you, Felix, all those lines are still in my head. When all this is finished, I will return to the stage.'

'You do realise, Oliver, that you are quite mad. You will be in prison when all this is finished.'

'They'll never catch me, Felix, I'm good at this.'

'Maybe not, but at this rate there's going to be nobody left to act with.'

Oliver laughed. 'Plenty more where they came from.' Oliver sat up in his deckchair. 'Did you bring a flask of tea?'

Felix nodded. 'And some Jammie Dodgers. Shall I be mother?'

Oliver nodded. 'Thanks, Felix. I'm getting the impression that you're not very happy about something.'

Felix snorted. 'You'd be right. Was Tabitha really necessary? Poor girl wasn't on the list.'

'I didn't kill her, I told you what happened.'

'You kinda did. You convinced her to take a swim whilst the balance of her mind was disturbed. Don't you feel bad about that?'

Oliver nodded. 'I do, I forgot to tell her that Terry Fibs was Rosencrantz.'

'Bloody hell, Oliver, you're turning into a monster.' Felix passed Oliver a cup of tea and held out the open pack of Jammie Dodgers.

'I'm ready for this, killing gives me a real appetite.'

They sat quietly for a couple of minutes, Oliver contentedly dunking his Jammie Dodgers in his tea whilst he basked in the happy knowledge of two days, well spent, on his campaign of revenge.

Felix, on the other hand, sipped nervously at his tea, his mind a maelstrom of emotions. He knew that Oliver had been wronged by these people but he had set in motion events that he now did not know how to control. With Oliver in this frame of mind, one wrong word could find him added to the list. How on earth could he pour oil on the burning waters of Oliver's revenge?

'Have you considered the possibility that now you have struck a fatal blow at the swine responsible for your father's death, that now may be the time to sit back and take stock?'

Oliver shook his head. 'Nope.'

'But you could lie low for six months, let all this settle down, then return triumphant to the stage. You could step into the void that the death of Desmond Tharpe created.'

'And do what, play second fiddle to that buffoon, if I come back with Morris Oxford still alive, I'm just going to be his sidekick again. If I kill him, I can step into his shoes, literally.'

Felix shuddered. 'Do you think they will fit?'

'I'll make them fit, I'm a new broom, I'm sweeping everything away.'

'But where does it stop?'

Oliver thought for a moment. 'King Claudius and Guildenstern, they must die before this play is complete.'

'Sir Morris and Gerard Soames?'

'The very same.'

'Then you are Hamlet?'

Oliver nodded. 'At your service.'

'But Hamlet dies.'

'Not in my version.'

'And then what?'

'Othello.'

'What does that mean?'

'It means that phase two will have begun. You gave me a list, Felix, there were a lot of women on that list and I haven't killed any yet.'

'What about Tabitha?'

'She killed herself.'

'But you talked her into it.'

'You can't be found guilty of killing someone in a leap from a cliff if you only said jump, you have to actually push them.'

'I understand that you are upset by the actions of these women but they were probably working under direct orders from Sir Morris.'

'They still looked the other way, said nothing, and turned a blind eye when my father died, and I was destroyed.' Oliver shook his head slowly, anger curling his lip into a menacing snarl. 'No, when this play is finished, Othello will walk the stage once more, justice will be done.'

'But these women.'

'Were all on the list you wrote me. Don't you see, if I become Othello then you are my Iago.'

'I have not whispered poison into your ears, I told you the truth.'

Oliver smiled reassuringly at Felix. 'I know you didn't, you could never be Iago, you are a true friend. I have many lights to put out before the daylight breaks once more.'

'Tonight?' asked Felix, startled by Oliver's words.

Oliver laughed. 'I was thinking aloud. The ladies from Othello are for another day, first I must finish my Hamlet.' Oliver put a whole Jammie Dodger in his mouth and bit down gleefully.

'You want some Custard Creams?' asked Felix.

Oliver nodded, unable to speak.

Good, thought Felix, maybe he could slow Oliver down with diabetes.

'So, it's Sir Morris and Gerard next and then you take a break.'

'Maybe.'

'What does that mean?'

'Just what it says. I may just leave old Morris hanging for a while, let him know it's coming. I mean, he would make a really good Macbeth would he not, with my traitorous mother at his side. A Lady Macbeth if ever there was.'

'No,' Felix almost shouted. 'Beatrice has no guilt in this, I told you.'

'You did, but I need to resolve this to my own satisfaction, not yours, Felix. At some stage I will talk with her and then I will know.'

'I assure you, your mother is an innocent party, she has been badly used by Sir Morris.'

'Maybe, but my father is dead and I was ruined, yet she landed on her feet, or back, and is now with dear Uncle Morris. Doesn't look good, does it?'

It didn't. 'Please, Oliver, as your friend, I beg you to tread carefully. Beatrice is a good person but she's vulnerable. She is as much a victim as you.'

Oliver nodded. 'I hear you, I will take my time, hear her out and then decide.'

'Promise you won't do anything without speaking to me first.'

'Very well, I guess I owe you that much. Without you, none of this would be happening.

Felix smiled weakly. 'I'm well aware of that, Oliver, it's more than I bargained for.'

'Too late to turn back now, old son, the play has begun and we are merely players in it.'

Felix finished his tea as Oliver finished the last Custard Cream. Apart from one Jammie Dodger and two custard creams, Oliver had eaten both packets. Maybe diabetes would slow him down, thought Felix, knowing full well that it wouldn't. Oliver had changed, his mission had obsessed him and he was living the part of avenging angel. His twisted mind shaping that revenge to mirror the plays of Shakespeare and bend their scenes to the vision of his madness. He watched Oliver chewing thoughtfully on the last remnants of the custard creams, and wondered what thoughts were going on in that mind, a mind that his letter had forever altered. Oliver looked up at him questioningly. Here it comes, he thought.

'Any more tea in the flask? I'm a bit parched after all those biscuits.'

'That's all you have to say after what you have done during the last forty-eight hours?'

'Killing is thirsty work. Rehydration, Felix, you need it to be at your best.'

'I'll bear that in mind when I'm feeling a bit murdery.'

Oliver chuckled. 'You could never kill anyone, you're too nice. A firm push is about the most you could manage.'

'You used to be nice before I poisoned your mind.'

'How can the truth poison a mind? The truth sets you free. I can see my way forward now, there's a future out there. I just have to kill a few folks to get to it.' Oliver thought for a moment. 'Quite a lot actually.' He gulped down his tea. 'We done here, Felix? I need to get back to Stratford before the cock crows.'

Felix nodded slowly. 'We're done, but please,' he held up a hand and Oliver paused, 'slow down a little. Think about what you are doing.'

'If I thought about it I'm not sure I could do it, mate.' Oliver smiled wistfully and then turned on his heel and disappeared into the shadows of the tower.

Felix sat and listened as his footsteps disappeared down the stairs until he could hear them no more. This would not end well. The storm was rising and before it had finished, everything that stood in its path was in peril. Even he wasn't safe. He sipped the remains of his tea and heard the gate clang gently as Oliver passed through it on the way to his car.

He walked to the battlements and watched Oliver's moonlit shadow float ghostlike across the pathway towards the southern car park.

'Goodnight, sweet Prince. And flights of angels sing thee to thy rest.' Felix knew there would be no rest for Oliver, not now, or ever.

Chapter 39
The Lady Of Shalott

Kinky Bernstein leaned against the wall behind the chain ferry. It was going to be another lovely day but the late May morning was still chilly. From the river, a hazy mist floated above the water like the memory of a fire that had long ago been extinguished. He loved the early mornings. With his lifestyle he got to see them often. His current lady friend had a husband who worked the night shift at Land Rover. He was a big man and he would be back from his shift at eight. Julia wanted him out long before that to hide the evidence of their passion.

Kinky seemed to have a type and that type mainly had husbands with nightshifts, no commitment and something to hide. They could never be seen in public with him; Stratford was a small town. Kinky never had to take them out for meals, buy flowers or commit to anything more than sex. It was a soulless but perfect plan. Kinky could be kinky, and that's why the ladies loved him. It was also why he was often walking the quiet streets of Stratford in the early hours.

He gazed down towards the weir. There was a log floating back up stream, caught in an eddy pushing it against the prevailing flow. He watched, unconcerned, as it floated gently towards him. It still had foliage on it that rippled in the light current. As it got closer, he realised it also had eyes. For a moment it didn't register, apart from the fact that it was a strange tree and then, like the Lady of Shalott, Tabitha Tharpe floated gently up to where he leaned against the wall by the chain ferry. He recognised her, he had interviewed her just the day before but, in his head, a little voice spoke.

'Out flew the web and floated wide
The mirror crack'd from side to side
The curse is come upon me, cried
The Lady of Shalott.'

Chapter 40
The Siren's Song

Toby looked down at Tabitha Tharpe's lifeless body, her blue eyes searching for something they would never see. The torment had gone, her face now just a mask of lost opportunities and thwarted dreams. He hated gazing at the newly dead; he always felt that their spirit was watching him, begging him to help, find their killer, bring them peace. Death was so … final. The last great leap into the unknown where all will go but none return.

'Blue remembered hills?'

He turned, and there was Fred beside him gazing sadly at Tabitha.

'Yeah, something like that, sir.'

'The happy highways where I went and cannot come again.' They stood there silently mourning for a life they could not have saved, for a girl they barely knew. 'You know something, Toby, sometimes this job is the absolute pits.'

'It is, sir.'

'You two just going to stand in my way quoting Houseman all bloody day, or can I have a look at the deceased?'

They turned to see the amused face of Alf Butcher smiling at them.

'Morning, Alf, going to have to get a fishing licence if we keep meeting by the river like this.'

'I hate fishing, the fish are too …' he thought for a moment, '… fishy.' He bent down to look closer at Tabitha Tharpe's body. 'Pretty girl.'

'She was. It was her father who was murdered by the river two days ago.'

Alf stared closely at her. 'There is a family resemblance. I do hope her poor mother is dead.'

Toby hadn't really thought about that. He turned to Fred.

'Long dead, but the father did have a girlfriend. Ginger interviewed her yesterday. Not a grieving type, apparently, they had a big falling out and Tabitha took her dad's side.'

'Still, doesn't pay to fall out with your sugar daddy's daughter.'

Fred shook his head. 'Not according to her. When Ginger asked about her relationship with her Tabitha, she said, and I quote, "That little bitch made her choice, she's dead to me."'

Toby looked shocked. 'Should we make her a suspect?'

'You know me, Toby, everyone's a suspect until proven otherwise.'

Fred glanced down to see Alf placing a thermometer in a place it was never expected to be, he looked away. The poor girl was dead but he felt bad about having to treat her so discourteously. There was no dignity in death. Toby and Fred stood watching as Alf Butcher carefully went about his work. After about five minutes he stood up, straightening his stiff back as he did so and flexing his shoulders to loosen his neck muscles.

'If only more victims would die on a table or park bench, make my job a lot easier.'

'Yeah, well we arrested the Park Bench killer back in sixty-six, so you're out of luck.'

'Really?'

'No, you daft sod.' Fred smiled and looked back at Tabitha. 'Initial thoughts, Alf?'

'Drowning.'

'Any signs of a struggle?'

Alf shook his head. 'No, not a mark on her. It would seem she entered the water unaided. I could smell the alcohol on her and I assume, given what has been going on in the last few days, she would have been prescribed tranquilisers. Not a great combination, but toxicology will reveal all. I'll have a report on your desk by tomorrow morning.'

'But not murder?' asked Toby.

'Doesn't look like it.' Alf Butcher repacked his bag and removed his surgical gloves. 'There is a clear link to the other two though, this case is getting a bit real. I expect Beeching's losing his mind.'

'That he is. Old Wilson is breathing down his neck so hard his underpants are on fire.'

Alf picked up his bag and headed back towards the road. 'See you at the next one, gents.'

'You think there's going to be another?' asked Toby.

Alf shrugged. 'Don't you?'

They watched him walk away, silently agreeing with him.

Twenty minutes later they were back in the CID room in Guild Street, and Inspector Beeching's pants were indeed on fire. 'Williams, get in here. You too, Marlowe.'

Fred threw a look at Toby that said, 'Say nothing.'

'Morning, sir.'

'Never mind that, Fred. Shut the door, we have got to get a grip on this. I am getting a lot of pressure from the chief constable. He's told me that DI Mel Townsend will no longer be assisting you.'

'Well, that's good news, sir.'

'No, it's not, he's putting her in charge. She'll be here in twenty minutes and she's bringing some of her team. We're losing control of this, Fred. If we clear this up, he's going to claim the credit.'

'Does it matter, sir? As long as we crack the case.'

Beeching looked at Toby like he had just spat at him. He instantly regretted his observation.

'You have a lot to learn, Marlowe; we want to make this collar, crack the case. It's on our patch. If Coventry come in and crack it, all the credit goes to Wilson and his team. Tell him, Fred.'

'What Inspector Beeching is saying is that this is our case and we need to solve it.'

'Exactly, so don't co-operate with DI Townsend.'

'We don't have a choice do we, sir?'

'Listen to me carefully, lads. We have to look like we are sharing information but we can hold back certain things that we feel are not relevant.'

'Like what?'

Beeching looked conspiratorially from Toby to Fred.

'Like clues, facts, you know. The information that can solve a case.'

'Isn't that a bit morally ambiguous, sir?'

'Wow, somebody swallowed a Thesaurus today,' said Fred.

Beeching leaned menacingly towards Toby. 'I'll tell you what's morally ambiguous; my reaction to young DCs that don't actually do what I ask. Do you understand?'

Fred stepped between them. 'I'll explain it to him, sir.'

Beeching nodded. 'And you'll keep DI Townsend in the dark, Fred?'

'Like a mushroom.'

'Good.' There was an uncomfortable pause before Beeching smiled and then sat down behind his desk. 'And the girl this morning?'

'Tabitha Tharpe, sir.'

'Desmond Tharpe's daughter.'

'I'm afraid so, sir.'

'Another murder?'

'Looks like suicide.'

Beeching nodded gravely. 'Poor girl must have been in a state, her father murdered and then seeing the Fibs fellow butchered in her hotel.'

'It's connected though, sir,' said Toby.

'Well of course it's connected, her father had just been murdered, a family friend has been butchered in the room next door. Poor girl must have been out of her mind with grief.'

'We don't know how she ended up in the water yet, not until we have the pathologist's report.'

For a moment, anger coloured Beeching's face. He took a deep breath.

'You may be right, Marlowe, but for now the official line is suicide. If we find evidence to throw doubt on this, we can keep it to ourselves.'

Before Toby could reply, Fred's hand came to rest on his shoulder. 'We understand, sir. As soon as we know something, I'll let you know.'

'Very good, Fred.'

As Fred and Toby headed for the door, Beeching continued.

'Like a mushroom, Fred, in the dark and fed on ...'

He didn't need to finish the sentence.

Toby was seething with anger. 'Can you believe that, sir.' Fred grabbed his elbow, steered him towards the exit and out into the car park.

'Time for a smoke.'

'I don't smoke.'

'Then it's a perfect time to start.' Fred didn't let go until they were on the car park. 'You need to calm down, young Toby.'

'But ...'

'Shut up and listen.' Fred's words were harsh. Toby fell silent.

'You know that Beeching wants promotion, he's a career pen pusher. He won't be happy until he gets back to London. If we don't solve this case, he's going to look bad.'

'Well, he is bad.'

'What part of shut up didn't you understand.' Fred fixed Toby with a firm but friendly smile. 'Are you ready to listen now?'

Toby nodded. 'This job is all about results and who gets them, if I didn't get results, I would have been chucked out long ago. I think we both know that Beeching is an idiot, but he's our idiot. We need to help him to help ourselves. This job is all about intuition, gathering information and then trying to work out how it all ties together.' He hesitated for a moment before continuing. 'Tabitha. What do you know?'

'I know she drowned, sir.'

Fred nodded. 'That's information. Now what do you think?'

Toby thought for a moment. 'There's something not right about it.'

Fred nodded and smiled. 'That's intuition. We both know that Tabitha Tharpe didn't end up in the Avon unaided. The facts all point to it, but there's just something not right. Drunk and drugged, distraught with grief. It wouldn't have been hard to help her on her way. No struggle required.'

Toby nodded in agreement. 'It doesn't feel right, does it?'

'No, it doesn't. So, let's assume that this is the third murder. We don't tell anyone, especially Beeching. We play him at his own game. Not for promotion but because we want to solve this case and catch the killer. You in?'

Toby nodded. 'Yes, sir.'

'Good, now here's what we do. You need to go back to see Whomper.'

'He doesn't know anything about this case.'

'I know, but Chief Constable Wilson is sensing a chance to muscle in, so we need to give him something to worry about which makes him back down on Beeching. If he thinks Beeching has the goods on him, he can't take the risk of imposing his team on the case. We then have a clear run at solving it.'

Toby nodded in agreement. 'Wow, that's very Machiavellian.'

Fred shrugged. 'I have my moments.'

'And what about DI Melanie Townsend?'

'Ah, the Blonde Bombshell.'

'I heard that you and she were once an item.'

Fred gave Toby an amused smile. 'Our paths may have crossed.'

'Putty in your hands then, sir.'

Fred shook his head. 'Far from it, the song of that Siren has lured many a criminal onto the rocks. She's a bloody good detective. If you lie to her, she will know.'

'So how do I hold information back?'

'Tell her the truth, just be economical with it.'

'I'm not sure I follow?

'If you tell her that Tabitha drowned, that's the truth. Just don't tell her anything about our suspicions.'

'I hear you, sir.'

'Good, get up the Green Dragon and see what you can get from Whomper.' Fred gave Toby a crisp ten-pound note. 'Buy Whomper lunch and as much beer as he wants.'

'You want a receipt?'

'At the Green Dragon? Good luck with that.'

Chapter 41
The Ploughman's Lunch

As Toby entered the stygian gloom of the Green Dragon bar, he stood for a moment to let his eyes adjust. It was like a throwback to a bygone age when London and all the big cities still had pea-souper fogs and you could taste the air you breathed. In the Dragon, you could at least see it.

In the far corner, what seemed to be a damp fire was burning creating an almost impenetrable fog bank. Somewhere in there was Whomper. Toby silently apologised to his lungs and headed in. He saw the glow from Whomper's Gauloises first, above the glow he caught a glimpse of one of Whomper's beady eyes watching him intently.

'DC Marlowe, you're just in time to buy me a pint.'

'But your glass is nearly full.'

Whomper picked it up and drained it in about six seconds. He belched and wiped his lips on his shirt sleeve. 'Like I said, you're just in time.' He held out his empty glass. Toby took it.

'Same again,'

Whomper nodded.

'You want something to eat?'

'Wining and dining. Somebody wants something.'

'I'd like a chat about a mutual friend.'

'Chief Constable Wilson, no doubt.'

Toby just stood there wondering how Whomper did it.

'We can talk about The Blonde Bombshell later.'

There was no point trying to second guess Whomper. Toby walked over to the bar; the barman was there but he was studiously ignoring him.

'Excuse me.'

The barman held up his hand. 'Don't break my concentration I'm close to cracking the crossword.'

'What you stuck on?'

'Three down, four across.'

'Can you give me a bit more.'

The barman nodded. 'Drinking establishment, three letters, middle letter u.'

Toby smiled, thinking the barman was joking. The barman did not respond. 'You're kidding.'

'Nope, I thought it was bar but that u ruined everything.'

'Pub,' said Toby. The barman looked at him as if he was the Messiah.

'Brilliant! Why didn't I think of that?'

Toby shrugged. 'Too obvious.'

The barman nodded. 'I think you're right. Sometimes you can be too close to something to see it.'

'If you say so. How many you got so far?'

'That one and the one with the u in it.'

'Just started it then.'

'Yeah, it's the Sun quick crossword.'

'How long you been at it.'

The barman looked at his watch. 'About forty minutes.'

Toby nodded. 'Early days then. What's the other word, the one with the u in it?'

'Insolvunt.'

'There's no u in insolvent.'

'You sure?'

'Positive. What was the clue.'

'What do you call somebody whose bank has closed their account.'

'Bankrupt,' said Toby, forgetting to pause.

The barman counted along the line; the u was in the right place. He beamed. 'That's brilliant, two before twelve p.m. Never done that before. What can I get you?'

'Two pints of bitter, please. What's on the menu today?'

The barman pointed towards the specials board. 'Ploughman's Lunch.'

'Anything else?'

'Pork scratchings or a pickled egg.'

Toby considered treating himself but decided to play it safe. Pork scratchings and pickled eggs didn't seem conducive to longevity.

'Two ploughmen's then, please. Do you have any brown bread?'

The barman looked at Toby like he had just spat in his pint. 'We don't do that sort of thing in the Green Dragon, sir; we have our reputation to think about.'

Toby smiled weakly. 'Could I have a receipt, please?'

The barman gave him a withering look, clearly the question was unworthy of response.

Toby returned to Whomper's micro climate with the beers. 'I've ordered two ploughman's.'

Whomper nodded approvingly. 'Great.'

Toby sat down opposite Whomper.

'What can I do for you, DC Marlowe?'

'Chief Constable Wilson.'

Whomper nodded. 'Ah, he's sending in the Blonde Bombshell.'

Toby didn't know what to say; how could Whomper know this?

'It was bound to happen sooner or later. Stratford is a small force, and three murders in three days ...'

'Two,' Toby interrupted.

'You don't believe Tabitha Tharpe drowned herself without some help, do you?'

'How do you even know about Miss Tharpe?'

Whomper smiled indulgently at Toby. 'I have a friend who

runs the chain ferry, he keeps me up to speed with events on the river. Stratford is like a village, everybody knows everybody.'

Toby didn't know where to start. 'Listen, Tabitha Tharpe isn't official yet, Beeching's going to announce it this afternoon. Can we keep it between us? I don't know how your friend knew.'

'He didn't, you just confirmed it.'

Toby paused. 'You tricked me again.'

'Only a little, I was told a young woman was fished out of the river and that you and Fred Williams were in attendance. I just guessed it was Tabitha.'

Before Toby could drop himself in it any further, the ploughman's arrived. If anything, the lump of cheese was bigger than before.

'You want me to take half of it?'

Toby nodded and Whomper sliced off about two thirds of Toby's wedge of cheddar.

'Can you help us?'

Whomper took a bite out of the cheddar he had just liberated from Toby's plate. He chewed it thoughtfully.

'Let me get this right. Beeching is panicking because Wilson has put his own DI, the afore mentioned Blonde Bombshell, onto the case and you and Fred will now have to report to her and this would have the effect of putting Wilson in charge. Beeching doesn't want that because Wilson will then get the acclaim for solving a huge case. To prevent this, you need to put pressure on Wilson to back off by blackmailing him with his indiscretions, none of which you can prove. Would that be about right?'

Toby nodded; he couldn't help but be impressed. 'Something like that.'

Whomper laughed out loud, emitting a fine spray of Cheddar into the already dense atmosphere of the Green Dragon. Toby stopped buttering his cottage roll, he had lost his appetite.

'You mean, exactly like that.' He fixed Toby with an unblinking stare, one eyebrow raised questioningly.

Toby submitted with a nod. 'Yes.'

'Well, that's good because I don't like Wilson. He's corrupt.'

'That's a bit like the pot calling the kettle black.'

'Oh no, DC Marlowe. Wilson swore to uphold the law; I never took that oath. He is taking my taxpayers money to uphold the law and he's not doing it.'

'Have you ever paid tax?'

Whomper shrugged. 'That's beside the point. Wilson is a fraudster and I don't want someone more corrupt than me upholding the laws of the land. It upsets the natural balance.'

Toby took a sip of his beer while he contemplated the moral ambiguity that Whomper seemed to be raising. Unable to decide whether he should be offended, he opted for co-operation.

'So, will you help us?'

'Course I will, I'm all about natural justice. Are you familiar with the Merchant of Venice?'

Toby nodded. 'Yes, I studied it for A level.'

'Well, our Tommy …'

'Tommy Vaughan?' asked Toby.

'The very same, he's a bit of a Shylock, if you follow my drift.'

'A money lender.'

'Yes, no paperwork, no license. He's using cash from the punter's bets. Undeclared profits being used for illegal loan sharking. It's wrong on so many levels.'

'You disapprove?'

'Not at all, free market in action. But when he lends the money to someone like Wilson, a public servant with a duty to uphold the law of the land …' Whomper leaned back in his chair, 'that's where I draw the line.'

'Good to see that your moral compass is still working, Whomper.'

Whomper winked at Toby. 'It's always working but sometimes it chooses to look the other way, if you know what I mean.'

Toby knew exactly what he meant; he was putting it all together in his head. 'So, Wilson is being bled dry by his spendthrift new bride and goes to Tommy for a loan at favourable rates. He can't do it through his bank, because he can't afford for it to become common knowledge that he is strapped for cash.'

'Exactly, and Wilson has the goods on Tommy Vaughan. He knows that Tommy has been paying a local trainer, who shall remain nameless, to nobble the odd horse to increase his profits. Wilson has a friend who's a vet. He inspected one of the favourites that didn't win and found it had been drugged. Told Wilson about it in confidence.'

'Why didn't he report it to the racing authorities?'

'He was stopped for drunk driving and refused to give a blood sample and called Wilson. Wilson came to see him at the police station and kicked him loose.'

'In exchange for a juicy bit of information on Tommy.'

'You got it. He has Tommy dangling on a piece of string.'

'So, who attacked Tommy?'

'Who do you think. Wilson had him beaten up because he was threatening to put up his interest. You see, Tommy thought he had the upper hand until Wilson gave him the vets report and a beating.'

Toby was impressed, Whomper was a one-man CID unit. All this information was great but how would they get Tommy Vaughn to talk if Wilson had him over a barrel? 'Tommy can't afford to talk to us then.'

Whomper smiled. 'He can't afford not to. You just have to tell him everything that I've just told you. Then reassure him that it won't be used if Wilson agrees to back away from another case. Just don't tell him the case.'

'So, we tell Tommy that we will leave him be if Wilson plays ball.'

'Correct, and all he has to do his confirm to Wilson that you guys know about the illegal loans.'

It all made perfect sense. Toby didn't know whether to be appalled or impressed. Thanks to Whomper, he could now give Fred the tools to get Wilson to back off. Beeching would be delighted. There was just one question he needed to ask.

'This DI Townsend from Coventry, what's she like?'

A beatific smile spread across Whomper's face. 'Beauty and brains, which makes her a real problem. The Blonde Bombshell just knows when she is being lied to.'

'But what is she like?' persisted Toby.

'Like the first rays of sun on a snow-covered mountain, like the sweetest fruit you ever tasted. The beauty of Cleopatra and the aggression of Boudica.'

'And what about my boss, DS Williams.'

Whomper lit another Galois and looked longingly towards the one-armed bandit. 'Oh, she and Fred were an item some years back. Beauty and the beast. Aphrodite and Fred Flintstone. They were good together.'

'What broke them up.'

'Ambition; she had some. Tragic really, Fred could have been a CI by now if he had stuck with her and followed her lead.'

'But she's only a DI.'

Whomper shrugged. 'It's a man's world, DC Marlowe. The women's lib movement has a long way to go.'

The conversation with Whomper seemed to revive Toby's appetite and he realized he had munched his way through all of his bread roll, most of his cheese and half a pickled onion. Whomper had watched him eat and smiled.

'The cuisine here seems to be growing on you.'

Toby shrugged. 'It's not bad, just a bit limited and a little unhealthy.'

'Well, I've heard that one of those microwaves has been ordered, just like the one that Dick Mayrick has at the Dirty Duck. Pies will soon be on the menu.'

'Any chance of a salad?'

Whomper gave him a disgusted look and ordered another pint.

Back at Guild Street, Toby brought Fred up to speed on his conversation with Whomper.

'This is excellent news, let's go and find Tommy Vaughan and enlighten him.'

Toby hesitated. 'Shouldn't we be concentrating on the murders, sir?'

'Once we get Coventry off our backs, we'll be able to.' Fred headed for the door but, before he got there, it swung open and in walked a tall blonde.

DI Mel Townsend was everything that Toby had been told, and much more. He stopped in his tracks, as did Fred. She stood in the doorway like Boudica at the gates of London, magnificent and immovable. She surveyed the scene and then fixed her stare on Fred. 'Been a long time, Fred.'

Fred nodded. 'It has.'

'You want to bring me up to speed on the murders?'

'Of course, DC Marlowe and I have just got to pop out to do an interview on another case first.'

DI Townsend stared unbelievingly at him. 'Another case? During the biggest serial killing case you've ever had.'

'They're sort of related.'

'In what way,' snapped Townsend, clearly not believing a word of Fred's explanation.'

'We won't know that until we have interviewed him.'

'Interviewed who?'

'That's right,' said Fred, as he squeezed past her and made for the door.

'What's right?'

'You're right,' Fred smiled and made his escape down the stairs. Toby went to follow, but DI Townsend blocked his way.

'Who are you interviewing and how are they related to the killings?'

'I'm not sure ma'am, DS Williams doesn't share those details with me when he's working on a theory.'

Toby was trying to be as vague as possible and squeeze slowly past DI Townsend at the same time.

She grabbed him by the lapel. 'How are they related?' she hissed.

Toby shrugged. 'Like when cousins marry.' It was the first thing that came into his head but it had the desired effect. DI Townsend looked at him like he was mad and, in her moment of confusion, Toby edged towards the door.

Toby felt her grip relax and, with the athletic agility of a top-level scrum half, he slipped past her and down the stairs after Fred. When he reached the car, Fred already had the engine running and was laughing. Toby jumped in next to him.

'Like when cousin's marry,' he repeated, shaking his head with amusement.

Toby shrugged. 'Well, it worked didn't it.'

'Yeah, suppose it did.' Fred sped out of the car park as DI Townsend came striding out of the station, clearly intent on stopping Fred leaving.

Fred looked the other way and floored it. Toby smiled and waved weakly at her. Deep in his soul, he knew that DI Townsend's first impression of him was not a favourable one.

Chapter 42
The Sword Of Damocles

Tommy Vaughan hadn't been hard to find. He had a small cottage in the village of Barton, a few miles west of Stratford. The village was nestled by the river Avon and had a pub. The Cottage of Content, the quaintly named pub, was where Tommy spent most of his evenings when there wasn't a race meeting.

Fred gambled that, as lunchtime approached, he was more likely to find him there than at home. As he opened the door and walked into the pub, he was proved correct. 'Hello, Tommy, fancy seeing you in here.'

Tommy looked up over the beer glass that was clamped to his lips. He slowly lowered it. 'Yeah, fancy.' He clearly didn't share Fred's enthusiasm for their unexpected meeting. 'I suppose you've driven up from Stratford just to bump into me.'

Fred smiled. 'So cynical for one so young.'

'Bugger off, Williams, nothing you do is an accident. What do you want?'

He sat down next to Tommy. 'Well, let's start with a pint of whatever you're drinking. Can I get you another?'

Tommy looked suspiciously at him. 'What's it going to cost me.'

'Less than you'd think.'

'And what does that mean?'

Fred nodded to Toby. 'Get them in, Toby. Pint of Mild for me and Tommy and whatever you're drinking.' He turned back to Tommy. 'How's your head?'

'It's all right.'

'How would you like to get the bloke that had it done to you off your back?'

'Nobody had me done, I fell.'

'Course you did, Tommy.'

Toby returned with the drinks and sat down next to Fred. 'Tommy, here, has just been reminding me that he fell.'

Toby nodded solemnly. 'Must have been quite some fall to smash in the front and back of your head, Tommy.'

'Didn't we establish that Tommy had a rubber head? Must have bounced up after the fall, then he twisted in the air and fell flat on his face.'

Toby nodded at Fred's analysis. 'Yeah, rubber heads will do that every time.'

Tommy put down his pint. 'OK, why don't you pair of comedians get to the point.'

'Fair enough, Tommy. Where shall I start?'

'Wherever gets you to the finish quickest.'

Fred smiled. 'Very well, now you just listen until I've finished, OK?' Tommy nodded belligerently. 'We know that you lent Chief Constable Wilson money to fund his newly found domestic bliss.' Tommy went to protest but Fred held up a hand to silence him. 'Hold on, Tommy, I think you're going to like this.'

Tommy took a swig of his pint and gave the impression that he definitely wouldn't. 'Now, you had the chief on a piece of string with that little secret up your sleeve, so you decided to give him a little squeeze. You raised the interest on his loan.'

'Illegal loan,' added Toby.

'Thank you, DC Marlowe, I was forgetting we are talking about illegal loan sharking.'

Tommy's knuckles were turning white as his grip on his glass tightened and little bubbles were starting to froth in his beer.

'I think you're supposed to swallow, not blow, Tommy.'

Tommy scowled at Fred. 'Just get on with it, Williams.'

Fred nodded. 'Very well, now where was I?'

'Loan sharking, sir, the illegal kind.'

'Ah yes, thank you, DC Marlowe.' Fred turned back to Tommy. 'Now, Wilson didn't much appreciate this, did he, and he managed to get the goods on you over that race fixing.'

Tommy's beer frothed over his glass.

'Wilson got a confession out of the trainer, didn't he. He had you bang to rights.' Fred took a long swig of his beer and then placed his glass down. 'Thing is, Tommy, I have good news for you. We're not interested in you. Wilson is bent and we don't like that but, and this is the good part, we don't want to prosecute him, we want to blackmail him.' Fred let that sink in while Tommy eyed first him and then Toby suspiciously.

'What's the catch?'

'There is no catch. My boss needs to get Wilson off his back and under control. If you make a statement, that we'll probably never have to use, he will pay off his loan and back off.'

'I'm not making a statement. You think I'm stupid?'

Fred looked at Toby. 'What do you think DC Marlowe?'

'Definitely stupid, sir.'

'I'd have to agree, but we won't use this statement because the police never like to wash their dirty washing in public, bad for our image. So, what do you say?'

'I say no, that's what I say.'

'That's disappointing,' Fred turned to Toby. 'Read him his rights, please.'

'Tommy Vaughan, I'm arresting you under suspicion of illegal money lending. You do not have to say anything unless you wish to do so …'

'Hold on, hold on,' cried Tommy. 'I thought you said I wouldn't be charged.'

'That's if you make the statement. If you don't, we'll do you and Wilson in public.'

Tommy looked sullenly at Fred. 'That's a dirty trick, Williams.'

Fred shrugged. 'I'm giving you a way out; you get your

money, Wilson off your back and no charges.'

'What about my interest?'

'Don't push it, Tommy. Illegal money lending and blackmail, you're looking at five years.'

'Maybe eight if previous is taken into account.'

'I was found not guilty,' Tommy protested.

'Unproven, I think. On two occasions.'

'Speaks to character, or lack of it, sir,' said Toby.

Fred nodded sagely. 'My DC has a point, Tommy. They've been looking to get you for years, don't give them a chance now, not when you have a way out.'

Tommy seemed to slump in his chair. Toby could almost hear the cogs of Tommy's brain turning as he tried to figure a way out. There was none.

He took a deep breath. 'OK, so if I make a statement, this all goes away?'

'Pretty much, unless Wilson decides to contest it, and that's not going to happen, is it.'

'We got to go down the station?'

'Not necessary in this case, DC Marlowe here has already prepared your statement. All you have to do is sign it.'

Tommy scowled. 'Can you do that?'

Fred's smile told him he could. 'Would you like to read it, Mister Vaughan?'

He shook his head. 'Just give me a pen to sign it.'

Toby passed him a pen. 'Sign and date there, please, and DS Williams will witness it.'

'Shouldn't I have a solicitor?'

Fred shrugged. 'Only if you want to go to court.'

Tommy didn't want that. He signed. 'What happens now?'

'We finish our pints and you are free to do whatever you want, just try to keep it legal, Tommy, because DC Marlowe has your confession to a crime.' He turned to Toby. 'What was it you called it?'

'Sword of Damocles, sir.'

Fred nodded. 'That's it.'

'What the hell's that when it's at home.'

'Never you mind, Tommy, just know that if you step out of line again it's going to fall on you from a great height.'

Toby picked up the statement and nodded to Tommy. 'Good day to you, Mister Vaughan.'

He nodded.

'We put the drinks on your tab, Tommy,' said Fred, as he followed Toby.

Tommy shook his head and watched them go, unsure whether to be relieved or annoyed.

Chapter 43
Madness Creeps Like An Uninvited Guest

Oliver sat on a bench looking out across the river towards the theatre. Would he ever tread those boards again? Was it even conceivable that he could escape justice? Given the number of murders he was planning, it seemed unlikely.

Felix had told him, in no uncertain terms, that even if he did manage to complete his bloody revenge, he would need to disappear for at least another year before attempting a return. Felix was nervous; he had underestimated Oliver. He believed that Oliver had been betrayed, as had his father. He deserved a reckoning but, now the blood was flowing and the bodies were falling, it didn't sit so comfortably with him. Oliver knew this. Felix would have to be handled carefully; he couldn't alienate his only ally.

Another thought crossed his mind; a disturbing one. Felix was not indispensable. There, he'd thought it. Considered the unthinkable. It was there now, parked on a little shelf at the back of his mind. He could take it down from that shelf any time he needed.

He stood up, walked over to the edge of the river and looked down at his rippling shadow. He smiled. 'You've changed.' His reflection said nothing, it just smiled back at him, recognising the moment when any restraint that had governed his actions had lifted away. Revenge was everything, at any cost and regardless of the innocent. He would try to only target those who had wronged him but madness creeps up like an uninvited guest. The voices that now sounded in Oliver's head were no longer just his own.

Sitting in the Vintner restaurant on Sheep Street, Felix had reached the same conclusion. All he could do now was to try and curb Oliver's excesses. He also had to avoid becoming one of his victims. How he wished he had never written that letter.

Chapter 44
A Shift In The Balance Of Power

In Guild Street, Inspector Beeching smiled for the first time in over a week. He held Tommy Vaughan's statement in his hand. 'This is excellent work, boys. We've got Wilson by the unmentionables.'

'When are you going to confront him, sir, only ...' Fred nodded towards the looming form of DI Mel Townsend who was staring into Beeching's office, her face throwing a look that would have turned most men to stone. 'DI Townsend is getting rather impatient, she's here to take charge of the case.'

Beeching glanced out at her. 'Yes, she is looking a bit fierce, has she been fed today?'

'Only red meat ... raw.'

'OK, Fred, I'll give Wilson a call now and tell him she is going to be working under you.'

Toby sniggered.

Fred glared at him. 'You're better than that, son.'

'Sorry, sir.'

Beeching held up the statement and gave it a quick kiss. 'Come on, you little beauty. You and I are going to have a little chat with the chief constable.' Beeching walked behind his desk, sat down and picked up the phone. 'Hello, Rose, could you get Chief Constable Wilson on the line for me.' He looked up at Fred and Toby. 'That will be all for now, stand DI Townsend down.'

'What do I tell her?'

'Whatever you like Fred, after this call she will be working for you.'

Fred led Toby back into CID, closing the door of Beeching's office as he did so. Mel Townsend cornered them both by Fred's desk before they could make their escape.

'And where do you think you're going?'

Fred smiled genially. 'Well, I don't know if you've noticed but we seem to have a potential serial killer in town so, if you don't mind, DC Marlowe and I are going out to make some more inquiries.'

'That's what you think,' said Mel indignantly. 'Wilson has told me I'm taking over this one and you need to bring me fully up to speed.'

'I would love to, Mel, but things have changed. Inspector Beeching now thinks it would be better if DC Marlowe and I continued running the case as we are fully up to speed. We'd be glad of any help you could give in a support role though.'

Fred's words hit Mel Townsend like a straight left followed by a right upper cut. She swayed for a moment, speechless. She recovered quickly though. 'What the hell are you talking about? Wilson told me this morning that I am in charge.'

'New evidence has come to light, ma'am.'

Mel turned on Toby. 'What evidence?'

'Inspector Beeching is discussing it with Chief Constable Wilson now.'

They all glanced into Beeching's office. There was a broad smile on his face and he was reading from a file he was holding.'

Mel Townsend looked from Beeching's smiling face to Fred's.'

'What's going on here, Fred?'

'A shift in the balance of power.'

'But my orders …'

'Are about to be overruled. Trust me, Mel, there's been a

change of plan. I suggest you call Wilson as soon as Beeching has finished with him, it'll save a lot of explanation.'

A guarded smile crossed her face. 'This is your doing, isn't it?'

Fred shook his head. 'Above my paygrade, I just do what the boss tells me.'

'You've never done anything the boss tells you.'

DI Townsend had a point but Fred wasn't going to concede it. 'Look on the bright side, if this enquiry goes bad, you won't get the blame. Silver linings and all that.' Fred turned to Toby. 'Come on, DC Marlowe, we need to get to the theatre.'

'Yes, sir.'

As they pushed past Mel Townsend and her two detectives, Fred nodded over to where Kinky Bernstein and Ginger Dalton were pretending to work. 'DCs Bernstein and Dalton will bring you up to speed, won't you boys.'

They both nodded unconvincingly.

As they climbed into Fred's car, Toby could hear him chuckling. 'You enjoyed that, didn't you?'

'I have to admit, I did. DI Townsend is a fantastic detective but there was no way I wanted to be reporting to her. She has an unorthodox way of working.'

'By the book?'

'Precisely.'

'Well, we can't have that now, can we, sir.'

'No, we can't. Right, let's get to the theatre, I've arranged another interview with Sir Morris. I think after last night's events he'll be more willing to talk.'

'What will you say about Tabitha?'

'Let's call it a suspicious death for now, imply that we think it's another murder without actually saying it.'

Toby nodded. 'That should get his attention.'

Chapter 45
Kill The King
And Marry His Brother

Sir Morris was sitting in his dressing room waiting for DS Williams and DC Marlowe. He wasn't alone. Next to him sat a gentleman whose skin was like an old leather suitcase; he was well dressed in a suit and tie but his serpentine features carried the stain of years of smoking and drinking.

'Good evening, officers. May I introduce you to Gerard Soames, theatre critic for the Sunday Review.'

Toby recognised him from a BBC 2 documentary he had seen about Sir Morris. He had read many of his reviews, which tended to be caustic and pithy, except when it related to Sir Morris's projects.

He stood and gave them a forced smile. 'Good evening, officers, terrible business.'

'Indeed, sir,' said Fred, not bothering to smile back. 'We were hoping to have a private word you, Sir Morris.'

'Nonsense, sergeant, Gerard and Terry are my ...' he fell silent.

Soames put his hand on his shoulder. 'Terry was like family to us.'

As Fred gave Sir Morris a moment, Toby slowly began to feel there was something he was missing. This wasn't a normal relationship. Soames and Fibs were more like underlings to Sir Morris. Why would critics be so close to those they critique?

'Very well, but I'm afraid that what I have to tell you about Miss Tharpe is rather distressing.'

Sir Morris nodded. 'We have heard about her suicide, a terrible thing.'

'It is, sir. We do have a problem though.'

Soames looked up, the journalist in him sensing a story. 'What problem?'

Fred rubbed his chin. 'There are elements that are leading us to believe that Miss Tharpe's drowning was … suspicious.'

Sir Morris and Soames exchanged glances. 'She was murdered?' whispered Soames.

'Too early to say, sir, but between you and I, there are elements that make it look possible. These are being investigated as we speak. Until then, we must keep an open mind.'

Toby watched their faces change from shock to fear. Fred had done a masterful job and he wasn't finished.

'If this proves to be the case, we are looking at three murders in two days, of actors and friends that are closely related to you. We are starting to think that you may be the catalyst for these terrible events.'

Sir Morris turned to Soames. 'But who would want to hurt me? I am beloved. A giant of the stage.'

'Someone who likes musicals, maybe,' offered Fred.

Toby had to bite into his lip to stifle a laugh.

'Nobody likes musicals, sergeant, not if they have an educated palate.'

Toby recognised the patronising tone from Soames' column in the Sunday Review. He had disliked Gerard Soames' work since he first read it; churlish and mean spirited. Listening to him now, he had the opportunity to dislike the man as well.

'You don't need an educated palate to be a successful killer, sir, history has proved that. Given the pattern of deaths, we feel that you may be at risk.'

Sir Morris shook his head unable to comprehend that anyone could not love him. 'I am but a humble actor, who could want to harm me?'

'Another actor maybe,' suggested Fred.

'Another actor?' Sir Morris looked appalled.

'You are very famous, Sir Morris,' Toby said. 'You have been at the top of your profession for decades. DS Williams has a point. These killings seem …' He struggled for the right word.

'Personal,' said Fred.

'Exactly. Can you think of any actor who you've had a major falling out with who would harbour resentment against you and your company?'

Soames looked at Sir Morris. Toby saw it and in that moment he knew. Somewhere down the line, Sir Morris had made an enemy. His vaunting ambition had led him to undermine an actor who was threatening to upstage him with their talent. He looked again at the exchange of glances between Sir Morris and Gerard Soames and he was certain.

Sir Morris continued to bluster. 'I have always treated my people well, they are like a family to me, some have been with me for thirty years.'

Soames nodded enthusiastically. 'Sir Morris is like the father of a huge and talented family.'

'So, what are you doing here then?' Fred's question was blunt and direct.

Soames was a little taken back. 'Well, I don't tread the boards.'

'No, you don't, do you? You comment on those that do. Isn't that at odds with your job? Being on intimate terms with a company that you have to review independently, surely that must compromise your objectivity?'

'I've reviewed Sir Morris on many occasions. I'm impartial.'

'No, you're not,' said Toby. Sensing a break though, he had become as rude as Fred. 'I've read some of your reviews and they're hatchet jobs. You have closed shows after the first week. But never a bad one about Sir Morris, why is that?'

It was Sir Morris's turn to look offended. 'Dear boy, think

what you are saying. I am Sir Morris Oxford. I'm not capable of putting on a bad performance, it's just not in my blood.'

'Every actor gets a bad review; it goes with the territory.'

'For the mere jobbing actor, perhaps, but I am raising the playing of Shakespeare's plays to a new plateau.'

'And that is why Terry Fibs and I spend so much time on the road with Sir Morris, he is constantly reinventing the genre.'

'Some would say that Richard Jenkins was reinventing the genre.' Toby had read about the young Welsh actor who had taken Stratford by storm in the early thirties. He had also discovered something that would explode in Sir Morris's face if he lied; he hadn't even told Fred. He had used Richard Jenkins' name to get a reaction, and he did. Again, Sir Morris and Soames exchanged furtive glances.

'Sorry, I didn't catch the name,' said Sir Morris.

Toby could see that he clearly had. He looked flustered, guilty. 'Richard Jenkins. He won awards. The critics loved him.'

'Yes, that does sound familiar.'

'He was in your company, Sir Morris.' Toby's words sounded more like an accusation.

Sir Morris pretended to remember. 'Oh, the Welsh lad, he was quite good.'

'Quite good? He was a genius, what happened to him?'

Sir Morris shook his head. 'I'm afraid it all went wrong. He had the talent but just could not handle the pressure. Threw himself under a train up near Long Marston, very sad.'

'Did you feel threatened by him?' asked Toby, his questions now very direct.

Sir Morris shook his head. 'Of course not, I barely knew him.'

'Really, I find that hard to believe.'

Sir Morris looked shocked at being called a liar to his face. Fred Williams, however, was smiling; he could tell that Toby had something up his sleeve.

Sir Morris turned to Fred. 'Really, are you going to let your DC speak to me, a Knight of the Realm, in such fashion?'

Fred nodded. 'Yes, I think I am.' He nodded to Toby to continue.

'You haven't answered my question. Did you know Richard Jenkins well?'

Sir Morris had control of himself and replied calmly. 'As I said, constable, I hardly knew him.'

'But he played Mark Antony to your Caesar in 1934, he played Hamlet to your Claudius the following year. Are you sure?'

Sir Morris gave Toby his most patronising smile. 'Dear boy, when one has performed in as many plays as I, with as many great actors as I, they all tend to blur into one never-ending scene.'

Toby nodded, waited a beat, and then dropped his bomb. 'That's surprising. I'd have thought you would have remembered him; didn't you marry his widow?'

Fred's mouth fell open; it was followed by Sir Morris's.

'Well … er, it's not really …' his words dried up.

'Beatrice Smallman, the ex-Mrs Jenkins. Still married to her, I understand.' Toby stood triumphant, staring at Sir Morris and daring him to deny it.'

'Ahh, that Richard Jenkins.'

Toby burst out laughing. 'Come off it, Sir Morris, you're fooling no one. Tell me the truth.'

Sir Morris seemed to have lost his tongue. Gerard Soames spoke up for him. His voice as oily as a warm kipper.

'That was a long time ago, constable, it was a very painful period and I'm sure Sir Morris did his best to rectify the situation.'

'Interesting choice of words. Rectify. That would suggest that he had done something wrong.'

'Sir Morris did nothing wrong. Richard had a serious drink

problem and it started to interfere with his acting. When he couldn't do the job any more, Sir Morris had to let him go.'

'That must have been pretty traumatic, given that Sir Morris was also the uncle to Richard Jenkins' young son, Oliver.'

'He didn't marry Beatrice until long after Richard had died, he wasn't a real uncle to Richard's son. He just kept an eye on the boy to help Beatrice.'

Toby nodded approvingly. 'Very public spirited of you, I'm sure. But that's about as believable as a line from one of your fawning reviews of Sir Morris.'

Soames glared at Toby. 'My reviews have always been impartial. It's not my fault if Sir Morris is never less than brilliant.'

Sir Morris looked up. 'Too kind, Gerard, but true.'

Toby looked at Fred and he nodded for him to continue. 'Don't you think that someone might have a grudge against you for the death of Richard Jenkins?'

'Who? His family are all dead.'

'His wife isn't.'

'Beatrice?' Sir Morris looked amused. 'She worships the very ground I walk on.'

'I'll bet she does. Lady Oxford now, isn't she? Done very well for herself. How did that go down with young Oliver? Not well, I'm guessing.'

'Oliver never knew. He died before we married.'

'Died? You sure of that? Our records show he disappeared, never been a body found.'

Sir Morris glanced helplessly at Soames, who turned to Toby and gave him his oily disingenuous smile once more.

'You have to appreciate that Sir Morris is a very public figure, he can't be seen to speculate about these terrible events. It would just bring it all back into the public domain again, it's far too painful for Lady Oxford.'

'I can imagine,' said Toby. 'Her husband dead on a local

railway after being sacked from Sir Morris's company, then the son of Beatrice and Richard becomes a great actor himself, only to suffer the same fate.'

'Oliver never killed himself,' said Sir Morris indignantly.

'True, but you did sack him, just like his father. Becoming too good was he?'

Sir Morris slumped down on a nearby chair and put his head in his hands. Gerard Soames put a hand upon his shoulder and then spoke to Toby with malice in his voice.

'How dare you! Sir Morris loved that boy, he even changed his stage name to Lawrence to protect him from comparisons with his father. It broke his heart when he disappeared, broke his mother's heart too. That's part of the reason Sir Morris married her, to comfort her.'

'Very altruistic of him, I'm sure. It all worked out pretty well for Beatrice, didn't it. She got to be Lady Oxford, no more spear carrying for her. No more acting for her. Not that she could act.'

'How dare you,' spat Sir Morris. 'Beatrice was a wonderful actress.'

Toby shook his head. 'That's not what the reviews say, I've taken the trouble to read them.'

'You know what critics are like, DC Marlowe, they were hard on her because of her closeness to me.'

'That may be true, Sir Morris, but if she was any good, why did she never have anything but minor parts when she was in your productions? Surely you would have given her the chance.'

Sir Morris didn't have an answer.

'I haven't seen Lady Oxford around the theatre since all this started, has she got something to hide?'

'Of course not. My dear Beatrice no longer acts, coming back to the theatre only brings back bad memories.'

'Like the suicide of her husband after you sacked him.'

'No.' Sir Morris stared sadly into the middle distance, it was too convincing to be acting. 'I'm afraid her marriage to Richard was not a happy one. He was a flawed character.'

'Genius, according to the critics. Destined to become one of the greats. He was on the verge of eclipsing even you in that thirty-five season. Were you glad to see him go?'

Gerard Soames rose to protest but Sir Morris waved him back down.

'No, I was sad if you must know. You are right, he had it in him to be great, as an actor,' he paused, 'but acting, you see, it's about confidence, self-belief. Richard had stopped believing and he crumbled, like a tower with no foundations when the first storm comes, he could not withstand it.'

'Storm?'

'Bad reviews. He'd never had any before that thirty-six season. When they started to appear, he just crumbled. Forgot his lines and then ran away and hid in a bottle, it was horrible to watch.'

Toby turned to Soames. 'Must have been tough for you. I've read two of the reviews you gave him that season, proper hatchet jobs.'

Soames winced. 'I prefer constructive criticism; he had dropped off from the standards he'd previously set.'

Toby looked across at Fred. 'Everything points to Beatrice Smallman being the most likely suspect.'

Fred nodded. 'She would have a motive.'

'Don't be ridiculous, we have been together for nearly thirty years,' snapped Sir Morris.

Fred shrugged. 'A lot of resentment can build up over thirty years, that or guilt.'

'Lady Oxford's son, he was a fine actor too, and just like his dad he started getting bad reviews, mainly from Mr Soames and the late Terry Fibs.'

Fred looked at Toby. 'That right? You have been doing your research, DC Marlowe. So, was Oliver as good as his dad?'

'Some would say better, sir.'

'And where is he?' asked Toby

'Disappeared in 1957, believed to be dead,' said Soames.

'Terrible business, he would have been my stepson had he not disappeared. I loved him, you know. A great actor with the world at his feet.'

Fred looked at Sir Morris. 'Like father, like son.'

Sir Morris nodded sadly. 'I'm afraid so, just like his father. He had a few bad reviews and he just fell to pieces.'

'Convenient, when he was upstaging you.'

'Not at all,' snapped Sir Morris, 'He was like a son to me.'

'King Claudius wasn't too keen on Prince Hamlet.'

Sir Morris stared at Toby, perplexed. 'Hamlet is a play; this is real life.'

'Shakespeare reflected the times he was living in.' Toby leaned towards Sir Morris. 'Did you love your stepson?'

Sir Morris's mouth opened and closed like a landlocked fish. 'Of course I did. What kind of question is that?'

'He wasn't a stepson then, but Sir Morris treated him as if he were, they were very close.'

Toby nodded to Gerard Soames. 'And you would know that, Mister Soames, being a part of Sir Morris's entourage. Hard for you to be objective, I would imagine.'

Soames scowled at Toby, then turned to Fred. 'You going to allow your constable to speak to Sir Morris like that?'

'I thought we had already established that, but if it helps, I can assist. We are trying to prevent you or any of your colleagues being added to the list of victims, so we need your help. We are not trying to accuse you of a crime, we just need to know if anyone could harbour a grudge against you and your troupe.'

'I can assure you that my wife is beyond suspicion. We have been together for thirty years.'

'You didn't wait long after Richard Jenkins died, did you?'

Sir Morris smiled wistfully. 'Beatrice was very fragile; she had a young son and had just lost her husband. We gathered around her like a family; we are a family of sorts. One thing led to another and before we knew it, we had fallen in love. Something good came from those terrible events.'

'But you didn't marry until Oliver disappeared. Would he have objected?'

'Of course not, I was like a second father to him. I was protecting his future and helping his mother. As I said, she was fragile.'

'Is she still fragile, is that why she no longer acts?'

The smile disappeared from Sir Morris's face. He glared at Toby. 'I don't care for your tone or insinuations, my wife was at home with a friend when both murders occurred, she had nothing to do with it. As for young Oliver, he disappeared over fifteen years ago. Last known destination, a ferry to Tangier.'

'You think he's dead.'

Sir Morris rubbed his forehead, he seemed to be in pain. 'I believe he is. I can never say it aloud, his mother still has hope. Fifteen years is a long time to stay out of touch. No postcard, no telephone call, nothing. They were close, very close ... he must be dead.' The regret in Sir Morris's voice seemed genuine.

Toby looked over at Fred. 'So, if your wife has an alibi and Oliver is missing, presumed dead, we are back where we started. Someone is killing your colleagues and we have no clues as to who the perpetrator could be.'

All four fell silent. Toby had really hoped that the evidence of a family rift would have opened up the possibility of either Beatrice, or her son, being possible candidates.

'Let's leave it there for now, gents, we'll send someone over to take a statement from your wife tomorrow. If what you say is correct, we can then eliminate her from our enquiries.'

'And Oliver?'

Toby looked at Soames's serpentine features. He knew that there was something they had not told him. A secret they were withholding. A lie that would eat away at the very heart of everything they held dear. At that moment, he was sure that Oliver Lawrence was alive.

'He is a person of interest. If he is still alive, we will find him.'

Toby turned to leave and Fred followed, pausing momentarily to speak to Sir Morris.

'I suggest you stay in the company of others and don't venture out alone. The streets of Stratford are not safe for you or your colleagues until this maniac has been apprehended.'

Sir Morris nodded; he looked a broken man. 'Thank you, sergeant and please go easy with my wife tomorrow.'

Fred nodded and followed Toby down the corridor and out of the back stage exit. Once they were outside, Fred pointed to a bench overlooking the river at the back of the Swan Theatre.

'Let's get some fresh air before we go back to the station.'

'I'd rather get a cuppa.'

'In a minute, young Toby.' They sat down. 'That was impressive work in there, why didn't you tell me what you'd discovered?'

'I didn't know if it meant anything, I needed to see their reaction.'

'We saw that, all right, they definitely shafted Richard Jenkins.'

'You should read the reviews from Fibs and Soames, real hatchet jobs. Jenkins was getting rave reviews and then, suddenly, they started giving him bad reviews out of nowhere and Sir Morris gave him lesser roles.'

'The king felt threatened by the young Prince and got his hatchet men to stick it to him. Quite Shakespearian really.'

Something that Fred had said struck a chord with Toby. 'That's it!'

'What's it?'

Toby jumped up.

'Don't you see? Sir Morris is the King, Richard Jenkins

threatened his crown, so he had his tame critics start to undermine him with bad reviews. Fibs and Soames are his Rosencrantz and Guildenstern. They wanted to break Jenkins, remove him as a threat to Sir Morris, but they went too far. Out of guilt or remorse, Sir Morris becomes involved with his widow, Beatrice, and ends up marrying her.'

Fred held up his hand. 'Hold on, young Toby. You're adding two and two together and making five.'

Toby would not be stopped. 'I'm not, sir. Think about it. Desmond Tharpe was Sir Morris's right hand man. If Sir Morris was trying to undermine Richard Jenkins, he would have needed Tharpe in on the plot. That would make Tharpe, Polonius. Polonius was stabbed ... just like Tharpe.' Toby was frantically scribbling down the connections on his pad. 'And who was Polonius's daughter? Ophelia. Tharpe's daughter was Tabitha, and she drowned. Threw herself into the river and drowned herself, just like Ophelia.'

Fred Williams leaned back on the bench and smiled indulgently. 'So, what exactly, is the point you are trying to make?'

'This is Hamlet, sir. Sir Morris is King Claudius, he has killed King Hamlet, married his wife and stolen the throne. Prince Hamlet is looking to avenge his father.'

'And who is Prince Hamlet?'

'Oliver Lawrence, sir. He's alive and he's back.'

Fred scratched his head. 'Have you been drinking strong coffee?'

'No, sir, think about it. He's avenging his father, Richard, who could have been the next King of the Stratford stage. Tharpe conspired against his father and was despatched just like Polonius, stabbed. Tabitha Tharpe had conspired to undermine Toby and he drove her mad. The displaying of Terry Fibs was specifically to break her shattered mind.'

'So, who was Fibs?'

'Rosencrantz. He did the King's dirty work. I'm sure if I look into the reviews they will be as bad for Oliver as they were for his father. If Fibs was Rosencrantz, and Soames is Guildenstern, it can mean only one thing.'

Fred raised an eyebrow. 'I know I'm going to regret asking, but what does it mean?'

'Our killer is following the plot of Hamlet. Gerard Soames and Sir Morris Oxford are the next to be killed. Oliver Lawrence has cast himself as an avenging Prince Hamlet. It all fits, sir.'

Toby stood triumphantly smiling down at Fred. Fred pointed to him to sit down and waited while he did. 'Have you any idea how batshit crazy that sounds, young Toby?'

'Yes, sir, but that's the point. Oliver Lawrence probably is crazy. His father killed himself because of Sir Morris and his gang, he had his own career finished by the same people. He went away, but now he's back. It all makes sense.'

Fred nodded slowly and thought for a moment. 'It does all make perfect sense if you assume a man who has been missing for fifteen years is still alive, and has returned to Stratford to kill everyone who he feels betrayed him and his father.'

Toby went to speak but Fred shook his head.

'No, Toby, let me finish. Not only has he returned but he is also killing them to the plot of Hamlet. Now whilst I can't deny that you have made the deaths, and the facts as we know them, fit into Shakespeare's tragedy, you have to admit it's a bit of an intellectual leap. If I go to Beeching and tell him that Marlowe has cracked the case and it's Hamlet, you will be on traffic duty tomorrow, do you understand? You might be onto something with Oliver Lawrence but, for God's sake, say nothing about the Hamlet theory.'

Oliver looked dejectedly at the scribbled notes on his note pad. 'But it all fits, sir.'

'You've made it fit, it's good work. Don't spoil it by inventing a plot to fit your facts. Find all the facts and that will give you the plot.'

'You're right, sir, but didn't you tell me to follow my instincts?'

'I did, instincts are important to a good copper, but they're not always right. Follow them until you can prove them. If you can't, say nothing.'

Toby knew Fred was right. If he spouted his theory in CID, he would be laughed out of the station. He would do his research and he would prove his theory. Whatever anyone said, he was convinced that Oliver Lawrence was his murderer, a latter-day Prince Hamlet intent on revenge.

Chapter 46
Farewell, My Lovely

When Fred and Toby returned to Guild Street, DI Mel Townsend was waiting for them. Her beautiful face was masked by simmering rage and yet, there seemed to be a hint of amusement playing around her eyes. Toby stepped forward to greet her but she flicked her eyes towards the kitchen. 'Bugger off, DC Marlowe, the grown-ups need to talk.'

Toby had been around long enough to know when not to argue, this was one of those moments.

Fred watched him go. 'That was a bit harsh, Mel, Toby's a bloody good DC.'

'Cut the crap, Fred. I want to know what the hell you said to Beeching that got Wilson to pull me off the case.'

Fred tried to feign surprise but, despite being born and bred in Stratford, his acting skills were negligible.

'Don't play the innocent with me, you found something on Wilson, didn't you?'

'Maybe.'

'Spill.' It wasn't a request.

Fred smiled; he liked seeing Mel Townsend annoyed. 'I would love to but unfortunately the evidence provided to Inspector Beeching is of a delicate nature.'

Mel grabbed him by his balls. 'This delicate enough for you?'

Fred winced. 'Well, if you're going to put it like that, perhaps I could give you a brief outline.'

She squeezed tighter.

'OK, no need for police brutality,' Fred winked at Mel. 'Unless this is foreplay.' A further tightening of Mel's grip confirmed it wasn't.

'Well?'

'It's complicated …' began Fred, at a pitch that only dogs could hear. He pointed to his captive groin. 'Maybe ease the pressure a little.'

Mel shrugged and let go.

Fred took a deep breath. 'Wow, I'd forgotten what big hands you have.'

Mel smiled despite herself. 'Cut the crap, Fred. What happened?'

Fred looked around the office, they were alone. 'All right, but you can't repeat any of this.'

Mel nodded.

'OK. You are probably familiar with Wilson's current marital status.'

'What, little miss ever-ready.'

'I think it's Heather Reddy, but I can see where you're coming from. Seems she's quite the shopper. Poor old Wilson is struggling to keep up with her on the expenditure front, despite being on a chief constable's salary.'

'Man's a laughing stock at HQ. Silly old fool is being milked for everything he's got.'

'And more.'

Mel looked at Fred sharply. 'What does that mean?'

'The old fool has been taking illegal loans from a local bookie cum loan shark. When he tried to blackmail the chief and put his rates up, he had him worked over. Tried to make it look like a robbery.'

Mel Townsend shook her head in disbelief. 'Geez, I knew he was dumb but this takes the biscuit.'

'Oh, levels of dumb you could only imagine. We got the bookie to make a statement and gave it to Beeching.'

'And he phoned Wilson and got me taken off the case.'

Fred nodded. 'Pretty much, Mel. Beeching's a glory seeker, doesn't want Cov HQ stealing his glory.'

'I don't imagine you're too disappointed either.'

Fred shrugged. 'I can never tell a lie.'

'Yes, you can,' snapped Mel.

'True. I never asked for you to be off the case, I want you on it, but I want to lead. Toby and I are getting close. I want you to help me, Mel, you're a great detective.'

'Keeping all the glory for yourself then.'

'Or all the stick. Three murders and no arrests, the pressure is on.'

'Three?'

Fred nodded. 'We think the girl was helped into the river.'

'You have signs of a struggle?'

'No, but everything the killer did was aimed at driving her mad. The way he laid out the body of Terry Fibs for her to find. Eyeballs out, tongue out. Seems like it was planned.' Fred paused for a moment. 'We have a theory.'

'Go on.' He paused. He couldn't tell Mel Townsend what Toby had suggested, she would laugh him out of Stratford. The only problem was, he was beginning to think it could be true.

'Well?' said Mel impatiently.

'I can't say anything yet, there are a couple of things that need to be confirmed first.'

Mel nodded. 'I see. You don't want to share.'

Fred nodded; he really didn't want to share Toby's theory. 'I can't, Mel. Beeching has ordered me to keep you behind the scenes. I have to appear to do what he tells me.'

'How? By doing just that?'

'No, I just have to be discreet. He didn't even want you to stay, I persuaded him. Trust me, Mel, you will be a part of this team. By the time this thing is played out, we are going to need all the help we can get.'

Mel looked at him for a long time, clearly trying to decide if he was telling her the truth.

'You think there is more to come?'

Fred nodded slowly. 'I think this is just the beginning.'

He could see that not leading this investigation was a bitter pill for her to swallow. 'This whole case could go really badly; it might be better to stay in the background. Unsolved murders are real career killers for homicide detectives.'

'OK, Fred, you win. What do you want me to do?'

'How about dinner tonight at my place?'

'I didn't think you could cook.'

'I can't.'

'Then why would I come?'

'The sparkling conversation.'

'And.'

'I think I have half a pork pie and some pickled onions at home.'

'You know the way to a girl's heart, but no.'

'You want me to come to yours then?'

Mel Townsend chuckled. 'Ever the trier, Fred. Aren't you forgetting something?'

'Like what?'

'We broke up ten years ago, everything you do irritates me.'

'Give me a chance.'

'Have you changed?'

'No.'

'Then why would I?'

'Perhaps you've lowered your standards.'

Mel sighed. 'Not that far, Fred.'

Fred nodded philosophically. 'Fair enough. It's probably for the best, I've an image of you in my head that you could never live up to.'

Two hours later, Fred and Toby were back in with Inspector Beeching. Despite his outmanoeuvring of Chief Constable Wilson, he didn't seem happy.

'So, do we have a chief suspect?'

Fred looked at Toby. 'Toby has a theory.'

'Go on.'

'Turns out that Sir Morris did have some enemies. He sacked Richard Jenkins back in thirty-six; he went on to kill himself.'

'Didn't he jump off a bridge in front of a train near Long Marston?'

'He did.'

'I remember. I was only about twelve. He was pretty famous, wasn't he?'

'He was, sir, headed for the top and then Sir Morris sacked him after a couple of bad reviews, reviews he had commissioned himself.'

Beeching nodded. 'Feeling threatened, was he?'

'We believe so, sir. He shacked up with Jenkins' widow and took Jenkins' son under his wing. He became a rising star soon after. Oliver Lawrence was his stage name. You've probably heard of him.'

'Oliver Lawrence, I saw him play Hamlet, he was brilliant. Whatever happened to him?'

'We believe that Sir Morris once again felt threatened and sabotaged his career, just like his father.'

'My God, can you prove this?'

Fred nodded. 'Toby put it all together, sir. Bad reviews from Fibs and Soames, Morris's tame critics.'

'And where is Lawrence now?'

'Nobody knows, sir. He had a nervous breakdown and disappeared in the direction of Morocco, never to be seen again. Toby thinks he's back.'

Beeching looked at Toby. 'He'd certainly have a reason to be angry, wouldn't he. Anything else?'

Toby nodded. 'He seems to think that he is Prince Hamlet, sir.'

'What?'

'He thinks he is Prince Hamlet, sir.'

Beeching looked surprised. 'What on earth are you talking about, Marlowe. Prince Hamlet?'

'I think what Toby is trying to allude to is that like the character, Prince Hamlet, he feels he and his father have been betrayed by his stepfather. Now obviously Sir Morris has broken no laws but if I was Oliver Lawrence, and I was still alive, I think I would be pretty bitter and twisted.'

Beeching nodded. 'That makes sense, Fred. Have you got any pictures of him?'

'The theatre is getting us some; obviously they are over fifteen years out of date but it's something.'

'He's following the play, sir,' blurted Toby.

Fred laid a hand on Toby's shoulder. 'Toby has a theory about where he will strike next.'

'Based on what?' asked Beeching.

Before Toby could answer, Fred squeezed his shoulder hard enough to make Toby wince.

'Toby believes he has worked out who was in on the plot to finish both Lawrence's and his father's careers. It's tenuous but it all stacks up.'

Beeching nodded approvingly. 'It's thin but it does make sense. Finally, a suspect with a reason to kill our national treasure. I want Lawrence found; if he's dead, we need to confirm it.'

'I'm on it, sir,' said Toby.

Beeching smiled. 'Good work, DC Marlowe. You get on with finding this Lawrence while I have a word with DS Williams.

Toby jumped up enthusiastically and headed back into CID, intent on proving his theory. Beeching waited until the door closed and nodded to Fred.

'Is he all right?'

'He's good, sir. The lead he's come up with about Lawrence is the first that makes sense. Hard to find a decent suspect when we are talking about killing a national treasure.'

Beeching snorted. 'Morris Oxford? He's more a pantomime dame than an actor. Saw him in Coriolanus couple of years back, he was bloody awful. This Lawrence chappy would be doing us all a favour if he killed him.'

'I have heard others saying that Sir Morris is past his best.'

'He never had a best. He just speaks slowly and loudly, like the front end of a pantomime horse. Prances around the stage like a fool.'

'You may be right, sir, but it wouldn't look good if we let him get killed on our watch.'

'True, Fred. We better try and save him then. Theatre's loss will be our gain.'

Chapter 47
O'er Hasty Marriage

Toby had enjoyed the drive down the Oxford Road from Stratford. May had just given way to June and summer was in full bloom. He slowed the MG as he descended the hill into Woodstock. The address he had been given was on Park Street.

He changed down into third and the motor hummed up the climb into the heart of the town. It was a beautiful place, famous for the magnificent Blenheim Palace, which sat in the heart of Woodstock, and was the birthplace of Winston Churchill.

Toby had only been here once before, on a school trip, back in the early sixties. He wished he had time to have a proper look around but Fred had been very clear; Interview Lady Oxford and press her on the death of her first husband and the disappearance of her son.

He turned right into Park Street and drove slowly down the road. There were shops, pubs and a couple of expensive looking hotels but, as he went down the street, they gradually gave way to big town houses, all built in the warm tones of Cotswold stone. Sir Morris's house did not have a number so it would be hard to locate.

He pulled up and decided to walk, it would be much easier to find on foot. The first house he looked at had a nameplate, Elsinore. Toby smiled, maybe he would have time for a quick look around. It was an impressive pile, clearly the theatre had been kind to Sir Morris. Elsinore seemed a strange choice given its association with the Shakespeare tragedy, but it was in Hamlet that Sir Morris had made his major breakthrough, an understandable conceit.

Toby stood at the front door, took a deep breath and pulled

the brass bell-pull. He heard the ring echo inside what must be a very large hallway, and waited. After about twenty seconds he was about to pull it again but the door swung open. Toby took a step back.

'Can I help you, sir?' There before him stood Sir Morris's butler. He looked at Toby as if he were something he had just found on the bottom of his shoe.

Toby held up his warrant card. 'DC Marlowe, Stratford CID. I'm here to interview Lady Oxford.'

The butler's forehead furrowed in a look of questioning condescension. 'Wait here, I will see if madam is available.'

He went to shut the door but Toby remembered Fred's advice. He planted his foot in the doorway. 'Madame will be available; this is a murder investigation and she has been informed that I will be here to take her statement.'

Anger coloured the cheeks of the butler. 'I'll thank you to step back while I enquire within.'

Toby smiled and pushed past him. The hallway was indeed huge and led to a magnificent stairway, Toby could have put his whole cottage in there. He turned back to the butler, whose gaunt features were now puffed up in outrage.

'Would you like to show me to Lady Morris or shall I find her myself?'

'That won't be necessary.'

Toby turned and there, at the top of the stairs, stood Beatrice Oxford. She was a striking looking woman. She descended towards Toby, appearing to float on a cushion of air. Toby swallowed hard; he hadn't expected her to be so beautiful. Despite being in her early sixties, her skin was smooth and unwrinkled and her figure was that of an athlete.

'I'm terribly sorry, madam, the officer entered uninvited.'

She smiled. 'That's all right, Seyton, I've been expecting officer Marlowe.' She reached the bottom of the stairs and nodded to Toby. 'Shall we sit in the lounge?'

Toby nodded. 'Yes, Lady Oxford, wherever you like.'

'Very well, follow me.' She glanced across at Seyton. 'Could you bring us some tea please, Seyton.'

'Yes, madam.' He shot Toby a look of disgust and disappeared down the hallway.

'It's this way, officer.' Lady Oxford was headed in the other direction. She glanced back at Toby. 'You must forgive Seyton, he's very protective of me.'

'That's all right, Lady Oxford, we have far worse to deal with.'

As they approached the end of the hallway there were two doorways. Lady Oxford opened the one on the left and it led into a huge lounge; at the far end were magnificent French windows that led out onto the gardens at the side of the house.

Toby nodded approvingly. 'This is an amazing house.'

Lady Oxford nodded. 'Yes, it's very nice. Not far from Stratford but well on the way to London. Sir Morris quite often uses the Oxford Playhouse for early performances of new plays, before he takes them to London or Stratford. It's very convenient. Take a seat.' Lady Oxford pointed to a leather armchair.

'Thank you.'

She sat down in another chair facing him. She crossed her legs slowly and then fixed him with a smile that masked a cool stare. 'So, DC Marlowe, how can I help you?'

She was cool but Toby sensed she was nervous.

'As you are aware, we have a terrible situation going on in Stratford.'

'Ghastly. First Desmond, then Terry and now poor Tabitha. Who could be doing this, officer?'

'Well, we do have a theory.'

Lady Oxford leaned forward. 'Pray tell me what it is, we need to end this living nightmare.'

Toby supressed a smile. Beatrice Oxford was a truly terrible actress. In just two short sentences she had given herself away; she definitely had something to hide. Toby decided to go in hard. 'Your first husband, Richard Jenkins, killed himself after Sir Morris sacked him. Is that correct?'

Lady Oxford looked flustered. 'That's a very harsh way of putting it, officer.'

'It was a very harsh act.'

'You weren't there. Richard was a great talent but very unstable. He had peaks of brilliance but troughs of despair. When things didn't go well for him, he would drink.'

Toby nodded. 'I understand that, Lady Morris.'

'Do you? Have you ever had to live with an alcoholic? It's not a pretty state of affairs.' Her words were terse, bitter.

'Affairs never are pretty,' said Toby.

Lady Morris stared at him. 'What the hell do you mean by that?'

'After Richard died, you and Sir Morris moved in together with, some would say, indecent haste.'

Lady Morris's mouth fell open; she clearly hadn't been expecting this level of questioning. 'How dare you, officer! What are you implying?'

Toby shrugged. 'I'd have thought that was clear. Your husband's death happens shortly after he is sacked by Sir Morris, you then become the lover of Sir Morris within weeks. I cannot imagine that your son took that well. He idolised his father, by all accounts.'

'He did, he was very young then. When his father died, Sir Morris took him under his wing, treated him like his own son.'

'Probably the least he could do, given his role in Richard's death.' Toby watched as the colour drained from Beatrice Oxford's face. 'Were you and Sir Morris secretive about your relationship after Richard died?'

'Well ... I ... I don't really know how to respond, are you accusing me of something? I feel like I'm on trial here.'

'No, you are not on trial Lady Oxford. We just need to get at the truth. We believe that the murderer is harbouring a great deal of resentment towards Sir Morris and his company. You were part of that company.' Toby watched the emotions pass across Beatrice Oxford's face; she would have been a terrible poker player. He decided to play his ace. 'We believe the killer is your son.'

Her mouth fell open.

Toby waited.

She slowly shook her head. 'Oliver is dead.'

'There is no evidence for that.'

'He went missing over fifteen years ago, he must be dead.'

'So, you've written him off then? Not very motherly of you.'

Her features turned from shock to anger. 'Look, here, I don't much care for your tone. Who the hell do you think you're talking to?'

'To the mother of a very dangerous serial killer, who will undoubtedly kill again if we don't stop him. You and Sir Morris, in our opinion, are at risk. These questions are tough but we need to establish motive.'

'Motive? Why would my son want to kill Sir Morris, or me, or anyone else come to think of it? You're barking mad, officer.'

'Really. I tried to put myself in your son's place. Sir Morris sacks his father and then his father kills himself. Not long after, you move in with Sir Morris and then you marry him.'

'Not until after Oliver disappeared.'

Toby smiled. 'Clearly, you thought it would be inappropriate until then.'

Beatrice didn't have an answer to that.

'Look, we are not accusing you of a crime, Lady Oxford, we are just trying to establish motive. If I thought my mother had moved in with the man I felt contributed to his death, I would be bitter.'

'It wasn't like that.'

'Maybe not, but it doesn't look good. Then we move on fifteen years and Oliver is now a great actor and, once again, Sir Morris sacks him. We know that members of Sir Morris's entourage conspired against both Richard and Oliver, undermining them, getting them bad reviews. Oliver ran away knowing all this.'

There was a tear in Beatrice Oxford's eye, the first piece of decent acting she had done since the interview started. 'This is most unfair; it wasn't like that. I loved Oliver.'

'But not more than Sir Morris, not more than being Lady Oxford.' Toby looked about the huge lounge. 'Things have worked out pretty well for you, haven't they?'

'How dare you!'

Toby ignored her and continued. 'I tried to imagine how I would feel if I came back to Stratford, fifteen years later, to find my mother now married to the man who helped kill my father, and then cast me aside in a similar fashion. Very Hamlet, isn't it? Father is killed by a rival for his crown who then moves in with his mother. Later, he forces him out when he becomes a threat and he ends up in exile. He uses his courtiers to undermine him, all sounds very familiar, doesn't it.'

Beatrice just stared at Toby. He had her on the back foot but she was being careful, afraid that the wrong response would reveal her guilt.

Fred had told Toby to follow his instinct and he went for the kill.

'We believe that Oliver has returned and he is out for revenge. We also believe that in his disturbed condition he has decided he is Prince Hamlet and is acting out the murders to fit the play. You have to admit, the circumstances that have created this situation are remarkably similar.'

Beatrice laughed in his face. 'Is that it? All those officers and information and the best you can come up with is, "It's just like Hamlet." If that wasn't so pathetic it would be laughable.'

'Desmond, Tabitha and Terry aren't laughing any more, are they?'

'Really, I've a good mind to speak to your superior.'

'Please do, he agrees with my theory. There is something wrong in the state of Denmark, Lady Oxford. We found no evidence from the moment that your son disappeared that you or Sir Morris did anything to try and trace him. Nothing. Almost as if you had just written him off, just like Richard before him. Makes a pretty good motive for revenge, don't you think?'

Lady Oxford jumped to her feet. 'Get out, get out now!' She shook with indignation.

Toby nodded. 'Very well, you don't want to give a signed statement then?'

'Get out!' She was screaming now, all pretence at civility gone. 'I'll have your badge for this.'

Toby shook his head. 'I don't think so, Lady Oxford, I'm just trying to establish the facts so we can find the killer and stop him. Listening to you, I'm pretty sure that we know who that killer is and why he is doing it.'

'Get out!' She wasn't listening any more. Red in the face, she was pointing to the door. 'Get out of my house, you horrid little man.'

Just then, Seyton came rushing in, his gaunt features animated in a way they had not been in many years. 'Madame, what's wrong.'

She pointed at Toby. 'Him, he's wrong. Get him out of here. Now!'

Seyton glowered at Toby, like an embalmed cadaver sprung back to life. He gesticulated towards the corridor. 'You heard madam, sir, get out!'

Seconds later the door slammed behind him and Toby was back out on the street. If he had been any doubt as to who his killer was, it was gone. Oliver Lawrence was his man.

Inside Elsinore house, Lady Oxford stood at the sink in the kitchen, washing and washing her hands. They would never be clean.

Chapter 48
A Constant Friendship

Evening had descended on the quiet streets of Stratford. The theatre was still closed and the absence of theatregoers had rendered Waterside a mere shadow of its normal bustling self. As Oliver approached the Dirty Duck, he saw that the patio at the front was empty. Why not, he thought. He had been busy the last few days; time for a rest. Take a deep breath and reflect. Everything was going according to plan.

Dick Mayrick was behind the bar. 'Evening, what can I get you?'

'Pint of mild, please, Dick.'

Dick started to pour his beer; he nodded in the direction of his empty bar. 'All this death is bad for business, never seen it so quiet at this time of year.'

'Swings and roundabouts, Dick, when it's all solved you will get coach loads of folk eager to see the site of the gruesome murders. Probably grow your business in the long run.'

Dick nodded approvingly. 'Never thought of it like that, let's hope he kills someone even more famous than Desmond Tharpe then. I could name a cocktail after him.'

They both laughed. Oliver paid for his pint and then headed for the outside tables.

He sat there enjoying the peace of the early summer evening. Things were going better than he had planned. Who next? That was the question.

The garden at the Dirty Duck was raised about ten feet above the pavement and offered a great view through the park to the riverside. Were it not for the trees and the wall around the graveyard at Holy Trinity, he could have seen the bench where he had ended Desmond Tharpe's life, and persuaded poor, demented Tabitha into the inky black waters of the Avon.

He felt no remorse; these people had been his friends and had betrayed him, death was their reward and he had delivered it. As he looked in amongst the trees, he saw the figure of a woman wearing jeans and a T-shirt walking towards the pub. She moved like a panther, loose limbed and sinuous, he knew at once who she was; Suzy Tench.

He felt a lurch in the pit of his stomach. When they had been on stage together, just sixteen years ago, they had both been marked for stardom. Suzy had become a star and he, well, lost opportunity, lost years. Those times were nearly behind him now. He felt himself tensing as she came closer. She looked up and smiled.

'You look lonely up there.'

Oliver tried to smile but it looked more like a nervous tick. 'Yes, death and mayhem seem to have thinned out the crowds somewhat.'

Suzy Tench climbed the steps to his table. 'Put me out of work.'

'Could I buy you a drink, Miss Tench.'

Suzy smiled at him. 'You know who I am then, seems I'm at a disadvantage.'

Oliver nodded, he was starting to relax, playing a part. 'My name's Francis.'

Suzy extended her hand. 'Pleased to meet you, Francis.' She looked at him. 'You know, you do seem familiar. What's your surname?'

'Bacon,' said Oliver. It was out before he could stop it.

Suzy grinned broadly.

'My dear, I'd keep that quiet around here.'

Oliver shrugged. 'No matter, it's just a name.'

Suzy began to laugh. 'No, silly, some historians have

suggested that Francis Bacon wrote some of the plays attributed to Shakespeare.'

'Give someone an advance and they'll write anything' replied Oliver, silently berating himself for not thinking through a proper cover story. Francis Bacon, for God's sake.

'Can you run to a gin and tonic?'

'Don't see why not, single or double?'

Suzy looked at him reproachfully. 'Double.'

Oliver was about to head for the bar but Dick Mayrick appeared on the patio. 'Good evening, Dame Suzy, can I get you a drink?'

'My friend Francis here is getting one for me.'

Dick looked at Oliver and winked. 'I'll get it for you.'

'But you don't know what it is.'

'Gin and tonic, double,' said Dick, as he disappeared back into his empty pub.

'He's good, isn't he,' said Suzy.

'He is.'

Suzy sat down opposite Oliver. 'So, Francis Bacon, what brings you to Stratford.'

'The theatre, I love Shakespeare. Just my luck, I arrive and the actors start dying.'

'Yes, it's a bit of a worry.'

'Oh, you'll be fine, Suzy, nobody would want to hurt you.'

'Can you guarantee that?'

Obviously, Oliver could, but he wasn't about to explain why. 'I'm sure you'll be fine, should I call you Dame Suzy?'

Suzy sniggered. 'No, that would be ridiculous.'

'When did you get the title?'

'New Year's honours list, this year.'

Oliver nodded his approval. 'I bet Sir Morris didn't like that.'

'He wasn't best pleased, apparently giving it to one so young who also happens to be a woman has devalued it.'

'Don't worry, Suzy, comments like that are the reason he is

far more likely to be a victim of the theatre killer. I can't foresee a world where you could be under threat.'

She didn't seem reassured. 'Desmond and Tabitha were harmless. Not likeable, but you can't like everybody, can you.'

'What about that Terry Fibs character, what was he like?'

'Nothing like them. If you drew up a list of the people most likely to get murdered, he would be at the top, man was a total arse.'

'Sounds like you could have killed him.'

'Oh, I've thought about it on many occasions but if I didn't get it right, he would have given me a terrible review, awful person. Real hatchet man, he's ended a lot of careers.'

Oliver nodded. He knew only too well the truth of Suzy Tench's words. 'So, why do you think it's happening?'

Suzy leaned back in her chair. 'Who can tell. Sir Morris has built an entourage around himself over the years, if your face doesn't fit you've got a problem.'

'You're not part of his gang and you've done fine.'

'I've got an Oscar, pretty much makes me untouchable. The old boy hates it. He never managed to crack film.'

'I can imagine,' said Oliver. 'He did have that TV series though, didn't he?'

Dame Suzy snorted with derision. 'Coffee and Cream, no that was Desmond and Theo. Morris got a regular guest spot as a shouty landlord, what a pile of excrement that was,' she thought for a moment. 'Apart from Theo, he was very good.'

'Theo Cumberbatch?'

Dame Suzy nodded. 'You know him?'

'I know of him. Always thought he was the best actor in Sir Morris's company.'

'You're right. He acted the pants off Desmond and Morris in that series. He knew how to reduce everything, play directly down the lens of the camera as if he was talking to just one person. Subtle, lots of delicate shade to his performance. All that whilst Sir Morris is lumbering round in the background like a drunk pantomime Dame, and poor old Desmond was striking poses and delivering his lines like he was playing Greek tragedy. I like to get drunk and watch them when they get replayed on telly, it's bloody hilarious.'

Oliver took a sip of his beer and watched Suzy Tench laughing uninhibitedly. He had just realised how much he missed her, missed this. Being part of the company, playing the great roles and then relaxing at the bar afterwards. Sir Morris and his gang had robbed him of a that. They would pay, all of them.

Dame Suzy stopped laughing and noticed Oliver watching her. 'Are you sure I don't know you? There's something about you,' she looked him up and down. 'I feel like I've known you all my life.'

'A previous life perhaps.'

'Oh, I don't believe any of that claptrap. Dead is dead.'

'We won't be seeing Fibs or the Tharpes again then?'

'No, can't say I'll miss them either. Fibs was a viper. Desmond was a pompous old git and his daughter was a spoilt brat.' She hesitated and smiled at Oliver. 'I'm making myself sound like the murderer.' She leaned forward and touched Oliver's knee. 'You won't dob me in to the rozzers, will you?'

'No, I won't be doing that. You're too good an actor to be banged up. Besides, we need to you keep Sir Morris in his place.'

'Are you an actor, Francis?'

Oliver hesitated for a moment. 'I was, many years ago, in a different life.'

'I knew it!' exclaimed Dame Suzy. 'I could tell by the way you carried yourself. Have our paths crossed?'

'Sadly, no. I trod the boards at Birmingham Rep for two seasons, it was as close as I got to Stratford.'

Dame Suzy looked disappointed. 'I never worked for Birmingham Rep.'

'Well, you were too busy down here, and on the TV and big screen. The Rep was brilliant but I couldn't hack the eight shows a week. Guess I just fell out of love with it.'

'That's a shame, I think you would have been rather good.'

Oliver smiled; he was beginning to enjoy himself. He had always liked Suzy and she hadn't changed. Despite her fame, she was still the friendly, speak her mind woman he had so admired all those years ago. Without warning, the beautiful spell that Suzy was weaving was shattered.

'Bloody hell, Suzy.'

They both looked down and beaming up at them from the pavement was Clarissa Pigeon. 'Fancy meeting you here.'

Suzy raised her eyebrows and whispered to Oliver. 'Dear God, it's the ghost of Christmas past.' She turned back to Clarissa, all smiles. 'Clarissa, darling, I wasn't expecting to see you here this season.'

She climbed the steps towards them. 'I wasn't expecting to be here but, with Tabitha dying, Terry Corridor called me up. He's asked me to take on Portia.'

She reached their table and kissed Dame Suzy on both cheeks without actually touching them. She then turned to Oliver and looked at him like a cat would a mouse. 'And who are you.' She moistened her lips with her tongue.

'Francis,' said Oliver, desperately trying to hide the distain he felt for her.

Clarissa was a diva and had treated him very badly as a young actor. Then, when he had started to gain fame, she changed. She swooned over him like an unwanted vest. He had always fought her off but she would never take no for an answer.

'You don't look like a Francis.' She turned to Dame Suzy. 'Does he?'

Suzy shrugged. 'I dunno, what does a Francis look like?'

Clarissa turned back to Oliver. 'Not like this.' She licked her lips. 'You got a girlfriend?'

'I might have.'

She smiled. 'That's a no.' She pulled up a chair and sat down next to Oliver. 'Mind if I join you?'

'Do we have a choice?'

'No.' Clarissa smiled at Dame Suzy. 'So, where did you meet Francis?'

'Right here, about ten minutes ago.'

Clarissa chuckled. 'Looks like I got here just in time.' Before she could climb onto Oliver's lap, Dick Mayrick appeared with Suzy's drink.

'Sorry about the delay, couldn't find the tonic.' He glanced down at Clarissa. 'Hello, Miss Pigeon, I didn't know you were here this season.'

'Always find my way home, Dick, Pigeon by name, Pigeon by nature. Been drafted in to replace the late lamented Tabitha.'

It was clear she didn't lament her at all. Dick Mayrick smiled. Clarissa Pigeon had a huge appetite for everything in life; business was about to pick up.

'What can I get you?'

She looked at him with mock severity. 'Champagne, of course, and none of that cheap rot you sell to the tourists.'

'Got some Pol Roger.'

'That'll do nicely.'

Dick turned and headed back into the pub, the sound of cash registers beginning to ring in his ears.'

'I'm playing Calpurnia,' said Dame Suzy.

'I know, isn't it wonderful? We've got the old team back together for another season.'

'Wonderful,' said Dame Suzy unenthusiastically.

Clarissa never noticed; her attention was focused, once more, on Oliver. 'You look very familiar, have we met.'

Oliver shrugged. 'I don't think so, I'm sure I would have remembered.'

He did remember. He hated Clarissa. She had treated him

terribly and, when his star had begun to wane under the terrible campaign that Sir Morris had orchestrated, she had piled on like a vengeful ex. Vilifying him at every opportunity. Hell hath no fury like a woman scorned, but it did. His fury was straight from hell and she would feel its full force. Not tomorrow, or tomorrow, or tomorrow, but soon, very soon.

Oliver rose from his seat. 'Regrettably, ladies, I must take my leave of you.'

Clarissa grabbed him by the arm. 'And where do you think you are off to?'

Oliver eased his arm from her grasp. 'I have a dinner appointment.'

'We could come, where are you going?'

'To a friend's house in Welford. We used to go to university together. As there is no theatre, we decided to have dinner and catch up.'

'That will be lovely, it's so nice to meet up with old friends,' said Suzy. She got up and gave Oliver a big hug. 'It's been so lovely to meet you.' She pulled him even closer and whispered in his ear. 'Run for it, I'll keep her talking.'

Oliver held her close until she let him go, feelings that he hadn't felt in years washed over him. How he had missed physical contact. He gazed into her eyes.

'Thank you, Suzy, it's been lovely for me too.' Oliver nodded at Clarissa curtly. 'Nice meeting you, Miss Pigeon,' he said, and then turned on his heel and descended the steps to the street, turned right and disappeared in the direction of old town.

'Well,' said Clarissa. 'He couldn't have made that any clearer, could he.'

Suzy laughed. 'You did come on rather strong, frightened the poor man to death.'

'He didn't look very frightened to me and he made it pretty plain that he fancied you.'

Dame Suzy smiled. 'Yes, he did, didn't he.' As Dame Suzy gazed towards the river dreamily, Dick Mayrick appeared with a bottle of Pol Roger and two flutes. He placed them on the table. 'Shall I pour?'

'Please, darling,' said Clarissa distractedly, clearly sulking at her recent rejection.

Dick passed a glass to Clarissa. 'Is Francis coming back?'

'I really don't care,' said Clarissa. 'He's gone for a dinner appointment.'

Dick nodded, looked around his empty beer garden and then smiled at the two famous actors.

'Would you like me to join you?'

'No,' said Clarissa bluntly.

'We would love you to, Dick, but we just need to go over some notes that Terence Corridor has given us on the play. Maybe when we have gone through them.'

'That would be lovely,' said Dick. He retreated back into his pub reinforced in his belief that Dame Suzy was wonderful and Clarissa Pigeon was a bitch. On the upside, she was also a spectacular drinker and really good for business.

Outside on the patio, Suzy was not happy. 'Do you have to speak to people like that? Dick Mayrick is a lovely man.'

Clarissa shrugged. 'He's a looker, I'll grant you that.'

'Nice body too, plays rugby.'

'I know, but he's a scrum half. He'll get you into bed and then give you a running commentary about how well he's doing.'

'At least he's not a prop, most of them can't even form a sentence.'

Clarissa took a sip of her Champagne and smiled at Suzy. 'But that's what I'm looking for. A man that gets on with it and just gives the occasional grunt.'

They both burst out laughing. Suzy didn't like Clarissa but, in small doses, at the right moment, she could be fun.

Chapter 49
Gruesome And Clean

As he turned into the Churchyard at All Saints, Oliver could hear Suzy and Clarissa's laughter.

'Psst,' a voice hissed at him from behind the first tree on the left. Oliver looked at the tree. Felix stepped out from behind it. 'It's me.'

'Really, I thought it was a talking tree. What do you want?'

'We need to talk.'

Oliver pointed towards the pathway that led between the row of trees and the outer wall of the churchyard. 'We can sit on the bench down there.'

'Are you mad? That's a double murder scene.'

'As the guilty party, I'm well aware of that.'

Felix stepped forward, grabbed him by the arm and led him back out onto the street.

'You can't keep coming back to the scene of the crime, someone's going to notice.'

Oliver hadn't really thought about that. 'You always hear those stories about killers returning to the scenes of their crimes and getting caught. You think that's a thing?'

'You're doing it,' hissed Felix angrily.

'Yeah, I suppose I am. I'm going to have to watch that.'

They started walking towards Trinity Street.

'Cup of tea at my place?'

Felix nodded. 'Please, let's get you off the street and make Stratford a safer place.'

Felix tapped Oliver on the shoulder as they walked around the gentle curve of the wall that ran around All Saints towards Oliver's house.

'I saw you.'

'I know, in the churchyard.'

'Talking to Dame Suzy and Clarissa Pigeon.'

Oliver smiled. 'Isn't Suzy lovely.'

'Are you mad, she knows you. She's been on stage with you,' snapped Felix.

'She doesn't know me now, neither of them did. I'm fifteen years older, my body is bigger, stronger than it was back then. My face is chiselled and my skin has darkened after years in the north African sun. Even my voice has deepened.'

Felix shook his head angrily. 'You can't chance that. Clarissa is a bitch; she was one of the gang that helped to ruin you. Do you really want to give her another chance?'

Oliver looked at Felix and smiled. 'No, that's why I'm going to kill her.'

Felix froze in his tracks. 'Her too? I thought it was just Sir Morris and the others.'

'It is,' said Oliver reassuringly. 'It's just taken me some time to realise how many of them there are.' He grinned secretively at Felix. 'I have a cunning plan; my revenge is going to be set over three acts and dear Sir Morris is being saved until the end.'

Felix clutched his head in his hands. He had created a monster. He took a deep breath. 'Look, Oliver, you've already killed Desmond and Terry,' he paused for a moment. 'You've killed three times if you throw Tabitha in.'

'I didn't throw her in, she jumped.'

'Pedant,' snapped Felix. 'You persuaded her in, it's pretty much the same thing.'

'The end result maybe.'

'Three of Sir Morris's gang are dead thanks to you. It's all happening so fast. You have to slow down, be more careful.'

'On the contrary, I need to speed up. The police don't know if they're coming or going. They haven't got time to really dig into the cases. I mean, look at me, Felix.'

Felix did look at him. He looked relaxed, happy. Oliver was clearly going mad, happily killing his ex-colleagues with gay abandon. Swatting them like flies on a window without compassion.

Oliver gestured back towards the town. 'I've killed three people in three days and I'm walking the streets in plain sight. I'm talking to fellow actors and they don't recognise me. I'm invisible.' Oliver smiled reassuringly at Felix. 'Let's have a cup of tea and I'll tell you who's next.'

Felix let out a deep breath. 'Bloody hell, Oliver, you're going to be the death of me.'

'No, I'm going to be the death of Gerard Soames. He's my Guildenstern.'

Felix nodded his approval. 'Now that I can agree with, man's an absolute snake. Worse than Fibs, slaughtered your father in the press and did the same to you. How will you get him?'

Oliver shrugged. 'I don't have a plan. I'll just wait for an opportunity and then see what inspiration brings me. It's worked so far.'

'I disagree. The stakes are getting higher with every death. Stratford is crawling with police. This needs to be planned.'

'What do you suggest?'

'Let me lure him out for you. He knows me.'

'He doesn't like you much though, does he.'

'He doesn't need to. I'm going to offer him a ride on my boat.'

'You have a boat?'

'I do, a nice river cruiser. I've got it moored by the boathouse. I'm going to invite him round for a little cruise down to Welford.'

'Do you think he'll come?'

Felix smiled. 'He will if I tempt him with a scoop.'

'Have you actually got one?'

'Oh, yes. I know who the killer is.'

Oliver stared at Felix. 'You can't tell him that.'

'I'm not actually going to tell him, I'm just going to invite him round for a cruise, with a suggestion that I have a theory about who might be the killer.'

'Do you think he'll believe you?'

Felix gave Oliver a reproachful smile. 'Are you forgetting that I too have been a fine actor?'

Oliver nodded. 'Yes, I was forgetting that.'

'Bugger off, Oliver. I'm going to invite Gerard down to the Ferry at Alveston for a drink. We can go in the boat. I'll moor up in a quiet spot near Alveston and then you can turn up and I'll offer you a ride back to Stratford. Once we are underway, you'll have him trapped in the middle of the river on my boat.'

Oliver nodded. 'That does sound like a workable plan. Do you think you can persuade him to come on board?'

'I think so. It has to be worth a try. And, of course, it fits in nicely with your plot.'

'How so?'

'Guildenstern was killed on a boat.'

Oliver grinned. 'He was, wasn't he. The Avon isn't the North Sea but it's cold and it's wet.'

'Can I just ask one thing?'

'Anything.'

'Could you not stab him. I had it refitted last year. All the seats have been reupholstered and the cabin has been freshly painted in Mediterranean Pastels.'

Oliver winced. 'Sounds lovely.'

'It is.'

'Very well, I'll think of something gruesome but clean.'

'Gruesome and clean would be perfect.'

Chapter 50
I Never Liked You

In the bar of the Garrick, Gerard Soames was quietly getting drunk. He had decided that this was the best way to remember his friends, who had all so recently been taken from him. He was only two gin and tonics into his quest when Felix Richards entered the bar.

'Jesus Christ, that's all I need,' sighed Gerard.

'Mind if I join you?'

'Yes, I bloody well do.'

'Thanks,' said Felix, and sat down opposite him.

'Did you not hear me? I said, no thanks.'

'I heard you, Gerard, but I know you don't mean it.'

Gerard nodded vigorously. 'Yes, I bloody do.'

'I thought you liked me.'

'I never liked you. Always thought you were a liberal poser.'

Felix leaned closer to Gerard and spoke quietly. 'Never mind about what you think I am, Gerard; you need to listen to me for a while. I think I have worked out who is doing all this killing.'

Gerard put down his drink. 'Go on then, Sherlock, enlighten me.'

'Be happy to, Gerard, but let's get out of Stratford first, this place is too depressing at the moment.'

'Where do you suggest?'

'I've got my river cruiser moored by the boathouse. Let's chug down to Alveston. I've got plenty of food and drink on board.'

'Is it a nice boat?'

Felix nodded. 'Twenty-eight-foot cruiser, quite a shallow draught but we will be fine.'

'I need food and drink; are you sure you can provide that?'

'Yes. I have a roast chicken, salad and a freshly baked cottage loaf.'

'Got any salad cream?'

Felix flinched. 'Surprisingly, yes. A friend of mine brought some on board last month.'

Gerard nodded his approval. 'Good, because that would have been a deal breaker.'

'Drink up and let's get aboard.'

Gerard drained his glass and stood up. 'Before we go, I just want to reiterate that I don't like you, Felix, you're a liberal lefty of the worst kind.'

'And you're a fascist, Gerard, but we can't let a bit of politics affect a beautiful friendship, can we.'

Gerard eyed him suspiciously. 'I'm not one of them, you know.'

'One of what?' asked Felix innocently.

'You know, a jolly boy.'

'Nothing jolly about me, Gerard. I'm strictly the miserable heterosexual type.'

Gerard nodded. 'Good, don't want any of that stuff with my chicken salad.'

Felix and Gerard walked down Sheep Street to the theatre and headed towards the bridge. Felix was casually glancing round to make sure no police were watching their progress. The water front was very quiet; performances were still postponed and Stratford had taken on the out of season feel of a seaside resort in October.

They crossed the bridge and made their way down to the boathouse where Felix's boat was moored. Felix looked anxiously around for witnesses but, apart from an old boy walking his dog and a couple dressed in tweed jackets with elbow patches, they were alone.

Felix peered at the couple. They were just sitting, gazing down river, two love struck geography teachers in search of the source of the Avon perhaps. The only thing that mattered was that they were paying no attention to him.

'This is it,' said Felix.

Gerard eyed it suspiciously. 'Must have cost a packet. How can you afford this?'

Felix smiled. 'Voice-overs, dear boy, I'm making a bloody fortune. Beats acting.'

They climbed on board and Felix quickly fired up the motor and cast off. He drifted it out into the channel and headed east towards Alveston. 'The bar's just inside the cabin, why don't you mix a couple of G&Ts.'

Gerard nodded. 'Will do.'

He disappeared into the cabin and Felix powered up the motor until they were doing four miles per hour. As they floated past the big houses on the Tiddington Road, Felix realised that he could actually afford to buy one and decided that, if he didn't get caught, he would use some of his recently acquired wealth to do just that. Gerard reappeared from the cabin with the drinks.

'There you go, old boy.' He passed one to Felix and clinked glasses. 'Chin chin.' His mood seemed to have lifted.

'You've cheered up.'

'I know, it's good to get out of Stratford. What with all these murders and no theatre it's turning into a bit of a ghost town.' Gerard looked around at the boat. 'Voice-overs are obviously paying well. Which ones are you?'

Felix smiled. 'I'm the plumber in the toilet blue advert. Yellow pages taxi driver, that's me too. Oh, and I'm the vicar in the Sherry advert.'

'Blimey, those are on every night.'

'I know, there's about another sixteen going on at the moment.'

Gerard looked impressed. 'That lot must pay well.'

'They do. I get repeats too, residuals they call it. Beats eight shows a week and a matinee for union minimum.'

'Maybe you're not such a lefty, more a champagne socialist.' Gerard nudged him in the ribs. 'So, where's the food, I'm bloody starving.'

'Chicken is sliced and in the fridge with the salad. I've already carved it and put a vinaigrette on, you can plate it up while I moor the boat.'

'This thing has a fridge?'

'And a loo, it's a proper little floating home from home.'

Gerard nodded approvingly. 'Maybe I've misjudged you, Felix.'

'Probably not, but why don't we put away our differences for now. I need to tell you something over supper.'

Gerard tapped his nose. 'This little secret about the killer. You know who it is?'

'I think I do.' Felix pointed to a curve in the river ahead. 'Alveston is just over there but we can moor up here and eat. Nice and quiet.'

They cruised steadily round the curve and, as the view ahead opened up, Felix saw the empty mooring. 'Just over there, Gerard. I'll get us in close and you pull us in. Use the mooring rope.'

'I can't tie knots. I'm a theatre critic.'

Felix couldn't argue with that. 'Just loop the rope over that pole and hold us in place until I get over and tie it off properly.'

Gerard picked up the rope with disdain. 'It's a bit rough.'

'I'm sure your cuticles can take it.'

Reluctantly, Gerard leaned out and looped the rope over the pole as they reached the mooring. 'OK, I've got it.'

Felix cut the motor and went to tie off. Once he had finished, he turned to Gerard and smiled. 'Right then, let's have supper while I share my theory with you.'

It was an idyllic setting; the church bells were ringing in Alveston and the evening sun was casting shadows across the meadows that lay between the river and the Welcombe Hills. The two men sat on deck eating their meals and sipping their drinks.

'You know, Felix, this is very agreeable. Getting out of Stratford, after everything that's happened, it's like a breath of fresh air.'

Felix nodded. 'It has been a bit bleak the last few days, hasn't it.'

Gerard sighed. 'Never known anything like it, I feel like I'm trapped in a Shakespearian tragedy.'

Felix smiled. 'I guess so. Someone is after Sir Morris and his group so it has to be someone he crossed.'

Gerard snorted derisively. 'Well, that's going to be a bloody long list, the old boy has been playing God for years. Pick any one from a hundred.'

'I pick Oliver Lawrence,' said Felix without hesitation.

The glass that was on its way to Gerard's lips stopped abruptly. 'Oliver? He's been dead for years.'

'Has he?'

'Course he has. Weak, just like his father before him. The going got tough and he ran away.'

'Nobody ever found a body, he just disappeared. The police think he took the ferry to Tangier'

'There you are then. He must be dead. Nobody would live in bloody Morocco if they could live in England, stands to reason.'

'There are other countries apart from England, Gerard.'

'I know, but they're full of foreigners. It was OK when we had an Empire but now …' He tailed off in disgust and took a sip of his drink to wash down the jingoistic bile that was rising in his throat.'

'You really are a terrible person. Is there anything or anyone that you like that isn't from England or related to the theatre?'

Gerard considered this for a moment. 'No. Not too sure I'm that keen on half the actors in the country either. All this method acting rubbish. Just learn your lines and say them as the playwright wrote them.'

'Like Sir Morris.'

'Exactly.'

'His performances aren't very nuanced though. I saw his Lear last year and it was like a recitation.'

'What's wrong with that? Shakespeare's words can stand alone, they don't need all this, "what's my motivation" crap.'

'Theo Cumberbatch really inhabits a character; he says almost as much with his pauses as he does with the text. He displays the inner monologue.'

Gerard slammed his glass down on the counter. 'Inner monologue! Pauses! The only thing they do is make you late for the bar.'

Felix smiled sadly at Gerard. Not only was he a terrible human being, he was also a terrible critic. Totally out of touch with the way in which classic works were now being interpreted for a modern age. 'I guess we are going to have to agree to disagree on that.'

'We certainly will.'

Felix should have let it go but this was probably the last chance he would have to talk to Gerard.

'Not a fan of Theo then.'

Gerard looked at him as if he had insulted his mother. 'Cumberbatch? Jesus! He ponces around the stage like a teenage girl. I don't know why Morris keeps him in the company.'

'He needs him.'

'Needs him? Are you kidding. Morris Oxford is a star of stage and screen.'

'Screen?'

'OK,' conceded Gerard. 'TV.'

Felix chuckled. 'Hard to Swallow is hardly classic TV.'

'The adventures of Lord Julian Swallow has many admirers, that's why it's in its seventh season.'

'Its sets are worse than Crossroads.'

'Doesn't matter, it's a hit.'

'It's cheap and it's hanging on by its fingertips, and only because it has a loyal following and the advertisers of cat food seem to think it's the perfect programme for their product. I watched an episode last year and the cats in the adverts out acted the cast of the programme. Must drive Oxford mad that Theo and Desmond, his supporting actors, have a prime time hit show.'

Gerard had to concede that point. 'It did rather rankle with him, between you and I, that's why he didn't let Theo play Othello last season. Said he wasn't black enough.'

'But he's mixed-race.'

'Exactly. Neither one thing nor t'other. Morris said it would confuse the audience because Othello was a Moor.'

'So, what happened?'

'Morris blacked up and played it himself.'

Felix shook his head in disbelief. 'He's way too old to play Othello.'

'He was very black though.'

'Jesus! He missed a chance there. Can you imagine a black actor playing Othello?'

'Mixed-race,' corrected Gerard.

'Whatever, it would have been preferable to a sixty-four-year-old, fat, white man playing the part.'

Gerard sneered. 'That's your problem, Felix. All these soft Liberal ideas and notions. Theo is too emotional; he would have been crying his eyes out when he strangled Desdemona.'

'He should be, he's just strangled the love of his life.'

'But he doesn't need to blub about it, and besides, the makeup would run.'

'Theo wouldn't have needed makeup.'

'Course he would, mixed-race isn't black enough.'

Felix gave up, he couldn't believe that he was still having this conversation in 1972.

'You really are an old dog, Gerard, you need to learn some new tricks.'

'Don't you worry about me, old boy, my column in the Sunday Review is syndicated to America and Australia. I'm as popular as Tynan.'

'Yeah, but he actually knows what he's talking about,' Felix paused for a moment. 'So, you don't agree with my theory about Oliver Lawrence being our killer?'

Gerard shook his head. 'No, he's dead. I bet he never reached Morocco. No moral fibre, just like his father. Probably threw himself off the boat in the Bay of Biscay.'

Felix looked out across the meadow and saw Oliver approaching from the direction of Alveston. Gerard would soon be learning the truth. He pointed him out to Gerard. 'Oh look, that's a friend of mine.'

Gerard peered at the figure Felix was pointing at.

'What's he doing out here?'

'Probably been drinking at the Ferry. I'll see if he wants a lift back into town.'

Gerard shrugged. 'Your boat, do what you like.'

Felix leaned over the side and waved theatrically at Oliver. 'Is that you, Francis?'

Oliver smiled. Felix was using the stupid false name he had invented in the Dirty Duck. He waved back.

'Yes. You going back to Stratford or staying here for the night?'

'Turning back if you want a lift?'

Oliver had nearly reached the jetty and saw Gerard, drink in hand, scowling at him. 'Great, you want me to cast off?'

'Please.' Oliver untied the boat, flipped the rope aboard and skipped athletically onto the deck.

'We've eaten all the food,' said Gerard.

Oliver smiled. 'No problem, I bet that there is still plenty to drink.'

'Help yourself,' said Felix, as he fired up the motor and began to swing the cruiser out into the river to turn back to Stratford.

Chapter 51
Styx And Stones

Toby sat in his car reading an old, well-thumbed paperback copy of Hamlet. He knew the plot; he had read it at least ten times. He'd played Polonius in his school play and then Hamlet in a university production. He knew there were resonances between Shakespeare's play and what was actually happening on the streets of Stratford.

He couldn't convince Beeching and the rest of the rest of Stratford CID that the murderer was following the plot of Hamlet, it was too far-fetched. He ran through it once more, this time jotting it on a pad as he did so.

Desmond Tharpe had been stabbed to death. Polonius had been stabbed to death in the play. Tabitha Tharpe appeared to have gone crazy with grief, mixed with alcohol and drugs, and drowned herself. Tabitha was Desmond's daughter. Ophelia was Polonius's daughter and she too had gone mad and drowned herself.

Terry Fibs had betrayed both Oliver Lawrence and his father, Richard Jenkins. Which character did he represent? Oliver thought long and hard. Fibs and Soames had both slaughtered Oliver and Richard with their reviews, betrayed their friendships at the instruction of Sir Morris. If Sir Morris is Claudius, this would confirm his theory that Fibs and Soames were Rosencrantz and Guildenstern. It all made sense.

But what about the quote written in blood on the pillow for Tabitha to see at the Falcon Hotel? He looked at his notes. 'Though this be madness there is method in't.' The quote came from Hamlet, Act 2 Scene 2, spoken by Polonius.

The butchering of Terry Fibs did seem like madness but

there was a method to it. The killer had wanted to drive Tabitha Tharpe over the edge. He butchered Fibs and then put him on display. He even used a quote from Polonius, who was Ophelia's father, to do it. Everything seemed to be falling into place. The removal of the eyes was straight from King Lear, but it was effective. And the tongue? Lawrence was an actor. Artistic licence, maybe?

Toby read and re-read his notes. It all made sense, but only if you assumed the killer was re-enacting Hamlet. After his meeting with Beatrice Oxford, he was sure that her son was doing just that. If that was the case, Gerard Soames was next. Rosencrantz and Guildenstern died before Claudius and Gertrude. He looked at his watch, it was seven p.m. He needed a shower and something to eat. First thing in the morning he would go and see Gerard Soames and get him to leave town.

Chapter 52
~~Three~~ Two Men
In A Boat

Oliver walked up to Gerard and offered his hand. 'Francis Bacon, pleasure to meet you.'

'I'm sure it must be.'

Oliver ignored the rudeness in Gerard's tone. 'So, what do you do.'

Gerard scowled. 'I'm Gerard Soames, theatre critic of The Sunday Review.'

'That's nice,' said Oliver, deliberately unimpressed.

Gerard rose to the bait. 'Nice? I'm the doyen of the English stage. Plays can rise or fall on my review.'

Oliver nodded. 'That's a lot of power for one man.'

'Not for me,' snarled Gerard.

'Can you break an actors' career as well?'

Felix glanced across at Oliver, he knew where this was going.

'Of course, my word is respected throughout the land when it comes to matters pertaining to theatre. I can make or break any play or actor.'

Oliver nodded thoughtfully. 'That's a huge responsibility, can you sleep nights?'

'I sleep very well; my comments are always based on performance and structure. If the play is well written the actors can shine, if it is bad then the playwright or director are at fault.'

'And you punish them.'

'I critique them so that they can improve.'

'Wow,' said Oliver. 'You're an arrogant little sod.'

Gerard spluttered, spitting out some of his drink. 'I beg your pardon.'

'You heard.' Oliver turned his back on Gerard and began to pour himself a Scotch.

Gerard snapped back at him. 'Who the hell do you think you are, to talk to me, like that.'

Oliver took a sip of his Scotch and turned back to Gerard. 'Oliver Lawrence.'

Gerard heard the words but they didn't seem to register. 'Who?'

'You heard. I'm Oliver Lawrence, one of those actors whose careers you helped to end. Richard Jenkins was my father and you and Terry Fibs destroyed him.'

'Oliver?' Gerard was confused. 'Oliver Lawrence, you can't be ... he's dead.'

Oliver raised an eyebrow quizzically. 'Do I look dead?'

Gerard shook his head.

Without warning, Oliver leaned forward and slapped him hard across the face. He squealed with pain and surprise. 'Do I feel dead?'

Gerard shot a glance at Felix. 'Are you going to allow this behaviour on your boat?'

Felix nodded. 'Yes, I think I am.'

Oliver and Felix stared into the face of Gerard Soames whose features, for the first time, began to register fear. He looked back and forth between the two impassive stares and began to realise that this was not a game.

'Who are you?'

'I already told you.'

'How can I believe that you are Oliver Lawrence.'

'Because, Guildenstern, I'm going to kill you.'

'I'm not Guildenstern, you're mad!'

'In my version of Hamlet, you are, would you like to hear it?'

'I know the play, I'm a critic.'

'Not my version, you don't.'

'Let him explain, Gerard, it'll all make sense.'

Gerard looked fearfully at Felix. 'I don't want to,' he trembled.

'Too bad,' said Oliver. 'You're going to.'

Gerard tried to get up off his stool but Oliver pushed him roughly back.

'Stay there,' he hissed. 'You see, like you, I love the Bard, and I have returned to make things right. Now, Desmond Tharpe, he was my Polonius, and we all know what happened to him, don't we.' Oliver looked questioningly at the trembling Soames. 'Hamlet stabbed him. Then there was Ophelia, Tabitha Tharpe. She drowned herself after Hamlet had killed her father and driven her mad. Are you getting the picture, Gerard?'

Gerard was; a trickle of urine ran down his leg and steamed gently on the floor of the cabin in the cooling night air.

Felix slowed the motor and watched, transfixed, as Oliver began to wrap the sins of the past around Gerard Soames like the coils of a serpent.

'Then there was your mate Terry Fibs, my Rosencrantz.'

There was terror in Gerard Soames eyes now and a terrible realisation that the past had indeed come back to haunt him. 'You killed Terry?'

'I did,' smiled Oliver enthusiastically. 'Unfortunately, I had to go off script and went a bit King Lear on him.'

'Gloucester's eyes,' whispered Gerard.

'That's right. You see Rosencrantz died at sea with Guildenstern, but I needed something gory to put old Tabitha over the edge.' Oliver turned to Felix. 'Sometimes you have to improvise.' He turned back to Soames. 'With you though, I can stick to the script.'

'But you're not a pirate, it was pirates in the play.'

'True, but I did board the boat back there and I am going to kill you.'

Soames was shaking his head from side to side, his mouth open in terror. Only a quiet whimpering could be heard.

Oliver rubbed his chin thoughtfully. 'Now, you're the eminent theatre critic, Gerard. How do you think Guildenstern died?'

'Old age,' joked Felix.

'Afraid not. He was at sea, in a boat. I'm guessing he was drowned.'

The trickle of urine increased to a gush.'

'You can clean that up,' said Felix disdainfully. Oliver shrugged.

'Whatever.' He turned back to Soames. 'Now, where was I? Oh yes, drowning. Now the Avon isn't very deep here, four foot maybe, so I'm going to have to improvise.' Oliver grabbed hold of Soames and pulled him upright. 'I could weight you down with a big stone.'

'Please, don't do this … please.' He was sobbing and did not resist.

From his pocket, Oliver produced some rope and quickly tied Gerard's wrists behind his back. He turned him back round to face him.

'Are you familiar with Greek mythology, Gerard?

He shook his head.

'Well, the river you have to cross from the land of the living to the afterlife is called the Styx and old Felix here is the Boatman.'

Felix bowed. 'Captain, if you don't mind.'

'You're mad … completely mad.'

Oliver leaned close to Gerard. 'You may be right, Gerard, but who made me mad?' He stared into the terrified eyes of his captive and then smiled. 'Before we proceed, would you like to unburden yourself? Admit your guilt?'

'I'm not guilty of anything,' Gerard whimpered.

'You lied about my father's performances, you lied about my

performances. Sir Morris had you all dancing to his little tune. He couldn't bear the fact that we were better than him, so he got you and Fibs to lie in your reviews. He persuaded Desmond, and some of the other actors in his inner circle, to feed him wrong lines to make him look bad. I know, because you did the same to me. Why not admit it? Confess.'

Gerard slowly shook his head with terror and soiled himself. Felix watched, transfixed.

'The sands of time are running out for you, admit your guilt. Confess, while you still can.' Oliver pushed Gerard towards the back of the boat and sat him down on the stern, his back to the river. 'You want to kill the motor, Felix? We don't want to give old Gerard a haircut as we put him in.'

The image was too much for Gerard. 'I did it, we all did it. You were right. Morris felt threatened and he hatched a plan to undermine your father.'

'And you all agreed to help,' said Oliver, not bothering to conceal his disgust.

'He's a hard man to say no to. We need his patronage.'

'You all took the thirty pieces of silver that Sir Morris offered. Judas's all.'

'Not all,' whispered Gerard. 'Theo had no part in it, nor Suzy Tench.'

Oliver turned to Felix. 'Judas does repent.'

'Trying to save himself.'

'Please don't kill me, Oliver. How … How was I to know that your father would kill himself?'

'How indeed, but he did, and then you did it again to me years later. Unrepentant and unashamed.' Oliver took Gerard firmly by the shoulders and stared coldly into his eyes. 'Time to pay the price for your treachery.'

Gerard tried to stand up, desperate to get away from the edge of the boat, but Oliver held him firm. 'The croaking raven doth bellow for revenge. Goodbye, Guildenstern.'

Oliver pushed Gerard backwards into the river but caught his legs as they came up. He jammed them onto the stern so that Gerard's calves were horizontal and his knees were bent, submerging his head and torso beneath the water. Gerard managed to do one sit up and screamed. Oliver pushed him on the forehead and he sank down again. Within a moment he was back up spluttering, Oliver pushed him under once more.

'Good god, Oliver, what if someone comes along?'

'Unlikely at this hour, Felix.'

'But he keeps coming up.'

'Not for much longer, those are the first sit ups he's done since school sports, I reckon he's got one more in him tops.'

He hadn't. Panic had set in and Gerard writhed like an eel caught on a line, his desperate attempts to breathe making the water bubble behind the boat.

'He does sound a little like a motor boat, doesn't he?'

Felix listened to the 'Bub bub bubbing,' of Gerard's filling lungs. 'Yes, he does a little.'

Very soon, the writhing stopped.

'I think he's done.' Oliver pulled Gerard back on board. His lips had turned blue and his eyes stared out into a world they would never see. Oliver turned to Felix. 'That clean enough for you.'

'I suppose, but you can mop up the piss.'

'Fair enough.' Oliver bent down, rolled Gerard over and untied his hands.

'You going to chuck him overboard?'

'No, I think it would be nice to give him one last view of the theatre.'

'Are you mad, I'm not taking a dead body back to Stratford in my boat, the place is crawling with cops.'

'I hear you, Felix, but I want to prop him up on the bandstand.'

'Why? It's crazy!'

Oliver shrugged. 'Guildenstern died at sea coming back home. Gerard can be looking across the water to his second home, the theatre. It's symbolic.'

'It's symbollocks,' snapped Felix.

'Look, it will be gone eleven when we get back to Stratford, we can take a look around. If it's clear, I will hop off and sit him down. You can chug on down the river to Welford, or wherever you want to moor up, out of the way.'

Felix didn't like it but he had seen Oliver despatch Gerard with clinical efficiency and didn't fancy putting himself on his list. 'Very well, but any sign of trouble and we dump him down river. Agreed?'

'Agreed,' sighed Oliver. 'Now, have you got any food? All this murdering makes me very hungry.'

Chapter 53
Gerard's Last Bandstand

DC Dave Dalton was up early. He enjoyed an early morning run, it cleared his head before the problems of the day began. With a serial killer in town, there were plenty of problems to clear.

The morning was bright and sunny and, as he reached the river, he could see that a gentle mist was rising where the sunlight was warming the surface. He took a deep breath and let it out slowly. It felt good to be away from the madness that had consumed the town for the last few days. He began to run faster, revelling in the warm air flowing across his body and the blood pounding in his veins.

It was barely six a.m. and he had the riverside to himself. At least, that's what he thought. As he passed the bowling club, he spotted a lone figure sitting up against the bandstand, gazing across the river towards the theatre. His heart sank, if it was a tramp, he wasn't stopping to move him on. Uniform could do that. He decided to run past and ignore him, it wasn't his problem.

As he got closer, he began to realise that maybe it was his problem. The man's head had been tied back to one of the columns to keep him upright. Maybe a stag do prank, he thought hopefully. Another ten paces and he knew it was no prank; he stopped and stared. The man was clearly dead. His lips and finger tips were blue and his skin was a deathly pallor. Dave Dalton stood there looking at the corpse. He knew this man; he had interviewed him yesterday. Gerard Soames. He turned and ran towards the boathouse. There was a phone in there, he needed to make a call.

Chapter 54
The End Of The Beginning

Toby was the first on the scene. He ran across the grass towards the bandstand. Ginger Dalton was still in his running gear. He looked up and shook his head.

'It's Soames.'

'Damn it. I knew he was next. I should have saved him.'

'How could you have known that, Toby?'

'Because he is Guildenstern.'

Ginger wasn't much of a Shakespeare fan. 'What does that mean?'

'Oh, nothing really, just a theory I've been working on. I think the killer is following the plot of Hamlet.'

'Interesting theory,' said Ginger, looking unconvinced. 'You shared this theory with Fred?'

'Not really,' lied Toby. He crouched down next to Gerard's body. 'Did you call in Alf? We need a cause of death.'

'He drowned.'

'How can you know that?'

'He's soaking wet and it didn't rain last night.'

'Fair point.' Toby walked around behind Gerard's body and followed the direction in which his head was facing. It was across the water, directly at the theatre. 'The killer's sending us a message.'

'Be easier if he left a note.'

'He's too clever for that, Ginger, he wants to play with us.'

A Ford Cortina sped across the Clopton bridge, it's blues and twos breaking the peace of the river bank.

'Looks like the gaffer's here. You mind if I get off home and get into some work clothes?'

Toby nodded. 'Yeah, I've got it from here. Better come straight back when you've changed though.'

'Will do. I'll let the gaffer know where I'm going.' Ginger Dalton turned and jogged off across the quiet riverside lawns towards where Fred Williams had come to a screeching halt.

Toby turned back to Gerard's body. Apart from the rope around his neck, tying him to the bandstand, there was no sign of anything amiss. No bruises, no cuts. Clearly there hadn't been a struggle. It had to be someone he knew. While Toby was still pondering the problem, Fred Williams arrived beside him and saw who the victim was.

'Bloody hell, Toby, looks like you were right.'

'No good being right if we didn't stop him being murdered, is it?'

Fred shrugged. 'True, it's not going to be much consolation to old Gerard here but it does give your theory more credence. I'm beginning to think that this Oliver Lawrence character is still alive.'

'Have we found anything on him yet?'

Fred shook his head. 'Nah, he got on that boat to Tangier and just disappeared. We have no confirmation that he got off. He could be at the bottom of the Bay of Biscay for all we know.'

'But he's not, is he. He's here.'

'I fear that he is, Toby. All we can do is get those photos out and plaster them around town and on the news. We're going to start a manhunt for a dead man.'

The next hour passed slowly as they waited for SOCO and then Alf Butcher to inspect the scene and gather evidence. The press had arrived and had been stopped from getting on the site by uniforms on the Clopton Bridge. The more resourceful members of the press had taken up residence on the other side of the river.

As Alf and his team worked, several cameras were snapping away taking photos they would never be allowed to use. Fred and Toby had stood between them and the bandstand while they waited for Alf Butcher to finish. It wasn't much but it was the only dignity they could offer the late Gerard Soames. At last Alf Butcher came wandering across to them.

'He was drowned.'

'Murdered?' asked Fred.

'I would say so, marks on his wrist suggest his hands were tied. Looking at the angle of the marks I think they were tied behind him. Probably by the same piece of rope the killer used to sit him upright against the bandstand.'

'Can you confirm this asap, Alf.'

'Yeah, my report will be on your desk tonight.'

'Thanks. We have a suspect and I'm going to announce it at noon. The sooner I can have that officially the better.' Fred placed his hand on Alf's shoulder. 'Hopefully this will be the last one.'

'You that confidant you have the right man?'

Fred smiled at Alf. 'We don't have him; we just think we know who he is. Catching him is going to be a lot harder.'

'Who is it?'

'You know I can't tell you that, Alf.'

'Off the record.'

Fred turned to Toby. 'You tell him, you worked it out.'

Toby wasn't sure. 'It's just a theory at the moment.'

'Maybe it is, but it all fits, just like you said, and Soames was the next on the list. Remember, I told you to follow your instincts. You have, and I think you're right.'

Toby leaned close to Alf. 'Oliver Lawrence, the actor.'

'The one who died?'

'He didn't die, Alf, he disappeared. His body was never

found. He had a reason to hate everyone that's died and he's following the plot of …' Before he could finish, Fred interrupted.

'His following some revenge plot he's dreamed up. All we've got to do is find him.'

'Good luck with that, gents, at the moment it's four nil to him. You're going to need to play a blinder in the second half.'

'He's clever, but he's taking risks. Propping him up on the bandstand in the middle of this park, that's madness. The night patrols could have caught him.'

'Do you have night patrols?'

Fred looked sheepishly at Alf. 'No, but if we did, they'd have caught him.'

'I'm sure that's a great consolation to the widow.'

'He wasn't married, confirmed bachelor.'

Fred looked down at Gerard's bluish, pink features. 'He wasn't much of a catch, was he.'

'Probably why someone threw him back,' said Alf.

'He was murdered because he betrayed Oliver Lawrence, they were all murdered for that.'

'How many do you think?'

Toby shrugged. 'The company was about thirty strong but the main group that were there when he and his father were betrayed is about half that number.'

Alf shook his head. 'You do have a big problem. Any one of them could be your next victim.'

Toby shook his head. 'Not all of them, we've already ruled out Theo Cumberbatch and Dame Suzy.'

'And, of course, the four that are dead.'

Fred nodded. 'And the ones that weren't in the company when Jenkins and Lawrence were around. Leaves us with about twelve possible victims.'

Alf Butcher let out a long breath. 'I'd better get back to the lab before he strikes again.'

'Sod off, Alf.'

He winked at Fred and did as instructed. Toby watched him go.

'He's right though, isn't he. We think we know who our killer is, but we can't even prove he's alive. We have pictures of what he looked like sixteen years ago and no idea if he still looks the same. All we can do is put all the survivors from Sir Morris's company into protective custody until we get him.'

Fred smiled at Toby. 'You may have something there, let's do just that.'

'You can't be serious.'

'I can, you've given me an idea. They're all here in Stratford. Why don't we get them back into the theatre, start the shows again? We can put a shadow on each one of them, draw the bugger out.'

'You mean use them as live bait? I'm not sure about that, sir. And where will we get twelve detectives from for a surveillance operation of this size?'

'DI Townsend would help.' Fred smiled. 'She'd jump at the chance.'

'You want to bring Coventry in?'

'No, I want to bring Mel Townsend in. She's a good cop, we can trust her.'

Toby didn't look convinced. 'What if we do this and Lawrence manages to knock one of them off? Can you imagine the fallout if the press got hold of it. Not that it matters, Beeching would never approve it.'

'Who says we're going to tell him.'

Toby turned to Fred. 'Are you crazy, sir? He'd hang you out to dry.'

Fred shrugged. 'You got any better ideas? Sometimes you have to take a chance, follow your instincts. Folks are dying here and it's our job to try and stop it. I can't look myself in the mirror if we don't and another victim gets killed on my watch.'

Toby knew that Fred meant every word, he was prepared to risk his career to stop the killer. 'I don't like it, sir.'

'You don't have to, Toby, it's my call. I'm going to find DI Townsend and put it to her.'

'You want me to come with you?'

'Best I do this alone, son. If this goes wrong, you don't want to be within a million miles of it.'

'So what should I do?'

Fred put his hand on his shoulder. 'Follow your instincts, son, follow your instincts.'

One hour later, Toby's instincts had brought him to the Green Dragon where Whomper did not seem surprised to see him.

'I was wondering when you'd be back, DC Marlowe.'

'Well now you don't have to wonder any more.' Toby went to sit down.

'You can't sit down there, DC Marlowe.'

'Why not?'

'Because if you sit there the implication is that you want to talk to me.'

'I do.'

'I know, but how can a man converse at length when his larynx is caught in a moment of terrible dehydration.'

'What?'

'Do I have to spell it out … I'm thirsty.'

The penny dropped. 'Pint of mild?' asked Toby.

'Better make it two, I've a feeling this is going to be a long conversation, what with the body of Gerard Soames being found by the bandstand this morning.'

Toby looked at Whomper with wide-eyed amazement.

'How the hell do you know that?'

Whomper smiled. 'I didn't, but you just confirmed it, again.'

Toby shook his head and turned away. There was something very strange about Whomper Smith.

When Toby returned to the smoky recess of the lounge that Whomper had made his own, he was no longer alone. On either side of him were two ladies, both seemingly in their forties. They were attractive and they were dressed in a fashion that Toby could only identify as 'hooker chic'. He put down Whomper's two pints and sat down opposite the three of them clutching his bottle of Fentimans Ginger Ale.

'You going to introduce me?'

Whomper glanced from side to side. 'These, are my weird sisters. This is Valerie and the other one is Denise.'

Toby nodded politely. 'Pleased to meet you both.'

They smiled warmly at him. 'Pleased to meet you, too,' they said in unison, so alike and so perfect in their synchronisation that they sounded like a Greek chorus.

Toby was stunned for a moment. 'I told you they were weird,' said Whomper.

Toby looked closely at them; they did look very similar.

'We're twins,' said Whomper.

'But there's three of you,' observed Toby.

'I can understand why you'd think that.'

'Our brother is a bit obtuse,' they said again, together.

'He's also about ten years older than you.'

Whomper held up his hand. 'We don't have time to discuss the finer points of our family tree, DC Marlowe, just take it from me, we three are twins, with all the special powers that can bring, and we want to help you.'

'You do?'

'We do,' echoed the twins. Whomper joined them in perfect pitch and harmony.

The whole thing was getting very weird, Toby tried to get the conversation back on course. 'How did you know that there had been another death?'

'My sisters foresaw it.'

They nodded together.

'You saw the body dumped there?'

'No, they foresaw it.'

'Like in a dream?'

'Perhaps I should let them explain.' Whomper turned to his sisters. 'Girls, tell DC Marlowe what you told me.'

They smiled and then began to speak in perfect harmony, word for word. 'A man of letters will write no more. He will drown but be found on dry land. He was the author of his own downfall.'

Toby just sat there; this was weird but strangely accurate. 'A man of letters will write no more.'

'Soames was a man of letters,' said Whomper.

'He will drown but be found on dry land.'

'Tied to the bandstand, I believe.'

Toby looked from twin to twin and then at Whomper, the alleged third twin. 'He was the author of his own downfall?'

'Now that's the really interesting part, isn't it.'

'In what way?' asked Toby.

'In a way that means the murderer believed that Gerard Soames had betrayed him.'

It all made perfect sense. Whomper and his twin sisters had basically confirmed information they had no way of knowing. These were indeed strange times.

'So how on earth do you girls know all this? The body was only discovered by DC Dalton a few hours ago and there has been no police statement.'

The sisters shifted uncomfortably. 'By the pricking of our thumbs, something wicked this way comes.' They spoke the lines together. Toby recognised them at once.

'The three witches from Macbeth. Is this a joke?'

'It's no joke, the girls can sense something evil out there. The visions they are getting are merely reflections of the events that have happened. The violent taking of a life leaves ripples across the firmament and they are tuned to receive them. Disbelieve them at your peril.'

Toby laughed bitterly. 'I can't disbelieve them, they're right. All I wish is that they could tell me something before the next murder happens.'

Whomper's sisters leaned towards their brother and they began to whisper amongst themselves. Like a murmuration of starlings, their whisperings ebbed and flowed, rising and falling and creating tiny rhythms that intertwined and made them unintelligible to anyone who was not a part of the conversation. After about a minute they fell silent and Whomper looked up.

'They're off to the shops, apparently the Italian deli on Church Street is doing two for one for fresh ciabatta.'

'Is that it?' asked Toby indignantly.

Whomper nodded. 'Yes, they said it was lovely to meet you and they look forward to the next time.'

'When will that be?' asked Toby.

Valerie and Denise rose from their seats and leaned over Toby, Valerie to his left ear and Denise to his right, and spoke in unison. 'When the hurly-burly's done. When the battle's lost and won.' They left without another word, drifting through the mists of cigarette smoke and into the dark recesses of the WC.

Toby just sat there.

Whomper's features spread into a wide grin. 'I did warn you that my twin sisters were a bit weird.'

'Weird doesn't do them justice, they're madder than a box of frogs.'

'Kinda cute though and very fond of the Bard.' Whomper drained his first pint. 'They do know stuff though; they were right about Soames, weren't they.'

Toby nodded. 'Yes, he was my Guildenstern.' The moment he said it he regretted it.

Whomper didn't laugh, he nodded. 'You think our killer is following the plot of Hamlet. Makes sense.'

'It does?'

'Of course. Desmond Tharpe was stabbed, his daughter went crazy and drowned herself. That's got to be Polonius and Ophelia. Fibs and Soames betrayed the murderer and he got them before they got him. Rosencrantz and Guildenstern.'

As he listened to Whomper say it, any doubt he had about his theory melted away. 'You think I'm right?'

Whomper nodded enthusiastically. 'I'm certain you are.'

'So, what now, who's next.'

'Whoever is Claudius.'

'I thought of that. Sir Morris Oxford is my bet.'

Whomper grinned. 'That old git could do with killing, probably improve his acting.'

'Then Gertrude and Laertes, whoever they are.'

Whomper paused and scratched his ear, his enthusiasm for Toby's theory suddenly calmed.

'What is it, Whomper?'

'I just had a horrible thought.' He looked at Toby, doubt etched across his face. 'Your theory is good; I think it's right but what ...' he trailed off.

'Go on,' urged Toby.

'What if the scores he has to settle are too big for one play, this could just be the first act.' The smoke that hung about the room seemed to thicken and enclose Toby and Whomper in a claustrophobic fog. Could this be just the beginning?

'Othello,' whispered Toby.

'Good play to get rid of the ladies in his life.'

'Macbeth.'

Whomper nodded.

'Everybody dies.' They both sat there, staring through the smoke at a nightmare they had just imagined, fearing that it could become reality.

Toby was the first to break the silence. 'Think we are getting a bit carried away?'

Whomper nodded. 'Absolutely. Probably never happen.'

'Never, we'll catch him long before then.'

They both nodded vigorously, keen to put space between the unthinkable scenario they had just envisioned, both aware that they could never unthink it.

Chapter 55
When Shall We Three Meet Again?

Fred Williams was sitting at his desk in Guild Street waiting for Mel Townsend. He needed her help and hoped that the past would not cloud her judgement. The door to CID burst open and she strode in like Boudica freshly dismounted from her chariot after sacking Camulodunum. She was a magnificent woman.

'What's so important that I had to come here to see you?'

'Hello, Melanie, lovely to see you too.'

There was a trace of a smile at the corner of her mouth. 'Go on, Fred, let's hear it, I know you want something.'

Looking at her, Fred did want something but this wasn't the time or the place to try and rekindle a romance that had been extinguished many years before. 'Come into the meeting room, this isn't for anyone else's ears.'

'Intriguing,' Mel grinned. 'Can I get a cuppa first?'

'There's a pot of tea already brewing in there.'

She looked at Fred with renewed respect. He looked back with renewed desire. He watched her pour the tea, she really was magnificent. She pushed a mug towards him and sat down.

'Well, let's hear it. If nobody else is here it can't be good, or legitimate.'

'There's been another murder.'

'I know, I heard it on the coms in the car. I heard he drowned in the river.'

'Was drowned in the river. Hands had been tied behind him

and someone had lowered him head first by the look of it.'

Mel nodded slowly. 'That would do it. Who is it?'

'A guy called Gerard Soames.'

'The theatre critic?'

'The very same.'

'So, it's another kill for our serial killer.'

Fred nodded. 'No doubt about it. He was a close confidant of Sir Morris and Terry Fibs. We believe he was done in by Oliver Lawrence.'

'The actor?'

'Yep.'

'I thought he was dead.'

'So do most people. He disappeared fifteen years ago and everyone assumed he was dead, but no body was ever found. We think he's back and settling old scores.'

He passed her the last photo that the theatre had taken of him for the 1956 programme. Mel looked at it. He was an athletic looking young man with a mid-distance runners build and dark brown hair. They were not to know that Oliver looked nothing like that now.

'He was a good-looking boy; you think he still looks like this?'

Fred shrugged. 'Who knows, but it's all we've got to go on.'

'Fifteen years is a long time, Fred.'

'I know. I've got the bloke at HQ trying to do an image from this photo but aged by fifteen years, hopefully he can get close enough so that someone will be able to identify him.'

'You think he's here?'

'He's here, walking amongst us, laughing at us. He's killed four people right under our noses and he's still laughing about it. He could be standing on that car park now staring up at us and we wouldn't know it.'

'What's your plan? You must have one or you wouldn't have asked me here.'

'Am I that obvious?'

'Always.'

Fred put down his cup and picked up a sheet of paper, there were twelve names typed on it. He slid it across the table to Mel. 'These are the twelve people we think are at risk, there may be others.'

Mel started to look down the list shaking her head as she did so. 'It's a lot of potential victims, why so many?'

'We believe that Oliver Lawrence is back to settle old scores. Every one of the victims was in Sir Morris Oxford's company when Lawrence's career hit the skids. Some were even there when Richard Jenkins, Oliver's father, was ruined. He killed himself.'

'Did Sir Morris and his people have something to do with it?'

Fred nodded. 'It seems that both Oliver and his father were becoming too good, outshining Sir Morris. He wasn't a sir then but he was a star. Fibs and Soames were two tame critics who were part of his coterie, they favoured him with great reviews. Before Richard and Oliver's careers crashed, they had always had glowing reviews but then these two, both influential critics, started posting bad ones, not of the play but of their individual performances. Those are a matter of record, we have copies. We've also had some actors and journalists, who were around at the time, admit that they were fed wrong lines or mistimed lines, little tricks to undermine their confidence.'

'You mean there was a concerted effort made to destroy their careers?'

'Pretty much.'

'Can't we pull Sir Morris in?'

'We could, but what's the point? He's broken no law. Being an insecure twat isn't an offence.'

Mel sat there gazing at the list. 'Some of these are household names.'

'I know, that's why the next bit is difficult.'

Mel looked up suspiciously. 'Is this the bit I'm not going to like?'

'Possibly.'

'Explain.'

Fred pointed at the names. 'They are all possibles according to our theory.'

Mel snorted. 'This I have to hear.'

'DC Marlowe. Toby. He's a bright lad. He thinks that Oliver is following the plot of Hamlet.'

Mel leaned back in her chair. 'Seriously?'

'Deadly serious, you familiar with the plot?'

Mel shrugged. 'A bit. A forest moves into his garden and his wife gets a spot.'

'That's Macbeth.'

'Sorry, I'm more of a Dixon of Dock Green girl.'

'Never mind, you need to trust me on this one. Our killer is following the plot of the play and we think the next to die could be Claudius.'

'There's no Claudius on the sheet.'

'No, King Claudius in the play.'

'And who would that be?'

'Sir Morris Oxford.'

Mel stared back at Fred. 'Jesus H Christ! That would melt the front-page presses.'

'It would, so we can't let it happen.'

Mel sat there quietly. After a few moments she looked up at Fred. 'You know this is the craziest story you have ever told me and you've told me a few. But you know what's even crazier?'

Fred shook his head.

'I think I believe you.'

Fred breathed a sigh of relief.

'Thanks, Mel, I thought you would think I'd lost my mind.'

'I've thought that for years but in this case … I dunno why, I believe you. Toby could be right. It's a crazy theory but this guy is crazy. How do we catch him?'

Fred looked behind him to make sure the door to the meeting room was closed. 'We think we know who the killer is but we don't know what he looks like now. Fifteen years is a long time. If he did still look the same, somebody would have surely seen him. He's obviously been walking the streets of Stratford.'

'Let's just stop everyone on the street and question them then.'

'We can't, this place is built on tourism. It'll destroy the trade. Beeching and the council won't allow that. I suggested a curfew two days ago and was informed that, "There will be no Martial Law in Stratford." We have to find him by stealth.'

'Go on.'

'I've got six detectives, including myself, and two uniforms who are bright enough to put into civvies for a few days. Can you match that with six from Coventry?'

Mel looked at Fred warily. 'I could, what would you want them to do.'

'There are twelve names on that list. I think we should allow the theatre to reopen and get a discreet tail on each one. Draw the sod out.'

'Use them as bait? Have you lost your mind! What if one of them gets killed? You want to explain that we were using them as bait to Beeching and the press? Count me out.'

'What other way do we have of catching him? The theatre is reopening next week anyway. A few days extra will give us a better chance.'

Mel knew Fred was right. What other way was there if they couldn't lock down the town and stop and question people? 'Would I be working under you on this one, Fred?'

He nodded; he knew where this was going.

'Following your orders?'

He nodded again.

'Can I have that in writing?'

He nodded once more. He had his detectives, now all he needed was some luck.

Toby got back to the station just in time to see Mel Townsend drive off, he would soon know how Fred had fared with his attempt to get Mel onside. When he entered the office, Fred was staring at the blackboard.

Without turning, Fred spoke. 'How did you get on with Whomper?'

'How do you know I went to see him?'

'I told you to follow your instincts, didn't I. If they're any good, that's where you went,' he turned to Toby. 'Did you?'

'Yeah.'

'And what did our Whomper have to say for himself?'

Toby sighed. 'It wasn't just him, sir, he had company.'

'Really? Was it a pork pie?'

'I wish it had been. Did you know he has twin sisters?'

The blood drained from Fred's face. 'Oh, Jesus.'

'What's wrong?'

'Whomper's sisters are witches and nobody knows if they are good or bad, they freak me out and …' Fred trailed off.'

'What is it, sir.'

'This is going to sound crazy, Toby.'

'Everything about this case is crazy, sir.'

'Whenever his twins appear, bad things happen. They're like portents of doom.'

'More like a Greek Chorus, they were speaking in unison. Even Whomper joined in.'

'Did he tell you he was a twin too?'

'Yeah, I almost believed it when they all started talking in unison, perfect pitch, all of them.'

'That's not as crazy as it sounds, they all used to sing in a folk band at the Cherry Trees a few years back. Very good at harmonising, they were. Did they put a finger in their ears?'

'Come to think of it, they did.'

Fred smiled. 'Good old Whomper, still working the old smoke and mirror routine. Did he say anything interesting?'

'He did.'

'Let's hear it.'

'He seemed to think that my theory about Hamlet was right, as far as it goes.'

'What does that mean?'

Toby shuddered at the memory of the conversation. 'We discussed the possibility that this could just be the opening play in a killing season. What if he can't fit all the killings into one play?'

'How many victims do you think he wants to kill, Toby?'

Toby bit his lip while he considered.

'Well?'

'Could be up to twelve, sir.'

Fred held up the list he had shown to Mel Townsend.

'This Twelve?'

Chapter 56
Alas, Poor Richard!
I Knew Him, Horatio

Two days later, Oliver sat in his kitchen drinking tea with Felix. 'I think this has all gone terribly well so far, don't you?'

Felix nodded. 'To be fair, far better than I expected, and far more.'

'Did you think I would just kill Morris? You must have known when you wrote me that letter how many guilty people there were.'

Felix took a sip of tea and thought for a moment. 'I suppose I am guilty of being naïve. I assumed you would just kill Sir Morris and that would act as a cautionary tale for the rest of them.'

'That is naïve, Felix. These people were terrible. Killing them was a kindness, both to them and the theatre. They should put up a plaque to me for services to Shakespeare.'

Felix smiled. 'When is enough, enough? At what point do you stop? There are four dead people and Sir Morris still lives. If you are true to the play, he must be next.'

'Surely Gertrude dies before Claudius?' he looked at Felix slyly.

'Don't be silly, Gertrude would be your mother.'

'I know, Felix. I am still not convinced of her innocence. She saw my father ruined, she saw me ruined and then she married that monster. How can she be innocent? It flies in the face of reason.'

Felix wasn't sure what to say, Oliver was no longer the man

he had welcomed back from exile. With each murder he had gone deeper into the role he had given himself. He had become suspicious of everyone. The play had become real to him and all the murders merely acts in the performance he was constructing.

'Your mother was not a gifted actress, Oliver. A spear carrier at best. She was around greatness with your father and basked in the reflected glory. They were a golden couple.'

'But my mother was beloved,' protested Oliver.

Felix shook his head. 'Not really. I had the pleasure of acting with her once. A Streetcar Named Desire by Tennessee Williams, think it was at the Oxford Playhouse. She was nervous and dropped the southern accent, slipping back into her native Brummie tongue. "I have always relied on the comfort of strangers," is not the same when done in a broad Brummie accent. How the audience laughed. After that it was spear carrying only.'

'My mother wasn't from Birmingham, she's a Stratford girl through and through.'

Felix smiled. 'Your mother worked on the principal that if you say something often enough it becomes the truth, but when the pressure was on, she would lose the accent and her roots would shine through.'

Oliver smiled. 'I find that vaguely comforting. I always thought she was a bit of a posh old cow, but to know she's from Birmingham ...'

'And not the nice parts either,' added Felix.

'Are you suggesting my mother is a little common.'

'Most certainly. I still think she is a good person, and she did carry a mean spear.'

Oliver waved him quiet. 'Let's say that, for now, I agree with your assertion that my mother is blameless.'

'Good, because she is.'

'Very well, but it's not really a matter of any import, she's not on my list.'

'What list?'

'This one,' Oliver pulled a sheet of paper from a folder on the table. Memory is a funny thing. All the time I was in Morocco it never occurred to me that I had been betrayed by people I considered friends, my mind hadn't allowed those thoughts to enter it. I had failed, it was my weakness that had led to my breakdown. When I read your letter, it was like a door into the past had been opened, for the first time and I could see it for what it was; betrayal. People I had loved had betrayed me.'

Felix was reading the sheet of paper that Oliver had passed him.

'What is this list?'

'Names, most of which you are familiar with.'

Felix scanned down the list. 'All of them, why are they here?'

Oliver chuckled. 'Come now, Felix, we both know why they are there. I've been remembering a lot more recently. I think being back in Stratford has unlocked the cage of memory, events I had pushed to the dark recesses of my mind have emerged. The truth can be a painful companion.'

Felix listened quietly to Oliver's words, realisation growing. 'You can't be serious.'

'Deadly.'

'There are eight names on here.'

'I left I few off.'

Felix looked down the list once more and then back to Oliver. 'This has to stop. Morris is the head of the beast, chop that off and be done with it.'

Oliver shook his head. 'He that killed my father and whored my mother. Oh, I want him dead, all right, but he needs to suffer. He is the tallest tree in the forest he has created, that forest has grown tall, fed by naked ambition and the blood of my father and the lost dreams of my career. I want to set fire to that forest. He needs to see it burn around him and fall in smoking ruins, leaving him alone, afraid and certain that he will be next.' The words had hissed from Oliver's lips and a fire burned in his eyes. Felix had no doubt about his friend's intentions.

'It's a fine speech, Oliver, but to use your analogy, aren't you afraid that if you try to burn down the whole forest, the great oak will escape? Another eight murders are just not feasible. Your luck will run out.'

Oliver licked his lips and nodded. 'You may be right, but look at those names and tell me none of them bears guilt for what happened.'

'They do, but the death penalty? Surely that bears no relation to the crime.'

'You think any of them are decent human beings?'

Felix shook his head. 'No, awful, every one of them. All toadies to Sir Morris's ambition, the world wouldn't miss any of them. If I was a bus driver and they were my passengers I'd drive it over a cliff.'

'Then you agree?'

Felix looked into Oliver's eyes; there was no warmth there. 'No, I have done you a disservice. I should never have written that letter. The past is another country; we can never go back. End it here, kill Sir Morris and leave. Give it a year and then return. Nobody will recognise you, start again. An unknown talent coming from nowhere to take the stages of England by storm. It will be a triumph.'

'Fine words from a fine friend, I must confess, it is tempting.'

'Then do it,' urged Felix.

Oliver smiled sadly. 'Too late, my friend,' he leaned towards Felix. 'The play's the thing. Wherein I'll catch the conscience of the king.'

Felix knew the quote. Hamlet Act 2 Scene 2.

Oliver continued. 'Don't you see, my friend? The play's the thing, and now it adapts to my direction. All the world's a stage, and all the men and women are merely players. They have their exits …' he paused and pointed to the list. 'It's a beautiful irony, don't you think?'

Felix sipped his tea; what he had put in motion he could not stop. For good or bad, the play must run its course, the ending had yet to be written.

Oliver glanced up at the clock, it was approaching seven p.m. 'Fancy a pint, I've had enough tea to last a lifetime.'

'Where you thinking?'

'Dirty Duck, of course. With a bit of luck, we may bump into Dame Suzy. She likes me.'

'She likes Francis Bacon; not so sure she'd be too keen on you if she knew who you were.'

'That's the point, Felix, we acted together several times and she doesn't recognise me. All I ever get is, "You seem familiar." I've changed. I can be her Francis.'

'You can't be serious; you've killed half the cast of the play she is currently in.'

'Don't exaggerate, I killed four, and Tabitha was so wooden they could replace her with a bit of scenery.'

Felix smiled; he couldn't help himself. Tabitha really had been a poor actress. 'I hope the understudies are ready.'

'I've been thinking about that too, maybe I could take over from Desmond as Mark Antony, I know the part.'

Felix was dumbstruck.

'Are you crazy, take over from a man you have just killed?'

'I could try, maybe I will ask Suzy to help me get an audition.'

Felix grabbed Oliver by the shoulders and shook him. 'For God's sake, Oliver, you're losing it. Forget acting for now.'

'Too soon?'

'Way too soon.'

'OK, let's get a pint.'

Felix followed Oliver out of the house, wondering how he would explain his friendship with Oliver once the inevitable happened and he was caught. His only hope would be if Oliver said he didn't know. It was a pretty slim hope but it was all he had. There was something else nagging at the back of his mind. He stopped on the pavement, just outside the gates of All Saints Church. Oliver turned back to him.

'Everything all right?'

Felix shook his head. 'I don't think so.'

Oliver walked the few steps back to him. 'What's wrong?'

'The other night, when you killed Gerard.'

'What about it.'

'I liked it.'

'You did?'

'I'm ashamed to admit it, but it was exciting. The way you talked to him and then killed him. It was like something from a Shakespearian tragedy. You were brilliant, it was your finest acting.'

Oliver smiled. 'I wasn't acting … nor was Gerard, come to think of it.'

'Gerard was an absolute sod, I couldn't feel any sympathy for him, but …' he trailed off.

'Go on.'

'I've never seen anything so thrilling, and so wrong. Does that make me evil?'

Oliver laughed. 'I don't think so. I reckon your mortal soul is safe from the fires of hell.' Oliver flicked his head towards the Churchyard. 'You want to pop in and say a prayer before the pub?'

'No, I think a drink would be of more use to me.' Felix was about to move off when he noticed that Oliver was now staring deep into the graveyard, not far from the place he had killed Desmond and persuaded Tabitha into the river. 'What is it?'

'There's a gravedigger, it's a bit late for that.'

'Big day tomorrow. Desmond and Tabitha are both being buried here, special dispensation.'

'Come, Horatio, let's take a look.'

Felix followed Oliver as he walked through the graveyard entrance, towards where the gravedigger was finishing the grave. He had called him Horatio. He realised that Oliver was back in the play. Surely there would be no Yorick, not in 1972.

Oliver reached the grave; it was dug and the grave digger was dressing the edges with a green cloth.

'How now, gravedigger.'

The gravedigger had not heard his approached and jumped.

'Bloody hell. Don't do that, I nearly had a heart attack.'

'I'm not surprised, that's a really big hole.'

'It's for two; a father and his daughter, you've probably heard of them. The two that got murdered from the theatre.'

Oliver nodded solemnly. 'Yes, very sad. I'm sorry we startled you.'

The gravedigger wiped his brow. 'It's all right, second time this evening. My mate left a skull just under the soil, nearly jumped out of my skin when it came out. Here.' He bent down and retrieved a skull from the bottom of the grave. He showed it to Oliver.

'Is it real?'

'I think so.'

'Who is it.'

The gravedigger shrugged. 'I'm pretty sure it ain't Yorick, my mate probably bought it in an old junk shop. Bet it belonged to a medical student once.'

Oliver opened his hands. 'May I hold it?'

'If you want to, mate, just don't report me to the council.'

'My father is buried here.'

'What was his name?'

'Richard, I knew him well.'

'I would hope so, sir.'

Oliver stared into the empty eye sockets. 'He was a fellow of infinite jest, of most excellent fancy, he hath borne me on his back a thousand times.'

'That's dads for you, sir.' The gravedigger shot Felix a look. 'Your mate knows his Shakespeare.'

'He does,' agreed Felix. 'He's also a bit of a luvvie.'

'That much is obvious.'

Oliver handed the gravedigger back the skull. 'Imperious Caesar, dead and turned to clay.'

'Might stop a hole to keep the wind at bay,' said the gravedigger, finishing the line for him.

Oliver smiled at him. 'You are a well-read man.'

'Not a lot of choice in this town, sir.'

Across the graveyard the bells rang. 'You hear that, Horatio? The pub is calling.' He turned back to the gravedigger. 'Goodnight.'

'Goodnight, gents.' he watched them walk away across the graveyard towards the street. There were some weird people in Stratford.

As Oliver and Felix walked down the street towards the Dirty Duck, Felix spoke.

'You do know you were calling me Horatio back there, don't you.'

'Was I?'

'Yes.'

'Sorry, I was in character. Hamlet's truest friend was Horatio and you, my dear Felix, are my Horatio.'

'Lucky me.'

'You want a change?'

Felix did not understand the question. 'What do you mean?'

Oliver turned to Felix and stopped. 'I am done with Hamlet; the play is at an end.'

For a moment hope flickered in Felix's heart.

'Is it over, are we finished?'

Oliver winced.

'Act one is finished. Now is the time for a new play and different players.'

Felix's heart sank. 'Which play?'

'Well, it's not A Midsummer Night's Dream is it?'

They both laughed. As they walked up the steps to the Dirty Duck, Felix persisted. 'Can you give me a clue?'

'Certainly,' Oliver turned to Felix, his eyes narrowed and he leaned conspiratorially towards him. 'O, beware, my lord, of jealousy: It is the green-eyed monster which doth mock the meat it feeds on.' He turned away, headed up the steps and disappeared into the Dirty Duck leaving Felix alone on the pavement. He gazed down helplessly at the cold unyielding stone. He knew that quote and recognised the path that he would have to follow.

'Farewell my tranquil mind, farewell content.' The words fell from his lips like tears shed for a cause that was already lost. 'Our wills and fates do so contrary run.'

Acknowledgements

Big thanks to my wonderful editor, Samantha Brownley. Friend, slave-driver and usually right. This book is better because of her.

Thanks also to Will Templeton for the final proof and set out of the book. It looks fab.

My man Pete Adlington has designed all of my covers and, as always, has done a great job. He's newly married so he needs the work.

Big thanks also to Rebecca Collins at Arch Pub for doing all the nitty gritty stuff with ISBN numbers, e-books, printers etc. All the stuff I'm not bright enough to do.

Once again into the breech, my wonderful PR Laura Lees. Always smiling, always enthusiastic, always knows best.

Finally, huge thanks to the lovely Lou Lancaster, my long-suffering wife, who has had to listen to daily readings from this novel for six months, and is still smiling. What a woman.